RAPE

Kitty stumbled into the kitchen, eyes
puffed by crying, lips swollen by slaps.
Her dress was ripped to the waist.

"You poor kid," Janie whispered,
"what'd they do to you?"

Kitty began to sob. Then she screamed.
"I never done it before! Never before!
I begged him to let me go!
He wouldn't—"

"God damn him!" said Janie.

"Emphatically a reading 'must'..."

Edwin J. Lukas, Executive Director,
Society for the Prevention of Crime (New York)

Published by Bantam Books

THE AMBOY DUKES

IRVING SHULMAN

BANTAM BOOKS · TORONTO · NEW YORK · LONDON

THE AMBOY DUKES

*A Bantam Book / published by arrangement with
Doubleday and Company, Inc.*

PRINTING HISTORY

Condensation appeared in OMNIBOOK *January 1947*
Doubleday edition published March 1947
2nd printing..........March 1947
Garden City Books (Sun Dial) edition published March 1948
Bantam edition published May 1961
2nd printing..........September 1963
3rd printing..............August 1965

*Bantam Books are published by Bantam Books, Inc., a subsidiary
of Grosset & Dunlap, Inc. Its trade-mark, consisting of the words
"Bantam Books" and the portrayal of a bantam, is registered in the
United States Patent Office and in other countries. Marca Registrada.
Bantam Books, Inc., 271 Madison Avenue, New York, N. Y. 10016.*

EVERY writer hopes to reach many readers. Usually, we must be satisfied with hundreds. I have been lucky enough to have had millions of people read my three books about crime in this country: THE AMBOY DUKES, CRY TOUGH! and THE BIG BROKERS. Yet, most of them have read abridged, altered versions. I am very happy that THE AMBOY DUKES is now going to reach the millions of readers for whom I wrote it in exactly the version that I intended it to be read.

IRVING SHULMAN

To My Daughters,
JOAN ANN
and
LESLIE JANE

Chapter 1

The bunches stood on the corners. The Bristol Friends, the Herzl Street Boys, the Amboy Dukes. Each bunch idled on its own corner, although members from Sutter Avenue bunches, East New York cliques, and Williamsburg gangs might be visiting and strengthening alliances. Off Pitkin Avenue were the unobtrusive but sinister poolrooms, barbershops, and fly-specked candy stores that served as hangouts and depositories for brass knuckles, knives, and an occasional gun.

The boys stood around on Saturday nights, ready for action. Between the ages of fifteen and twenty-two, they stood on the corners and discussed the deadly gossip of rackets: whores, guys who were cut up, and the dough you could make from one sweet job. Their voices, purposely brutalized and wildly boisterous, attracted little attention from the strollers on Pitkin Avenue, but as young men and women approached the corners they walked close to the curbs to minimize the jeers and dirty comments that were tossed at them. The bunches spoiled for a fight, and their technique was swift and murderous: a kick in the ankle, a hook to the groin, a clout behind the ear—then some well-placed kicks in the kidneys and head, and the victim was ready for the ambulance.

The boys were of one face and form, and their viciousness was not tempered by youth. Lean or fat, tall or short, their bodies were hard, their eyes narrow and cruel, their lips thin and bitter, and on their right hands they wore large cameo signet rings which served as cutting weapons.

1

Alert and tense, they smoked endlessly and spat constantly as they sought for the opportunity to begin slugging. The boys were careful of their dress, and since it was late spring they wore pastel tan, blue, and brown gabardine suits: three-button jackets, ticket pocket, center vent, deep pleated trousers with dropped belt loops, pegged from twenty-four inches at the knees to sixteen inches at the cuffs. Sharp. They wore open-collared sport shirts or white, blue, or brown buttoned-down oxford shirts, and their ties were tied neatly in broad knots. Nonchalantly they swung long key chains that hung from a right or left belt loop, and the keys spun in continuous enlarging and contracting circles. The boys sported ducktail haircuts: long, shaggy, and clipped to form a point at the backs of their heads. Their slick vaselined hair shone in the reflections of light.

Hour after hour they stood on the corners, jeering and spitting at strangers, and only speaking reverently to real mobsters who might pass by. Then they wondered when they were going to have the cash to promote a trim dish like the piece hanging onto Buggsy Stein's arm. Numbers and slot machines and the black market paid off. Not working like hell in school or in a bastard defense plant or shipyard where they had spotters who would turn you in for sleeping on the job or shooting a little crap in one of the storerooms.

Frank Goldfarb puffed hard on the cigarette and jingled the coins in his pocket. Then he looked at his new wrist watch. His father and mother had left it on the kitchen table that morning with a note that stated that the watch was to celebrate three things: his fourteenth birthday, his graduation from school next month, and for last year, when he had been *bar mitzvah* and they could not afford to buy him anything.

The watch was a beauty, and Frank held it to his ear to listen to the strong steady tick.

"Got a new watch?" one of the Dukes asked him.

"Yeah." Frank nodded. "My pop gave it to me."

The Duke held Frank's wrist and examined the watch. "Not bad, kid," he finally said. "Take care of it. Never slug

2

a guy while you're wearin' a good watch," he advised Frank. "First take it off and put it in your pocket. But you gotta do it fast. Remember, fast."

"Thanks," Frank said reverently.

The Duke winked at Frank and refused the cigarette Frank offered him. "Try one of these." He extended his open cigarette case to Frank. "They're reefers. If you're gonna smoke y'might's well get a kick outa it."

Frank recoiled.

The Duke's look became hard and brittle. "What's the matter?" he asked slowly. "Afraid? We ain't got room for guys in the Dukes who've got crap in their blood."

Frank hesitantly lit the reefer. The Duke winked encouragingly at Frank.

Hell, Frank thought, this is like smoking a regular butt. Frank smiled as he exhaled. This was the life. He pushed into the mob and walked along Pitkin Avenue, feeling the thrust and excitement of a crowd that moved with purpose.

Any night in the week, but especially Friday and Saturday nights, Pitkin Avenue was a packed and vibrant street, raucous with movement and color, and between Saratoga and Rockaway avenues there walked an intent mass of shoppers, strollers, and loungers who moved with purpose along the avenue, pausing to appraise the store windows, the arguments of the political speakers, and the appearance of other people.

Both sides of the avenue were lined with bright stores, restaurants, and chop suey joints. Radios from second-story repair shops blared into the street, and at the corner of Pitkin and Amboy a Socialist speaker, flanked by an American flag, stood on a ladder and hoarsely harangued the crowd. On Pitkin and Hopkinson the speaker was a Communist, on Pitkin and Bristol, a Socialist-Laborite.

The crowds swelled, eddied, and pushed along the sidewalks. The strollers entered restaurants and ice-cream parlors or stood at the open windows of candy stores and hot-dog stands, drinking nickel malteds, nickel ice-cream sodas, and three-cent egg creams. They ate frankfurters heavy with mustard, large dripping ice-cream sandwiches, cones filled with varicolored custards, and they nibbled on

3

large nutted squares of chocolate that cost three cents, two for a nickel. Occasionally a connoisseur would buy a candy-covered cherry for two cents, carefully bite into the chocolate shell that enclosed the cherry and liquid, and stand still, enraptured, as he savored the richness and fullness of sweet delight as the chocolate, liquid, and cherry melted and blended in his mouth.

Last year when Frank had been bar mitzvah the crowd had been a listless one. For in 1941 Brownsville was a wasted, hopeless neighborhood, with home relief and WPA employment as its principal occupations. But that was last year, and in 1942 the war hit Brownsville with a smashing impact that jarred this depressed and ruined slum area out of its hopeless lethargy. Jobs could be had for the asking, and employers no longer made demands for skill, experience, high school graduates, or Anglo-Saxon backgrounds. In ever-increasing numbers people in Brownsville left the WPA and home relief for the shipyards in the Erie Basin, on Staten Island, and Kearney, New Jersey, which hired any man or woman who wanted a job. At the New York Port of Embarkation and the Brooklyn Navy Yard there were jobs as laborers, porters, packers, warehousemen, stockmen, and clerks for all who applied. Huge ads and posters appeared in the newspapers and subways which insisted that it was every citizen's patriotic duty to take a job, and Brownsville went to work. The Lexington Avenue and New Lots expresses were jammed with people going to their jobs, and twenty-four hours a day the New Lots local disgorged at Saratoga and Rockaway avenues thousands of people who were returning to their Brownsville flats to eat hot greasy meals and drink gallons of seltzer, Dr. Brown's Celray Tonic, and Pepsi-Cola.

For Frank Goldfarb's father there was the job that he had always wanted: sewing-machine operator in a union shop that manufactured military uniforms; and somehow Mrs. Goldfarb found herself working in an ordnance plant, packing .50-caliber bullets in web belting. With all the overtime they wanted, the Goldfarbs began to eat better, pay off their debts, buy new beds and springs and mattresses, maple furniture for the kitchen, new clothes

4

and shoes and hats and suits and dresses and watches and rings and junk jewelry. Then the miracle of war bonds and a bank account came to the Goldfarbs, and at last they were economically stable, income-tax payers, solid, solvent members of a community which shook off the worn cloak of poverty.

With his hands thrust into the pockets of his blue pegged pants Frank sauntered along the avenue, enjoying his contact and association with the crowd. Occasionally he touched the tooled leather of his new belt, and as he passed mirrored store windows he paused to look at his reflection in the glass. This crowd had money, could pay for anything in any store with new crisp bills, bright shiny coins, or impressive government checks. It was good to walk along, feeling the heavy coins in his pocket and crackling the crisp dollar bills in his fist, and knowing that Miss Moscovitz, the home-relief investigator, would no longer be butting into his family's affairs. There was no longer a need for a home-relief allotment which kept getting less and less as the arguments at home became worse and worse, until their Amboy Street flat always seemed to have been filled with the loud voice of his father and the shrill screaming of his mother.

That was all gone, buried in a past that Frank did not want to remember but which he could not forget. And it was when he remembered the past: the cheap twelve-dollar bar mitzvah suit that Uncle Hershell had bought for him and for which he had had to take a thousand dollars' worth of crap about his father who'd rather remain unemployed and on relief than work in a non-union shop; it was when he remembered the past with its orange and blue food stamps, clothing tickets, and continual begging and pleading for a little more relief, a little more money for food, a little more money for the things that they needed, that Frank would seek refuge on the corner of his block and stand reverently with the little guys, the punks, and watch the big guys in the bunch. He would grin like an idiot fool when one of the big guys would nod to him or even ask him for a cigarette.

Now he was fourteen, and maybe the guys would permit him to hang around more often and listen to their

5

talk. Soon, he hoped, he would be considered one of the boys, in the gang, solid with the right guys, an accepted member of the bunch on his block.

One Sunday in April 1944, Alice Goldfarb leaned back in her seat on top of the Fifth Avenue bus and tried to count the stories of at least one of the tall apartment houses on Riverside Drive. But the bus moved too quickly and there was too much to see. To her left lay the green velvet stretch of park along the river; then there was the river, iridescent, bright, and magnificent in the early morning sun, and beyond the river the shores of another state, New Jersey. It was too exciting to concentrate on any one sight, and when the bus passed Grant's Tomb, white and proud in its marble, so splendid that the picture of the tomb in her history book was an injustice, she could only point at the dome of the tomb, unable to say anything. Only after the bus passed the mausoleum did she realize that the body of a real genuine President of the United States lay entombed there, and before she could communicate her awe and wonderment to her brother Frank she saw a trim white, black, and red yacht proudly moving down the Hudson toward the bay; and actually to see so many things which heretofore had existed only in books and the movies made Alice wonder if she really had lived before this Sunday morning.

As the bus was halted by the red traffic light she leaned forward to look into the streets that ran into the Drive. The buildings rose story after story, strong and proud of the wealth housed in their duplex apartments, with wood-burning fireplaces in the libraries, parlors, and master bedrooms. Blue and black limousines stood at attention along the curbs, and sitting smartly in the drivers' seats were the uniformed chauffeurs waiting patiently for the occupants of the apartments to descend to the street and to be driven to the churches and other places of smart assembly.

"Look!" Alice stuttered with excitement as she nudged Frank so that he might see the uniformed nursemaid slowly pushing a magnificent black-and-chromium baby

6

coach, while behind her, at a proper distance, walked a maid with a pedigreed French poodle.

"The dog is like a Persian-lamb coat." Alice's face was bright with joy. "That must be what they make Persian-lamb coats from," she concluded.

Frank squeezed his sister's thin shoulders. "No, baby," he said. "That's some kind of fancy dog. They make Persian-lamb coats out of lambs that come from Persia. I think."

"And look at that automobile!" Alice pointed at a black Rolls-Royce cabriolet with the canvas top down. In the back seat sat a dowager with her hair dyed platinum gray. The Rolls stopped close to them as the traffic light flashed red, and Alice stood up to lean over the rail of the bus. Silently she hoped that the light would not turn green again for at least a half-hour, so that she could fix forever in her memory the picture of the silent, regal old woman sitting erect, as if posture were the only worth-while thing in the entire world, aloof and unknowing of the bus which stood alongside her limousine. The bus groaned into low gear as the red light changed to green, but the Rolls, with a smooth and silent meshing of gears, drew away from the lumbering bus and disappeared into the traffic ahead.

Each block of the bus ride brought to Alice a new sight, a new joy. There were people walking arm in arm on the clean broad sidewalks; tall austere doormen resplendent in uniforms with brass buttons, who whistled imperiously at taxis to stop for people who waited with bored politeness under the canopies of apartment houses; gray limestone and marble mansions, with tall french windows in which hung heavy draperies that barred the sun and the prying gazes of the people who rode on top of the busses; unlittered parks with benches that were invitingly empty and private. And always the apartment houses that seemed to stretch and surge infinitely upward to end in roof gardens and penthouses, things so distant and remote from Alice's imagination that the word image could evoke nothing but a gasp, as if Alice had mentioned the forbidden name of Jehovah.

7

Alice turned her thin childish face to Frank. "We'll come back this way?"

"We oughta take the subway," Frank replied. "We want to eat something before we go to the show."

"I can always eat," Alice whispered, for she feared that she was speaking too loudly for the sacredness of Riverside Drive, "that's why I want to ride back on the bus."

Frank pinched her cheek. "You like this, don't you?"

"I never saw anything so wonderful. It's like a real dream."

"I'm glad you're having such a good time." Frank smiled.

Alice pressed his hand and then turned to look at the girl who strode along the Drive wearing pink whipcord riding breeches, brown boots that gleamed and were molded to her legs, a white blouse open at the throat, and a light tan camel's-hair polo coat thrown loosely across her shoulders. Blond hair fell to the girl's shoulders, and her mouth was a bright note in her lovely face.

"Look at her," Alice whispered. "She's so beautiful!"

"I've dated girls just as good-looking." Frank hated the lack of conviction in his voice.

He looked at Alice's thin rapt face, her large brown eyes catching every sight and motion on the Drive, her lips moving silently in admiration and wonder, and suddenly he hated everything about him. More than once he had taken this bus ride with a girl and had never noticed anything, for the bus ride was an inexpensive and convenient way of entertaining a girl on a Saturday night when he did not want to go to the movies. Now with Alice, for the first time he saw the wealth about him and he saw it through Alice's eyes, in its grandeur and magnificence, its opulence and majesty. But while her appreciation was almost a religious rapture, his reaction was one of bitterness and venomous irritation. In the quiet assurance of the handsome people riding in the limousines, standing under the canopies of the apartment houses, strolling with sedate dignity along the Drive, he saw only an affront to him. Somewhere, indistinctly, so far removed from his understanding that it was like a dim, vague dream that he had never had, he remem-

8

bered the harangues of the Communist and Socialist speakers on Pitkin and Hopkinson and Pitkin and Bristol. Somewhere in their talks to which he had never bothered to listen, he thought he remembered references to the joy and splendor which resided in certain streets of Manhattan and Brooklyn, and to the misery, poverty, and squalor that had rotted Brownsville, East New York, and Ocean Hill.

Why it was unfair, he did not know, but it was. Because his father had been unemployed and poor was no reason why they had had to live in a stinking, rotten tenement of carrion brick in a putrescent neighborhood, where he had known nothing but the despair that was attendant upon hopelessness and an enervating poverty. Now that they could get out there was no place to go, and the Drive stood clean, proud, and inviolate, an hour on the subway from Brownsville, a street upon which he was privileged to ride for a dime, but carefully guarded from him by doormen, massive draperies, and wealth. April was warm, and soon it would be June, July, and August. Soon the heat would make the oppressive rooms of their flat suffocating and stifling, and he would have to build once again a little makeshift fence around the open space on their fire escape so that Alice and he could sleep out of doors. In the morning he would awaken, stiff and cramped from sleeping in the small space, his back and hair damp. He would lie with his eyes shut to keep out the first rays of the sun which were welcomed as they entered the wide glass windows of penthouses and solariums but which meant to Frank another blistering day in Brownsville, another day of sitting in the movies or sweating it out on the crowded beaches of Coney Island, another day of drinking iced liquids that neither cooled him nor eased his thirst, another day of pushing back his plate at supper, unable to eat because of the small beads of perspiration that stood out on his forehead and the vile, evil cooking odors that seeped through the walls and entered the open windows of their flat.

Things were different on the Drive. There the sun and June, July, and August were no problem, for it seemed as if the sun were aware that this was residence of people

9

who stood for no nonsense from their employees, the stores in which they shopped, and the elements. There were no odors of cooked cabbage, cauliflower, and onions, of garbage cans, of moldering trash in the cellars and dark recesses of halls.

Alice tugged at his sleeve. "You're not listening to me, Frank. Look at the sailboat on the river."

"I was thinking." He obliged Alice by looking at the boat and nodding approvingly. "You sure would like to live here."

"I'd rather live here and die at the end of a year than live to be a hundred on Amboy Street."

"Don't say that," he said sharply. "These people ain't no better than we are."

"What does it cost to live here?" Alice stared at the river.

Frank's laugh was without mirth. "More'n we got. Stop knocking yourself out, baby. We haven't got a chance."

"Frank," Alice appealed to him, "Why don't we try to get into that housing project on Bergen Street? I know a girl who lives there. I was in her house once and it's beautiful. I bet as nice as these houses here."

Frank brushed a bit of white cotton from the shoulder of Alice's jacket. "We can't," he said. "I went with Mom once to the relief office when they were first opened, and the lady said that they only took in a couple of people who were on relief and let them live there and that where we lived wasn't so bad as other people's. Now," he sighed, "it's all filled up and Mom 'n' Pop are making too much money, so they can't live there even if there was an apartment."

Alice attempted to understand what Frank had told her. "You mean," she said, "that first we didn't have enough money and now we have too much?"

"Something like that."

"So what're we supposed to do? I hate it!" she exclaimed. "I hate it like poison!"

"Stop it, baby." Frank pressed her hand. "We're supposed to have a good time. Look, it's all the same the rest of the way up. So if we get off at the next stop I'll

10

take the bus back with you to Radio City, and then we'll be riding nearer the water and we can watch the boats instead of these lousy houses. We have just as much fun as these people," Frank bragged without conviction. "Most of them don't have any fun, and they're sissies who ride around in the backs of their automobiles, and what fun is that? It's more fun to drive a car, and you watch," he added, "as soon as I can get a license I'm going to get us a car and we'll go out to the country and every place. You'll see."

Frank extended his hand to help Alice from the bus, and they waited for the light to change so that they might cross the Drive.

"Let me count the floors in this house." Alice motioned to the apartment house on the corner. "Five"— she nodded and her lips moved as she counted—"twelve, fifteen, twenty-one, twenty-two, twenty-three. Twenty-three floors." She turned triumphantly to Frank. "At last I was able to count to the top of a house. The light's changed."

Frank led her across the street, and they strolled to the bus stop. Alice was busy counting the floors of another apartment house, and her face was radiant as she informed him that this building was taller by five stories. But Frank stared moodily at his shoes and did not answer her.

"I said this is a taller house," she repeated.

"Who cares?" he replied irritably.

The ride back was a silent one. For a few minutes Alice was dispirited, but this new world was too exciting for her to remain depressed, and soon her face shone again with excitement and joy. Frank's right arm was draped casually across the back of the double seat, and to Alice's exclamations he replied with a grunt.

The bus maneuvered into Fifty-seventh Street and lumbered toward Fifth Avenue. In the smart shop windows Alice saw the postured mannequins wearing furs and gowns with a grace that no girl or woman could ever hope to equal. In their inanimate yet superior faces were fixed for all time the expressions of women accustomed to the adulation of many men, and these slender inani-

11

mate dolls seemed to Alice to have partaken of more wonderful experiences than would ever befall her. For at least they were privileged to wear gowns, wraps, and furs whose soft luxury she could never hope to know.

Too quickly the bus was at Fiftieth Street, and again Frank extended his hand to her as she stepped from the bus to the sidewalk. Alice thanked him, and Frank nodded absently. She looked at her brother, only five years older than she and still so many more years apart in thought, action, deed, and experience. Frank had always been bitter, but that was because they had been poor; but even in his bitterness he had been her friend, and Alice still remembered the days when they had sat together on the fire escape and he had read stories to her and they had conjectured and argued as to how the hero was going to escape in the next episode of the serial they were following at the New Singer. He had looked after her and they had talked and wondered about many things. And then Frank had become fourteen and her mother and father had gone to work, and from then on he had no longer been the same brother. With haste and complete disregard for her baby worship of him, he had moved into the world of boys who seemed to live at a hysterical pitch of excitement. Suddenly Frank had begun to dress like a man, smoke, even drink, date girls who looked as if they thought, said, and did things which were to Alice little understood but nevertheless dirty; and now she saw him only in the morning before they went to school, and infrequently in the evening when he took her with him to one of the neighborhood restaurants for a supper which Frank would rush through in his impatience to leave.

Frank walked with Alice through the Radio City promenade toward the Music Hall. For an impatient moment he permitted her to pause and stare at the tall Easter lilies that nodded gracefully in the breeze. Then he took her hand and led her away, but as they walked Alice kept looking back toward the flower beds that she could no longer see.

With reverent silence Alice walked through the thick-carpeted lobby of the Music Hall. Above her—how high she could not guess—was the ceiling, and from the ceiling were suspended giant crystal chandeliers whose prisms caught and disbursed the soft light that fell in a warm glow over everything. As she walked she had to look down to be certain that the nap of the carpeting was not above the tops of her slippers. She walked past statuary, heavy mirrors in intricate black-and-gold frames, needle-point chairs, deep luxurious sofas, and gleaming tables which mirrored the reflections of the chandeliers. She did not envy Frank's calm and even bored acceptance of the marvels, for to her it was like stepping into an enchanted cave and suddenly coming upon wonders so startling, so breath-taking beyond description, so inconceivable, that she felt Aladdin would have had difficulty in duplicating them even though he owned a magic lamp.

Frank guided her to a seat in the balcony, and she experienced a quick spasm of fear as she saw the screen at so great a distance. But a quick glance about reassured Alice, and she gave herself up to the movie. Frank yawned in the darkness and wondered how Alice could sit on the edge of her seat, softly sighing and making sharp little exclamations of joy and sorrow as the motion picture plodded along. With a final burst of triumphant music the picture came to an end and the giant curtains closed over the screen.

Alice clapped her hands. "Wasn't that wonderful?" Her joy was so genuine that Frank did not dare disagree.

The orchestra platform moved upward, and Frank leaned forward to see better as the Rockettes swung into line and moved in flawless precision, as if they were controlled by one impulse. In perfect synchronization they moved into squares, units, alternating lines, their costumes bright and exciting, their rhythm and flashing legs accentuating the beat of the music. Swiftly and without effort, with a grace that was flawless and free, they danced, and now they were in one line across the stage, extending from wing to wing, and they moved forward until they stood almost at the edge of the stage above the orchestra, arms locked behind one another's backs, and kicking in a variety of steps to their right and left.

13

Spontaneous bursts of applause started through the audience, and as the Rockettes gave one final kick, dipped, stood still, and bowed, the applause cascaded toward the stage, and Alice stood up, wildly clapping her hands, until Frank forced her back into her seat.

"They were so wonderful!" she exclaimed. "So wonderful! I could stay to see them again."

Frank pushed a strand of hair back from Alice's forehead as she adjusted her hat. "You could ride on the bus forever and look at the gardens forever and now you could stay to see them again. Where are you getting all this time?" he asked her.

Reluctantly she followed him into the aisle and waited for the crowd to move up the steps. "I could still stay," she said defiantly.

"I believe you." Frank nodded. "Now look"—he leaned over to speak to her—"we gotta eat. So we'll go to the bathrooms here and wash. Wait till you see them. Nothing like what we got at home." Amboy Street and Riverside Drive flashed before him and he was bitter.

Alice caught the change in his mood. "Don't feel bad," she said. "Someday we'll move away."

Chapter 2

Next morning the alarm clock jarred into Frank Goldfarb's troubled sleep at seven o'clock. Frank pushed the plunger on top of the clock, shut off the alarm, and went on sleeping. But his sister Alice, lying in the other bed, sat up, stretched, and rubbed her eyes. Alice's bed was next to the window, and she looked out at a clean blue sky in which drifted a few wisps of white cloud. She leaned on the window for a moment, smiling, until she noticed that Crazy Sachs was staring at her from his window across the yard, and then as he caught her eye he

14

made an obscene gesture, the meaning of which was evi-
dent to her even though she was only eleven. She
clutched the cover to her and reached up to draw the
shade to the lower sill.

"Frankie," she called to her brother, "wake up."

Frank rolled toward the wall. "Let me alone," he said
sleepily. "I'm sick."

"You're not sick," she went on. "We've got to get up."

"I'm not going to school today," Frank said.

Alice shook him. "You're not going to cut again. Get
up."

"Get away from me," her brother warned her, "or I'll
kick you in the ass."

"You're a bum to talk that way to me." Alice's voice
quivered. "I hate you almost as much as I hate your
friends and that Crazy Sachs. Do you know what he done?"

"What?" Frank asked without interest.

"He was looking at me in my nightgown this morning
and he made a dirty motion at me."

Frank rolled over to look at her. "He couldn't see anything," he finally said. "So what're you griping about?"

"He made a dirty motion at me."

"So what?"

"Nothing, if that's the way you feel about it. Are you
getting up? I'll go into the bathroom to get dressed."

"If I gave you a half buck," Frank asked her, "would
you keep quiet about me not going to school?"

"No! You're going to get left back in everything. I
don't want to listen to you. So you'd better get up!"

Frank propped his chin on his hands. "And suppose I
don't?" he teased her.

She hesitated before going from their bedroom into
the kitchen. "You know"—she turned to him, her voice
pinched and complaining—"I wish we didn't have to
live here. Why can't Momma and Poppa find a better
place for us to live? They're both working and we could
afford the rent."

Frank swung his legs off the bed and stretched.

"Where the hell's my cigarettes?" he said before answering her. "Because, dope"—he tapped a cigarette out
of the pack and reached for his trousers which hung

15

across the back of the chair near his bed—"you can't find any place to live. We're lucky to have what we got."

"You shouldn't smoke before you wash your teeth," Alice went on.

"For chrissake"—Frank jammed the cigarette into the full ash tray that stood on the night table—"who the hell is asking you? Who the hell are you to tell me what to do, anyway? Remember, I'm older than you are. I'm sixteen."

"So what?" Alice retorted before she entered the bathroom.

"So plenty," he replied sullenly. "Oh, go on"—he gave her his spitting look—"get dressed."

"I wish we were still on relief," his sister said. "Then Momma would be home."

"Get dressed!" he yelled at her.

Alice slammed the door of the bathroom and Frank went back to his bed. She didn't know what she was saying. Just a kid who was always getting upset about not having her mother and father at home. But what the hell, they were both working and making good money, and once they completed forty hours and reached the overtime and the Sunday work, the pay checks were really something. So suppose they weren't home for supper and he and Alice had to eat at the Chink's or the delicatessen or at Davidson's? He liked it better that way. He could order what he wanted without his mother yelling that he was mixing meat and dairy. And when he ate at Davidson's he could go to the bar and order a manhattan or a martini or some other drink that he had never thought he would ever taste. He had started at the top of the list and gone from an alexander to a zombie. The zombie really had potted him, but the guys on the corner told him that he was funny as hell. Most of the guys who were members of the Amboy Dukes ate at Davidson's and the Yat Chow Inn, and it was a lot of fun. But what Frank liked best was that he did not have to carry his lunch along to school. Now he was able to walk into the cafeteria and order anything he wanted, purchase what pleased him, and if he wanted to eat two or three desserts he was able to buy them.

16

"Hurry up in there," he shouted to Alice. "If I'm going to go to school I don't want to be late."

"I'll be out in a minute." Her voice was muffled. "Are you going to make breakfast?"

"Sure, kid," he said and went to the icebox, knelt down to draw out the large pan filled with water, and carefully spilled the water into the sink. Then he opened the upper door of the icebox and groaned. The ice had melted down until there was only a small cake left, and now he would have to go for ice. Even the iceman was working in a war plant. "What do you want for breakfast?" he shouted again. "We've got eggs and sour cream and some cottage cheese. You want to eat that?"

Alice opened the bathroom door and came into the kitchen. She wore a neat plaid skirt and was drying her face. "We've got milk?"

"Yes."

"Then I'll eat a scrambled egg and some cottage cheese and sour cream and milk and cookies."

"You'll get fat if you eat all that." Frank laughed.

"I hate to eat out. That's why I eat so much in the morning. I wish Mom were here to make me my lunch like she used to."

"Shut up!" Frank brushed past her. "When she was home we didn't have enough to eat. I'll be through in a minute."

Rapidly he washed his hands and arms and soaped his armpits. The room in which they slept was close and he wanted to be clean and fresh. Then he turned on the cold water and put his head under the faucet until the base of his neck was cold and tingling. Now he was wide awake. He plunged the comb through his long black hair and made a straight three-quarter part. Then he placed the towel on his head and pulled it back to flatten his hair, and with his hands he cupped his hair behind his ears until the duck tail was prominent.

The first and most lasting impression of Frank's appearance was one of sullenness. His face was a bitter challenge, a pugnacious invitation to attempt to kick him, and in his slight, medium frame there was the hardness of bone and muscle which is the heritage of those

17

persons who do not succumb to the threadbareness of poverty and the hunger of their watered meals. Frank had fought with the desperation of a small boy who hungered to stay alive, and as the chemistry and physiology of the body built up tissue and bone and blood to combat illness, so did it fortify Frank's sullen spirit.

Frank looked at himself approvingly in the mirror. All right. No pimples or blemishes, and since he had shaved Saturday night, his face was still smooth and clean. He was lots luckier than Black Benny, who had to shave every day and had a faceful of blackheads.

"Get out of here," he said to Alice as he entered their bedroom. "I want to get dressed."

"Shall I turn on the radio for you?" she asked him.

"Sure," he said. "And look. Get my books together. I don't know which ones I have to take to school today. So get them all together and I'll be able to pick out what I need. Hurry up. Then I'll get breakfast started."

He opened his bureau and took out a white undershirt with short sleeves. Across the chest of the shirt was printed a crown, and underneath the crown Amboy Dukes. They were nice shirts, and Frank had a dozen of them. All the boys who were in the gang wore them, and later on when it became warmer they'd wear them without regular shirts. Then he examined the blue button-down oxford that he had worn on Sunday and decided that he could wear it for another day. He put on his shirt and then picked out a pair of blue-and-yellow-plaid socks and his cordovan shoes. A few strokes of the shoe brush made the shoes gleam, and then Frank yanked his light brown herringbone tweed suit from the closet. He really was going to knock them over today. Since he was wearing his cordovan shoes he'd wear his cordovan belt. Then he snapped his key chain to a belt loop, gave the chain a couple of twirls, and winked at himself in the dresser mirror. He caressed his cheeks with his right hand and squinted at his tie rack before he chose a matching blue knit tie. Dexterously he made a loose knot that fitted neatly under his collar, smoothed a stray strand of hair into place, and went into the kitchen. He

18

had to get Alice out of the house before he could continue dressing.

"Come on," he said to her. "Get the tablecloth and let's get started. And read me Pop's note while I'm making the eggs. And get the cream and cottage cheese out of the icebox. But first read the note."

Alice picked up the three dollar bills and the two quarters from the kitchen table and read the note which was lying under the money. "Poppa says that he and Mom'll be working late tonight and that we should eat out. As if we don't all the time."

Frank moved the eggs around in the frying pan to keep them from sticking. "Shut up and read."

"They said you should do your homework and not come home too late and that you should be sure to get some ice. And I should dust."

"For crying out loud." He scooped the scrambled eggs onto two plates. "Look, kid, there's three and a half dollars there. I was going to take two dollars and give you the rest. But I've got some money. So you go to the ice dock, get one of the kids who has a wagon, and give him a dime for carrying it upstairs. So I'll give you the two bucks and you'll come out ahead of the deal. How about it?"

"Won't you be coming home right after school?" she asked him.

"No."

"Where're you going?"

"None of your business!"

"I was only asking you."

"So I'm only telling you. You want the two bucks?"

Alice held out her hand. "Give it to me."

They finished their breakfast, and Frank told her to leave and he would do the dishes. As soon as she left the apartment he rinsed the dishes and put them on the washtub to dry. The flat certainly was getting dirty. The windows hadn't been washed in months, and the rooms were full of dust and fuzzy-wuzzies. No question about it, it was a dump. He looked at the alarm clock. Eight-twenty. He'd have to step on it. Frank made certain that the door to their apartment was locked, and then he opened the bottom

19

drawer of his dresser, reached back under a pile of under-wear, and removed a small metal box which he opened with one of the keys on his chain. He took out a packet of three Ramses and put them in his pocket, placed three reefers in his cigarette case, and removed his homemade pistol and five .22-caliber shells.

Frank hefted the gun in his hand. He had made the grip and stock in his manual-training class at New Lots Vocational, and he had sanded and stained the stock dark mahogany. The stock had been drilled through from end to end, and a five-and-a-half-inch piece of steel tubing with a three-eighth-inch bore had been inserted into the stock. Frank had removed the trigger and firing-pin assembly from a cap pistol, and he had filed the cap detonator to a sharp point, so that it now served as a firing pin. When he pulled the trigger a strong rubber band jerked the firing pin against the cartridge. The revolver was loaded through the muzzle, and there was no accuracy, but it could send a bullet a couple of city blocks. Frank's gun was one of the best in the Amboy Dukes. He squinted along the barrel before he placed the gun in his right hip pocket. The cartridges he dropped into the pocket that held the Ramses.

For the last time he stood before the mirror and adjusted his hat. Alice had piled his books on the night table, and he took two of them at random because he wasn't going to school. As he walked down the dark narrow steps of the tenement he felt as he always did. That he was in a prison and walking to his freedom, but instead of walking up to the light he was walking down. He passed the doors on the landings with their dirty opaque glass panels and ducked as he passed the electric-light fixture which hung awry and looked as if it might at any moment tear away from the ceiling. It was good to get out on the street, and he hurried up to the corner of Amboy and Pitkin because he saw two of the boys there. One was Black Benny, who went to Vocational with him, and the other was Moishe Perlman. Moishe worked in the Todd Shipyard in Red Hook and between being a calker, second class, and manipulating a hot pair of dice, he was making more than a hundred bucks a week. Frank envied him.

"Walkin' to the station with us?" Moishe asked Frank.

Frank looked at Black Benny. "Not going to school?"

"Want to go to the Paramount?" Benny replied. "They've got a good picture."

"Sure." Frank laughed. "We haven't cut school for a couple of days."

"I don't know why the hell you guys are wasting your time in school," Moishe said as they walked along Pitkin Avenue to Saratoga. "Why don't you get your working papers and make yourselves some real dough before the Army gets you?"

"I'd like to," Frank said, "but my old man won't let me. He wants me to get my diploma, and now he's even talking about my going to college."

"College!" Benny punched him in the ribs. "He must be nuts!"

Frank hit him over the head with his books. "Shut your hole about my old man. He's a hell of a lot smarter than you."

"I didn' mean nothin'."

"All right. Just watch your mouth."

Moishe began to run. "The bus is coming. Hurry up."

They pushed onto the bus, and Frank watched Black Benny and Moishe get a nice-looking broad between them and give her a rub. Moishe and Benny hemmed the girl between them, skillfully pocketing her and preventing her escape. In her eyes there was loathing and fear of the two hoodlums, who did not look at her but nevertheless pressed against her lasciviously, pinioning her against their rigid hot bodies. Moishe pushed against the girl's buttocks, thighs, and legs while Benny pressed against her stomach and breasts. The girl wanted to scream, to cry out, but she did not dare, for innocence shone in the eyes of Black Benny and Moishe, between whom no sign of recognition had passed, and she feared to create a scene. Frank watched them, the snicker of a dirty smile playing about his lips. As the bus lurched to a stop at Livonia Avenue, Benny fell forward against the girl, and his free hand, seemingly by accident, passed across her breasts.

The boys did not speak to each other until they stood at the station waiting for the New Lots train.

"She wasn't bad," Moishe said.

Frank laughed. "You sure gave it to her good. She didn't know what to do."

"That's a good way to start the morning," Moishe agreed. "And I've picked up a couple that way."

"Should we do it some more?" Benny asked him.

"No," Moishe said. "We'll talk."

As the train rocked through the tunnels toward Manhattan they stood in the vestibule of the subway car and spoke in low voices about Lenny Assante and the counterfeit gasoline coupons some of the boys were selling for him. It was an easy way to pick up some money.

"Hell," Moishe said, "he sells you A coupons that are so good that even the OPA can't tell them, and all he asks is twenty-five bucks for a hundred. Then you can sell them easy, for fifty or sixty cents apiece, and you make twenty-five. People'll rather buy the coupons than pay sixty cents a gallon without a coupon. I've been selling some down at the yard and they're going fast."

Benny looked at Frank. "How about it?"

Frank shrugged his shoulders. "Where can we sell them?"

"How about the poolroom?"

"No good," Frank said. "Then some of the guys'll want to get cut in on it."

"Let's think it over," Benny said to Moishe. "We've got to figure the angles. If we can get rid of them we'll buy some. How about selling me some for my brother's car? He doesn't mind my using his car, but he doesn't want me to use his gas. This way, if I give him some coupons, he won't bitch so much."

Moishe told them to hold his lunch and extracted a little booklet from a pocket of his denim shirt. He passed three coupons into Black Benny's hand. "I'm giving you these at a bargain price. One buck."

Benny gave him a dollar. "You're a white guy, Moishe. Thanks."

"That's all right."

"We'll let you know," Frank called after Moishe as he left the train at the Atlantic Avenue station.

Moishe waved to them.

Nevins Street was the next station, and Benny and Frank went up to the street and into Bickford's for a second breakfast. They had almost thirty minutes before the theater opened, and they sat at the white marble-topped table sipping their coffee and looking out of the large plate-glass windows of the restaurant. Flatbush Extension and Fulton Street were full of people and traffic, and Frank decided that this was a hell of a lot more fun than sitting over the drawing board at Vocational and making three perspective drawings of cones. School was a lot of crap, Benny agreed, but what the hell could you do when your old man and your old lady insisted that you get an education? Frank winked at some trim-looking kids who passed the restaurant, and two of them turned around and motioned for Frank and Benny to come along with them.

"Let them alone," Benny said as Frank started to stand up. "We can pick them up easy in the show. This way we've got to pay for their tickets."

"But they were nice-looking."

"The hell with that." Benny pulled a paper napkin from the container on the table and wiped his lips and hands. "You can't see them in the dark."

"Give me the checks," Frank said. "I'll treat."

Benny nodded. "Anything you say, sport."

For three and a half hours they sat in the Paramount balcony with the two high school babes who were also on the hook. First Frank necked with one of the girls, then he swapped with Benny. He liked Benny's babe better. She didn't kiss as wet and she smelled cleaner than the one he'd first had.

"Suppose I call you up," Frank asked her. "Will you meet me?"

"Sure," she said. "We can go dancing."

"That sounds pretty good." Frank's hand slipped into the neck of her blouse, but she moved away from him.

"Only on the outside," she whispered into his ear. "I don't like to get mussed up in the movies."

"And after we go dancing, then what?" he asked her.

"We can go to the movies." She giggled.

"Hell no." He shook his head "I can see the movies alone. I don't need any help."

She pressed his hand down on a breast. "I'm only kidding you. We can go anyplace you say."

23

"Down my club?"

"All right with me." She nodded.

"Look, babe," Frank said to her. "I'm a square guy. If you go out with me you've got to come across. I'm one guy that don't like passion cramps."

"I won't give you any, honey," she whispered to him. "Now be a nice guy and sit still and let me watch the show."

"Last kiss." Frank bent forward again. "I like you swell, babe."

The girl slid low in her seat and placed her head on Frank's shoulder. "I like you too." She placed his hand on her breast again and held it. "Now let's see the show."

It was half-past one when they walked out of the lobby into the street, and the bright warm sun made them blink. They stood in front of the theater, and now that Frank could see the girl he'd been necking he was glad he had swapped with Benny. She was about sixteen and wore high-heeled shoes with Betty Jane straps that came across her ankles, and the hem of her gray flannel skirt was above her knees. She had nice legs and she knew it. She wore a red blouse open at the collar, and Frank could feel himself getting warm when he imagined what it would have been like if she'd let him give her a real feel. The gray flannel jacket was so long that it almost reached the hem of her skirt. When she laughed her teeth showed white and even, and her lipstick was put on in a heavy carmine smear. She was a smooth-looking kid, fast, certain, sure of herself.

"Come over here." He pulled her to one side. "I want to write your phone number in my book."

"I'll give it to you when we get a soda."

"Sure," Frank said. "Hey, Benny, let's take the girls in for some sodas."

"Sure," Benny agreed. "Let's go."

Frank was glad they had someone to kid around with so that the time would pass more rapidly. The only thing he didn't like about going on the hook was that after he came out of the show he didn't know what to do or where to go. It wasn't any fun going to the poolroom in the afternoon because there wasn't anyone around. Frank could remember when he was a kid they would hardly ever let him into the poolroom, that the tables were always crowded. Any

24

time he would peek through the doors of the poolroom on Sutter and Hopkinson, there would be guys shooting a game and sitting around gabbing. And over at Beecher's Gym on Rockaway Avenue there was always a crowd to watch Bummy Davis work out. But now the poolrooms were crowded only at night. Everyone was out working or hustling, so it wasn't any fun to go to Katzie's in the afternoon. But sitting in Childs' with the two babes and kidding around and telling dirty jokes made the time pass so fast that it was almost four o'clock when they left the babes, after promising to call them up that night so they could make a date to see them the next day.

"Boy"—Frank rubbed his hands—"we're sure going to have a time with them tomorrow."

"I shouldn't have swapped with you," Benny said. "You got the better-looking babe. Aw, what the hell, Frank, you always get the better-looking women."

"Cut it out." Frank was embarrassed.

"Honest," Benny said, "I'm not sore. They're both all right. I'm going to ask my brother for the car tomorrow night, and we'll take them for a ride and then we'll take them over my house and we'll have a party."

"What about your folks?"

"They're on the swing shift this month. My brother Sam'll get home about midnight, but he's regular. If we get in we'll fix him up too."

"Must we?" Frank asked.

"Sure," Benny said. "Aw, what the hell, Frank, I'll fix him up with my babe. So stop looking as if I stepped on your feet."

"You're one swell guy, Benny," Frank said appreciatively. "One swell guy."

"So"—Benny tweaked Frank's cheek—"maybe you wanta kiss me to show your appreciation?"

Frank pulled away from him. "Stop clowning and let's get on the train."

They walked from the station on Saratoga Avenue and stopped to look into Davidson's Restaurant. None of the guys were there yet.

"I want to go home and drop off these books," Frank said. "Then I'll meet you on the corner at six. No, wait. I wanta eat with my kid sister. She gets sorta lonesome and she's upset today."

"What's the matter?" Benny wanted to know.

"Nothing. Something that happened this morning. You know how kids are."

"Then I'll see you down the club?"

"Sure. About eight-thirty."

As soon as Frank turned the corner from Pitkin into Amboy he stopped whistling. There it was. That dirty, stinking block. The ugly gray and red tenements, tombstones of disease, unrest, and the smoldering violence which has its birth in misery, were crowded close together and rose straight up on both sides of the street to shut off all but a narrow expanse of sky. It was as if nothing bright would ever shine on Amboy Street. Each tenement had before it a rusting iron fence against which leaned the twisted and dented garbage cans, and paper bags of refuse were piled against the cans. Women and children flanked the entrances to the tenements, and when Frank saw Alice talking to some girls on the stoop he motioned for her to follow him upstairs.

"You're waiting long, kid?" he asked her as he looked into the icebox and saw that Alice had got the ice.

"I stayed in school for a little while and then I went over to the weaving class at the Center."

"What're you making?"

"Baskets."

Frank laughed. "You like to do that?"

"I guess so."

"You're sort of lonesome, aren't you, kid?"

"No."

"Well, it's better for you to go to the Center," Frank said righteously. "I saw you talking to that stinker Fanny Kane. That kid's got ideas that're too old for her."

The color crept into Alice's face, and she didn't look at her brother as she spoke. "I'm not friends with her. She just came over to talk to us."

"Well, just see that you stay away from her. And another thing. When you get a kid to bring the ice up here don't shut the front door."

"I won't."

"All right then," he said to her. "Get washed and then we'll go out to eat."

While Alice was washing he thought about Fanny Kane. Too bad she was only twelve, for her face was wise and her eyes were knowing. If she were a year older he might've given her a break. But for a twelve-year-old kid she had plenty and she looked like she was willing to pass it out. What the hell, sometime when he didn't have anything to do and if he met her in the movies or some place he might get her to come down to the clubroom and then he'd see how far the kid would go. But he didn't want Alice fooling around with a kid who was definitely jail bait and on the make. If that happened, then he'd have to start watching out for her because he didn't want anyone talking about his sister. That bastard Crazy Sachs.

"Hurry up," he called to her. "I haven't got all night. And I want to wash."

Alice opened the door. "I'm finished. Oh yes, Frank. Mr. Alberg asked for you."

"Who's he?"

"You remember him. He's the gym teacher at the Center. He asked for you and told me to invite you to come down."

Frank wasn't interested. "Tell him I'll come around someday."

"He's very nice."

"I know. But come on. We've gotta eat, and it'll be crowded as hell when we get to the delicatessen. Delicatessen all right with you?"

"I suppose so."

At the delicatessen Frank looked quizzically at his sister. He wished that she didn't make him feel like such a heel. It wasn't his fault that their mother and father were working overtime, and she was too young to understand that it was the overtime that really counted. If his mother got sixty-five cents an hour for packing ammunition, it wasn't a hell of a lot. But when she got into the overtime and started to get ninety-seven cents an hour or if she worked on Sunday and got a dollar and thirty cents an hour, that really was money. And all this moping around about not eating home and not being able to have the folks at home

27

was damned inconsiderate of the kid. But then, he figured, she didn't know any better. She had been too young to remember. He wished he could forget.

"You've got to stop potting around, Alice," he told her. "I know it's tough on you and even on me, being alone so much. But if Mom and Pop don't make the dough now, who knows"—he shrugged his shoulders—"after the war's over there might be another depression and then things might be tough again. So this way they're making money and we'll have some left if times get tough. Gee"— he shook his head—"you're too young to remember what things were really like."

"I remember," Alice said slowly. "I remember when we were on relief."

"You can't remember, and I don't want to talk about it," Frank cut her short. "Finish your pie and I'll walk you home. Do your homework and go to sleep."

"Did you do your homework?" she asked him.

"I didn't have any." Frank thought that was funny and he had to smile. "I didn't get any homework today."

Fanny Kane was still hanging around their stoop when Frank said good night to Alice, and he could tell by the way she looked at him that she would give anything if he'd invite her to the Amboy Dukes. As he walked toward Pitkin Avenue he felt her eyes upon him, and consciously he swaggered a little, for he was a Duke, and the Dukes were tops.

The Amboy Dukes had clubrooms on East Ninety-third Street in East Flatbush. Above the entrance a small electric yellow-and-gold sign winked Amboy Dukes. To the right of the entrance door was a little room in which were located the meters of the house and which the Dukes used as a checkroom. The main room had a hardwood floor and was furnished with old secondhand nondescript sofas and easy chairs, a radio-victrola, some end tables loaded with ash trays, and floor lamps in which the dark red and blue bulbs made the dimness in the room a guarantee of privacy. At the far end of the room was another door which led into the small kitchen and toilet, and a closet in which the Dukes kept two folding cots. The club was similar to the dozens of other clubs in East Flatbush, and its purpose was certain and precise.

On any night there would be some of the boys in the clubroom, and one or two of them would be standing out front on the sidewalk to pick up the girls who regularly walked through the streets of the neighborhood looking for a place where they could meet some guys and dance. The Amboy Dukes were lucky, for they had a reputation as a sharp bunch of guys, and a string of steady girls came around in the evening for the dancing and necking. The Dukes had three rules which their members had to observe: they had to pay their dues promptly, be ready to fight for one another at any time, and stay out of the clubroom if they were stag. Stags could hang around the kitchen or sit on the bench in front of the basement steps which led to the clubroom until they picked up a date. Then they could enter, dance if they wanted to, or they could sit in the large chairs or sofas and neck. Each of the Dukes was an expert at minding his own business, and no one muscled in on another guy's date. The Dukes was a good club to belong to, and all the members knew it.

They realized it most when the Dukes threw a party. Then there was a band, guests from other gangs, maybe a real grown-up mobster and his date, and lots of babes who flocked to any dance the Dukes gave. The lights were still dim and private, but there wasn't any rough stuff. Any guy who became drunk and started a fight got a fast deal and was thrown out.

The only time when girls were not welcome at the club was during the meeting night, which was held every two weeks, and when the Dukes were lining up one or two girls on the cots. Before the meetings the members changed the bulbs in the floor lamps and later the boys played poker and pinochle. A case of beer would be brought in and the Dukes would have a good time without being bothered by babes. On the evenings when the boys would have a couple of amateur sluts or a professional at the club the sign would be cut off and the cots set up in the kitchen. Then the boys were not permitted to drink, nor were they allowed to have any visitors. The blue and red bulbs were in the lamps, and the kitchen was in total darkness.

As Frank walked along Ninety-third Street he could see the sign in front of their clubroom winking invitingly at him, and then it went out. Frank increased his gait and took the eight steps to the basement two at a time, knocked on the locked door in code, and the door was opened slightly.

"It's me, Frank," he whispered.

"Come in," Crazy Sachs said. "We've got a hooer in the back."

"I saw the sign go out."

"We just got her here."

"She ever been down before?"

"No," Crazy replied. "Two of the boys picked her up in Davidson's. She's about thirty. A regular bum."

"Ah," Frank sniffed, "she doesn't sound so hot."

"She's all right," Crazy said. "And all she's asking is a buck apiece."

Frank walked over to one of the sofas and flopped into the cushions. He took one of his reefers from his cigarette case and lit it. The boys weren't doing much talking, and one of them would walk into the dark kitchen as one of them came out. Frank wished he hadn't come down to the club. Maybe he should've stayed home with Alice or even taken her to the movies instead of sitting around and waiting for his turn. He never enjoyed paying for it, and so many guys ahead of him dulled his appetite.

Black Benny came out of the kitchen and Frank called him over.

"How was she?"

"So-so."

"Worth a buck?"

"Depends how you feel."

"What the hell makes you so fussy?" Crazy butted in.

Frank took a deep drag on the reefer and let the smoke drift slowly out of his mouth. "Get away from me," he said to Crazy.

Crazy spit on the floor and cursed him softly as he walked to the kitchen door and listened. "Hey, guys," he whispered to the room, "what d'ya say we all give the bum a lay and then we'll take back the money?"

Larry Tunafish, who was sitting in one of the dim recesses of the room, laughed. "You're nuts, Crazy."

"No, honest," Crazy insisted. "It'll really be good."

"Suppose she gets some gorillas to come down and clean us up?" Larry asked him.

"Forget it." Crazy walked toward him, his hands shaking with excitement. "We've got plenty of protection. She's just a bum, and I'll tell her I'll cut her up if she ever opens her mouth."

The boys sat tensely on the chairs and sofas, tasting and savoring Crazy's suggestion, seeing it in its rottenness but enjoying the thought of the whore deprived of her money. They had never done anything like it before, and it sounded like a good idea, except that it had been proposed by Crazy. The boys always thought over carefully anything Crazy suggested, and most of the time they did not listen to him, for Crazy was a right guy who was a little soft in the head and too ready to use a knife on a guy. In fact, some of the boys weren't too happy about having Crazy in the Dukes because sometimes he acted too nutty to suit them. Crazy walked with a stoop, and his black wiry hair grew out of a broad flat skull. His ears stuck out like the ears of a cup, and his face was dull. His eyes mirrored his helplessness and bewilderment at a world that read a newspaper with ease, wrote rapidly with agile fingers, and reasoned in a matter of seconds. But constant torment, jeers, and gibes had made Crazy dangerous, and within him there always smoldered a fury that changed him from a dull boy to a dangerous, maniacal street fighter. But this was a good idea, even for Crazy, and now they waited for the club president, Larry Tunafish, to make up his mind.

"How about it, guys?" Larry asked them.

"I'm in on it," Black Benny said.

"You, Frank?" Larry asked him.

The reefer was making Frank feel dreamy. "Anything you guys say."

Just then the kitchen door opened and one of the boys told Crazy to go in. Crazy giggled stupidly, made a slugging motion with his right fist, and passed through the door.

"Who hasn't gone in?" Larry asked the room.

"I haven't." A voice from one of the sofas spoke.

"Me too."

"Frank." Black Benny spoke.

"I don't want to," Frank said.

"Why?" Benny asked him.

"I just don't want to!"

"Frank's high," Benny said to the room.

"All right." Larry spoke decisively. "After you two guys get through we'll give her a deal. Mitch," he said to one of the boys, "get the bright bulbs out of the checkroom and start putting them in the lamps."

Now the boys were feeling good and they were impatient for the last two Dukes to finish with the whore as they waited in the bright room for her to dress and come out of the kitchen.

As she opened the door and came into the clubroom she blinked. She was closer to forty than thirty, and her dyed red hair was black at the roots. Her face was full, tough, and stupid, bruised by drink, dope, and the many beatings given her by pimps, and her eyebrows had been shaved off and replaced by two thin penciled lines. The plaid of her cheap suit did not match at the seams, and she carried a black shoulder bag. Already she showed signs of physical decay and the taint of disease which would finally kill her. She looked around and tried to grin at the boys who sat and stared at her.

"Well, boys," she tittered nervously, "everybody happy?"

"So-so," Black Benny said.

She tugged at her skirt. "Well"—she cleared her throat which was heavy with phlegm—"you can't please everybody."

"That's what we like about department stores," Larry said to her.

"What?" she asked him.

"That you can return the merchandise and get your money back."

The whore became uneasy. "What the hell are you guys talking about?" she asked them, and began to walk to the front door. Then she stopped as she saw Crazy push one of the large chairs in front of the door and sit down in it. "Let me out." Her voice became shrill.

"When you give us back our dough," Crazy said.

"Get out of my way." She stood in front of Crazy.

Crazy put his foot in the pit of her stomach and kicked her into the middle of the room. As she reeled backward on her high heels she screamed and collapsed, with her skirt above her thighs.

None of the boys spoke as she sat on the floor and sobbed. "Let me out of here, you dirty bastards," she wept.

"When you give us our dough," Larry said.

She stood up and looked at them. "You dirty bastards!"

"You want a kick in the ass?" Crazy asked her.

"You'll get yours!" she screamed at him, her eyes wild with fright and fury. "You'll get yours!"

"Stop your yelling," Larry warned her, "before I tell Crazy to go to work on you."

Crazy stood up and walked toward her menacingly. She backed away from him toward one end of the room, and suddenly a hard slap on her buttocks sent her staggering forward toward Crazy. Crazy grabbed her by the hair and spit full in her face. Then he twisted her hair until she fell to her knees.

"You no-good hooer." Crazy spit at her again. "You're gonna give us our dough?"

"Let go of her," Larry said to Crazy. Crazy kicked her shin and she winced with pain.

Frank stared at the ceiling and tried not to be part of what was going on. The whole thing made him sick. Crazy spitting in the whore's face and the whore sitting limply in the middle of the floor, clutching her pocketbook while she wept. It stank. Not at all like the kind of thing the Dukes would do. But that's what came from listening to that bastard Crazy. The guys never learned.

"Give me a break," she sobbed.

No one answered her.

"Give me a break." She hiccuped as she sobbed. "I took on eleven of you guys and you're not giving me a break. Don't you guys ever give anyone a break?"

"Sure," Crazy said, "we'll break your ass if you don't give us back our dough."

"Shut up," Larry said to him. "Listen," he said to her. "We've got you, so better give it back."

"I'll give you back a quarter each." Her voice was thick with tears.

Larry shook his head. "All of it."

"A half buck each," she replied desperately.

"No."

"Ain't you guys got hearts? Give me a break!"

"No."

"Please!"

"Cut it out," Larry warned her. "We're not bargaining. Get it up."

She put her hands to her face and wept bitterly. Black Benny shifted nervously and nudged Frank. "I don't like it," he whispered.

Frank continued to stare at the ceiling. "I think we're being a bunch of jerks," he said with disgust.

"It wasn't my idea," Benny went on.

"Mine either."

"Well?" Larry's voice was frigid and hard, and the knife scar on his right cheek glowed red. "You made up your mind? I'm gonna give you another minute to make up your mind, and if you don't you're gonna get a beating."

"Can't I even keep five bucks? Please"—she stood up slowly and approached Larry—"give me a break. This is work to me. I spent a whole night here with you guys. I gave you boys a good time," she appealed to them; "give me a break. Please, give me a break." Her voice trailed off in a whisper.

Larry looked at the boys and saw they were disgusted. All except Crazy, who started to yell that they shouldn't let her get away. The whore saw they were wavering and continued to plead, crying and blubbering for a break. She approached each boy and begged for a break, asking each of them if he wanted his dollar back, but no one replied to her question. She began to weep again, and the boys were ashamed to look at her or one another. All except Crazy, for the boys accepted so few of his suggestions that he hated to have this one flop.

"Stop your bawling," Crazy warned her, "or I'll clout you one in the teeth." He shoved her against the wall to emphasize his threat.

34

"You're the only one who doesn't want to give me a break." She turned on him. "I'll bet it was your idea!"

"Shut up!"

"Amboy Dukes are supposed to be regular guys"—she wept and clutched her purse with both hands—"not a bunch of chiselers."

Unwittingly she had struck the responsive chord. Larry stood up and pulled the chair away from the door. "Go ahead," he said to her. "You can blow."

As she realized that she was free to go she stumbled forward and then turned and walked toward the kitchen. "I want to fix my face," she said hoarsely.

After she left the boys leaned back and relaxed. They were glad it was over and that they hadn't taken her money. It hadn't been such a good idea. Frank lit the third reefer. It took three of them now to make him feel real high, and as he took the first couple of drags on the opiated cigarette the comedy of the episode struck him and he began to laugh wildly, stamping his feet and beating one fist into the other. Soon some of the other boys began to laugh, partly at him and partly as a release from the tension, and the clubroom rocked with laughter as Crazy wallowed and slobbered on the floor in the middle of the room and imitated the pleadings and weepings of the whore. In his stupid, vicious, and pornographic way Crazy was obscenely funny, and the boys were limp from laughing. This was really some night.

Benny looked at his wrist watch and saw that it was past eleven. "You're coming?" he asked Frank, and stood up. "We're going home," he addressed the others. "Anybody coming?"

"I'll go with you!" Crazy shouted.

"Aw, balls," Frank muttered. "I've had enough of that jerk for one day."

Frank left the clubroom with Benny, Crazy, Mitch, Larry Tunafish, and Bull Bronstein. On Ninety-eighth and Rutland they stopped into Katz's Kozy Korner for sandwiches and coffee, and when they left the restaurant they walked under the elevated structure on Ninety-eighth Street to East New York Avenue. It was past midnight, and

Frank was coming out of the marijuana jag and feeling lousy. Crazy Sachs kept yelling and laughing, and nothing they said could shut him up. Sometimes Frank wondered why the hell he had to be a member of the Amboy Dukes, but then he remembered that Crazy was one of the best guys they had when they got into a fight. It really wasn't his fault that he was dumb and crazy. So crazy that he didn't graduate from public school and too dumb to be anything but a laborer on a wholesale meat truck.

The fresh night air was clearing Frank's head, and the fatigue of excitement was being replaced by the natural fatigue that came from getting up early and going to bed late. Now his head no longer felt as if someone were flying around in it, and things were beginning to look life size again. But as the shape and smell and feel of things returned to normal he found himself becoming more and more irritable. That was why when he saw the three guys pass them on the sidewalk he stuck his foot out and tripped one of them, because as they passed Black Benny and him he identified them as being spicks who probably came from Ocean Hill. They wore zoot suits and felt hats with shallow crowns and large exaggerated brims, and one of them had a key chain which dangled to his knees.

They stopped and waited for the boy who had been tripped to get up. Then Frank approached him and looked at him steadily, his eyes still glittering from the marijuana. "Why don'tcha look where you're walking?" he asked him.

The Puerto Rican boy smoothed his hair and dusted off his hat. "What's the idea tripping me?"

"Because I don't like you." Frank's face twitched. "I don't like the way you look."

"And I don't like the way you look," one of the other Puerto Ricans said to Frank.

"Shut your goddamn mouth," Larry Tunafish advised the stranger. "No one's asking you what you like."

Crazy Sachs pushed his way forward. "Where you from? Where you guys from?"

"Fulton Street."

"Fulton near where?" Crazy wanted to know.

"Near Stuyvesant."

36

"Ocean Hill jerks," Bull Bronstein observed.

"What the hell makes you Brownsville guys think you're so hot?" the fellow who had been tripped asked them. Then he realized he had made a mistake and he clamped his lips together. They were only three against five, and Bull Bronstein, squat and powerful, with a prominent jaw that set off the heaviness of his cruel lips, looked like the kind of slugger who could take care of two ordinary guys by himself. And the guy who kept jiggling and hopping around in that nervous shuffling way looked as if he were slightly nuts and a cutter. "We don't want no trouble," he said, and motioned for his two friends to start walking. But Bull and Mitch barred the sidewalk.

"Just a minute," Mitch said. "What the hell are you guys doing out here anyway? Maybe you were looking for a *shul* to chalk up with some swastikas?"

"We never done anything like that!" The third Puerto Rican, who had been silent, spoke.

"How the hell do we know?" Frank asked belligerently. "Maybe you're the guys who chalked 'Dirty Jew' and 'Jew Christ Killers' all over the shul on Douglass Street last week!"

"We didn't do nothing," the Puerto Rican said.

"Maybe you didn't, but maybe your gang did," Frank persisted. "What's the name of your gang?"

They were silent.

"Come on." Frank pushed the fellow he had tripped. "What's the name of your gang?"

"Yeah," Crazy added, "talk up!"

"The Sharpsters."

"I never heard of you," Mitch said. "You must be a bunch of heels. Why'd you guys chalk up the shul? You guys know I got a brother in the Army? You know he was wounded in the Liri Valley and is still in the hospital? How do you think he feels about you guineas coming into Brownsville and marking up our shuls?"

"We didn't do nothing." The second Puerto Rican tried to edge away, but Crazy blocked him.

"That's what you say," Black Benny said. "You look like the guys who must've done it. What the hell else would you be doing out here?"

37

"We're coming from a party in Canarsie. Honest."

"So why'd you go around chalking up shuls?"

"We didn't!"

Crazy Sachs approached them and grabbed one of them by the tie and yanked him forward. "You calling us liars?" The Puerto Rican struggled to break free, and Crazy hit him a short jab in the stomach that knocked the wind out of him.

That was the signal. Frank went for the fellow he had tripped and kicked him in the right shin. As the fellow winced and doubled up with pain Frank's knee caught him under the chin and he was knocked cold before he even hit the sidewalk. Then Black Benny kicked him in the face, and they turned to gang up on the other two boys, who were trying to defend themselves. Bull Bronstein was slugging one of them with looping roundhouse rights and lefts, and finally they were down, bleeding from their noses and mouths.

"You see, you bastards," Crazy panted, "what happens when you get tough! Now I am gonna finish you off!"

He drew his spring knife and approached one of them and jabbed him in the arm and ripped down. The boy screamed with pain, and Crazy kicked him in the face. Then he started to run and the Dukes ran after him.

"You stupid son of a bitch," Mitch said to Crazy, "what did ya cut him for?"

"Because he's a guinea and painted swastikas on shuls."

"Aw, shut up!" Mitch replied, and saved his breath for running.

They ran for a couple of blocks, and when they felt safe they turned back up Douglass Street to Pitkin Avenue. Crazy was walking in front and singing to himself, and every once in a while he would skip a couple of steps and shake his head. Then he walked along with one foot on the sidewalk and one in the gutter and told them that he was crippled. Frank turned away from him with repugnance and dislike.

"Boy," Crazy said as they stood on the corner, "we sure had us a time tonight. Getting laid and everything. Though we shouldn't have let her get away with the dough."

Frank looked at him. "Can't you stop talking?"

38

"What the hell's eating you?" Crazy replied. "I'm not botherin' you."

Suddenly Frank hit him flush in the mouth and knocked him to the sidewalk. Crazy was dazed and shook his head, but before he could get up Frank hit him another smashing blow in the jaw, and as he fell prone Frank kicked him twice in the kidneys. Crazy was through.

"That," Frank said to them, "is what he gets for fooling around with my sister."

"Did he do that?" Larry asked him quietly.

"The son of a bitch, he did. This morning the kid was looking out of the window and she was wearing her nightgown, and Crazy saw her and did something. He can't do that to my sister."

Mitch helped Crazy to his feet, and Frank turned to him. "I'm warning you," he said to Crazy, "if you ever bother my sister I'm gonna cut you into ribbons. Understand?"

Crazy rubbed his jaw. "You hit me when I wasn't lookin'."

"I'll clout you again, you goon." Frank drew back his fist, but Black Benny held him. "You just don't bother my sister. If I ever catch you looking at her I'll ruin you. I'm just warning you and I'm not kidding." Then Frank shook Benny's hands from his arm and walked down Amboy Street to his tenement.

He felt lousy. Almost one o'clock in the morning and his eyes ached and he didn't know how the hell he was going to get up in the morning, and he knew that Alice was going to wake him to go to school.

The hall was dark and the musty smell was more pronounced since the weather had become warmer. Slowly he climbed the steps to the third floor and quietly opened the front door to the flat. He took off his shoes, tiptoed into the kitchen, and gently shut the door. He stopped to listen to Alice's even breathing and quickly placed the gun, cartridges, and Ramses inside the pillowcase on his bed, where they would be safe until morning.

Frank stretched and yawned as he put on his pajamas and then he shook Alice gently.

"Wake up, kid," he whispered.

39

"Frank?" she whimpered.

"Ssh," he said. "Listen, Crazy Sachs'll never bother you any more. I just clouted him around and warned him to let you alone."

"You been fighting!"

"Naw." He laughed quietly. "He didn't even get a sock in. Now go back to sleep. Good night."

"Good night."

Frank started to get into bed and stopped. He went back to the kitchen, lit a match, and approached the kitchen table. In the center of the table lay another note and some bills and change. That meant they were working late again tomorrow. Poor kid, Alice, he felt sorry for her.

Chapter 3

Frank had every intention of going to school Tuesday morning until he descended the tenement steps and saw Benny sitting behind the wheel of his brother's convertible Dodge, grinning so that his mouth seemed to cover his whole face. Benny was pleased with himself, and as he pressed on the horn the clear golden notes were a call to freedom, to swift driving in the sun, away from the dull red walls of the school. The car was a smooth-looking job: light blue, red leather seats, white-wall tires, fancy fog lights, and all the other extras that Benny's brother Sam could buy. With Benny sitting behind the wheel of the Dodge and twelve gallons of gasoline in the tank that had been purchased with counterfeit coupons, school was out.

With much laughter they had driven around Prospect Park, lain on the grass to get an early sun tan, and lunched in the Canton Inn on Flatbush Avenue, where they were able to kid around with a couple of good-looking girls who went to Erasmus and who were so impressed by the blue Dodge that they asked Frank and Benny to telephone them soon. These girls from Flatbush in their tweed suits and small jaunty hats had class and assurance, and Frank told Benny that they would have to work them easy, but Benny laughed and told him that there wasn't any difference. Three or four stiff drinks would soften up any babe, and if she smoked a reefer, that was all. And if she didn't smoke, a couple of aspirins in a rum cola would send her rocketing to the moon.

In many ways Frank was still naïve, and the thought of getting a girl drunk or high made him squirm. But a guy couldn't get along by being soft, and if he didn't take advantage of the situation someone else would. And anyway, he thought, giving a babe a reefer wasn't bad. Hell, he smoked three a day now, though he wasn't going to smoke any more than that if he could help it. Some guys were so hopped up on tea they were rocking on their heels. Reefers were like drinking or getting laid or anything else that he got a kick out of. But no matter what it was, nothing was going to get the better of him.

It was almost three o'clock in the afternoon when Frank and Benny opened the door of the Winthrop Billiard and Recreation Parlor and greeted some of the Tigers who were shooting a game of rotation on the first table.

"H'ya, guys." Black Benny placed his hat on a hook. "Wanta see the car I'm driving?"

The Tigers crowded to the open door and whistled.

"That's a smooth job," one of them said. "Boy, with a load like that, would I have me a time."

"Yeah," another one agreed, "a babe would have to come across to ride in that car with me. I wouldn't bother with nothing else. How about it?" He turned to Benny. "It must be easy to get tail with that car."

"It belongs to my brother," Benny replied, "and he doesn't have any trouble. So I guess we won't have any."

"You mean to say you haven't broken that car in yet?" the houseman asked Frank. "You kids're slow."

"Look what's talkin'." One of the Tigers laughed. "Feivel couldn't get it up with splints."

"Shut your mouth, stinker," the houseman warned him, "or I'll nail it shut with my fist."

41

"I was only kidding." The Tiger chalked his cue nervously.

Feivel, the houseman, grumbled and went behind the sandwich-and-cigarette counter. Feivel was a former pug, a lightweight who had battled it out with Lew Tendler and Abe Attell, and he had been a first-rate drawing card in his day. Under the counter he kept a scrapbook bound in leather with his name tooled in the cover, and each page of the book was carefully sheathed with white celluloid covers which protected the clippings and pictures. The book was the most valuable possession Feivel had left, for his money had been spent as quickly and as violently as he had made it, and his last deal, buying a third interest in a summer hotel in the Catskills, had cleaned him. All he had now were his job as houseman, his cauliflower ears and broken nose, his precious scrapbook, the bitter memories of his former glory, and an insane temper. None of the Tigers or other guys who came into the Winthrop fooled around with him the way they did with other housemen, because Feivel could still hit, and his hands were tough and hard, although he was now a scarred and stitched caricature of the boxer he once had been. He was only five feet four inches tall, but when he bobbed and weaved around for the guys, jabbing an imaginary opponent with short solid lefts, he still seemed to have plenty on the ball. But the boys said that Feivel had no sense of humor, for he got sore if one of the guys even gave him a little hot-foot, so they left him alone and practiced their jokes on more affable and less dangerous subjects.

"We'll be calling those babes soon," Benny said.

"Right." Frank nodded.

"Where'll we take them?"

"Your house?"

"Sure." Benny slapped him on the back. "That's what I said we'd do yesterday. Come on, I'll shoot you a coupla games o' blackball."

Feivel racked up the ball and Benny gave him a dime for the first game. Feivel still was muttering and grumbling under his breath, and suddenly he turned to the two strangers who were playing on the table behind them and told them to stop making jump shots.

"Cut it out," he said to them. "For a lousy sixty cents an hour don't think you're going to tear the cloth."

"Aw, shut up," the first stranger said. He was about eighteen years old and with a long scar on his left cheek that extended from his forehead to his chin. Ignoring Feivel, he stood hard and compact as he bridged his hand on the table for high right English on the cue ball.

Feivel approached the table and confronted the fellow who had answered him. "All right," he said, "put your cue in the rack and blow."

The fellow held his cue tight. "The clock says we've got this table for another forty minutes. Now cop a walk, you're screwing our game."

The poolroom became quiet, and Frank placed his cue on the table and stepped back. These two guys didn't know who Feivel was.

"I'm telling you to get out before you get hurt," Feivel said to the first stranger.

"Come on"—his partner placed his cue in the rack— "let's go."

"No," his friend said.

Feivel raised his voice and clenched and unclenched his hands.

"I'm telling you to blow before you'll be sorry. Get out!"

"What's the matter?" the stranger asked him. "Are you supposed to be a hard guy?"

"Hey, buddy," Black Benny interrupted, "I wouldn't pick an argument with Feivel. He's tough."

"Is he?" The fellow looked mockingly at the irate houseman. "He looks like a punch-drunk pug to me."

"You bastard"—Feivel tensed—"don't you call me punch-drunk! I can still lick punks like you with both hands tied behind my back!"

"Take it easy, Feivel," one of the Tigers taunted him, "or you'll strain a gut."

"Shut up!" Feivel swung around and then turned back quickly to the stranger. "I'm giving you your last chance. Are you gonna get out or do I have to knock you around?"

"Why don't you guys go?" Frank said to them. "Go ahead," he said anxiously to the fellow who had hung up his cue, "get your buddy out of here."

"Come on, Lenny," the fellow said, "let's go."

"I'm staying." Lenny took off his wrist watch and dropped it into a trouser pocket. "Now"—he turned to Feivel—"you son of a bitch, let's see if you can do anything besides talk!"

Feivel spit on his hands and clenched them tight. "You asked for it, you bastard!" He hunched his left shoulder and tucked his chin behind it. Then he began to shuffle forward, moving his fists in small circles, moving his head in short arcs as he advanced toward Lenny. His eyes were narrowed and he flicked his nose with his right thumb, but there was no spring in his legs, no swiftness of movement, no hint of speed or sudden change of pace.

Lenny watched him circle about and waited for Feivel to rush him. When Feivel moved in Lenny danced aside and clouted him on an ear. With a roar Feivel came in for a clinch, but Lenny maneuvered away from him and ran toward the front of the poolroom where there was more space. Again Feivel rushed him, and Lenny side-stepped and Feivel ran into the wall. For a moment he hesitated, and in that instant Lenny hit him a chopping blow in the back of the neck. Feivel's head rammed into the wall, and when he turned around his nose was a bloody mess and pain made his eyes wobble.

Now the guys could see that Feivel was worried. He wiped his nose with his left hand, and the blood left a sticky smear on his cheeks and chin. Slowly he shuffled toward Lenny, trying to recall the skill which he had used more than twenty years ago when he had been good and could have killed a kid like this Lenny in less than one minute of the first round. As he inched in he realized for the first time that he wasn't the man who had battled it to a draw with Lew Tendler. The ease of movement, the artful co-ordination of mind, body, legs, and arms, the swift smile of confidence as he had moved about the ring, happy in the knowledge of his skill and the power of his right hand—all were gone. All he had been doing for the last ten or more years was to talk about how good he'd been and to drag out the old scrapbook and show it to people. That had been enough to keep people afraid of him. But he hadn't had a workout since he had tried to manage Young Lerner way back in 1933. Now he knew he was slow and through, and what hurt most was not that his nose kept dripping and that the back of his head felt as if it had been rammed by a pile driver, but that the kids in the poolroom, those snotty little Tigers, were watching him take a beating from a kid, and not one of them said anything or tried to stop it. They wanted to see him get a beating—he knew that—for now they saw that he was just a bag of wind, a guy with a big mouth, a punch-drunk pug, a has-been. And that was why he was going to be careful and try desperately to beat the hell out of this kid who stood facing him the way he used to stand a long time ago, waiting for a nervous kid who was new at the game to step in close or rush him. He had to beat this kid, and he wondered if he could. He had to beat this kid or he would never know another moment's peace in the poolroom.

"What're you waiting for?" Lenny taunted him. "Come on, I'm waiting."

Feivel did not answer him. Now he realized how the raw kids who came up against him must have felt. He moved in slowly, his left out and his right moving in a small circle. He tried a tentative jab, but Lenny blocked it easily. Feivel tried the jab again, and in his mind the signal of hope flashed an alert as he saw that the kid covered up all right but that he dropped his right hand just a little. Again the jab, and again the block, and now he saw that Lenny looked a little nervous. In another minute he would try an offensive of his own. Now the kid was set up—about four feet from the wall and with his back toward the telephone booth. Simultaneously, as Feivel shot the left jab and Lenny lowered his guard, Feivel threw his right and the blow caught Lenny in the pit of the stomach. As he involuntarily bent over from the pain and shock Feivel's hard left fist smashed into his jaw. Lenny straightened up, and Feivel's right catapulted into his face and he fell against the telephone booth, glanced off, and was met by two driving fists that hit him in the stomach and jaw. Sick and blind with pain, Lenny tried to cover up, but Feivel's fists kept driving him into the wall, tying him up, smashing him

45

in the stomach and ribs and face, nipping and tearing into bone and muscle and flesh. Lenny's eyes were puffed and he was almost blind, and now his head was rocking wildly as the fists kept piling into him. Feivel was transfigured. Now he knew it: he could still battle, still hold his own and beat hell out of the stinkers that came into the pool-room, beat hell out of the amateurs who hung around Beecher's, still have something real like his fists and the remnants of his skill, his knowledge of what to do and how to do it and how to find out what a guy was a sucker for. He could still battle, and now this was going to be it. The right cross had everything he had in it. It started from his hip as he shifted for the punch, went up through his shoulder and into his biceps and forearm, and exploded against Lenny's chin. Then he stepped back and watched the kid slump to the floor.

No one spoke, and as he turned around and looked at Lenny's friend the kid backed out of the door, with his lips quivering and his face and eyes filled with horror and nausea.

Then Feivel turned to the Tigers and Frank and Black Benny. "See," he puffed, "what happens when a bastard like one of you kids gets tough with me? You thought he had me," he puffed, and wiped his face. "You thought he had me! You thought I was through and that he was going to knock the crap out of me!" He leaned against the first table and breathed heavily with his mouth open. "You thought he had me." He laughed. "Now look at him! How does he look? Maybe one of you guys wants to look like him? Huh? Maybe? All right, you snotnose little bastards. You little sons of a bitching bastards who think I'm too old to do anything. All right. Maybe one of you wants to do something?"

"No one wants to do anything," Benny said softly. "We ought to clean that guy up. He looks bad."

"Sure"—Feivel nodded—"clean him up. But not in here!"

"Be a sport, Feivel," Benny said, "we'll take him into the toilet and clean him up."

Feivel clenched his fists and gritted his teeth. "No, you

won't. All of you"—he suddenly began to scream hoarsely —"get outa here! Get out before I kill you! Get him out too!" Feivel's voice broke and he gasped as if to keep from crying. "Get him out before I kill all of you!" Then he turned and stumbled toward the counter.

Silently Frank held the door open while Benny and the Tigers carried Lenny into the street.

"You guys better take him down to your club," Frank suggested.

"Maybe a drugstore would be better," Benny said.

"No. Because maybe the druggist'll call the cops and they'll nab Feivel," Frank reminded them.

"The son of a bitch deserves it," one of the Tigers who was helping to carry Lenny said. "He's crazy."

"But we don't call the cops, do we?" Frank asked sharply.

"No," the Tigers agreed. "We'll take him to our place and straighten him out." They turned to Benny. "Can we take him in your car?"

"Sure," Benny said, "if you watch out that he doesn't bleed on the upholstery. Load him in. Coming, Frank?"

Frank shook his head. "No. I'll see you later."

"Will you call the babes?"

"That's an idea. What time'll we pick them up?"

"Say nine o'clock. Then we can take them for a drive and over to my place."

"Hey," one of the Tigers interrupted, "let's get started."

Benny started the car with a roar, and Frank stood there until the Dodge turned the corner. Then he walked to the candy store on the corner and called the girls. His date had a nice voice over the telephone and said that nine o'clock was all right with her, and because he wanted to kill time he talked to her two nickels' worth. Then he hung up and strolled out into the late afternoon sunshine and headed toward Brownsville.

He had hardly spoken a word to Alice in the morning because his head was splitting, and he had yelled at her. Now he was sorry and he wanted to make it up to the kid.

She was really a good kid, not like Fanny Kane. He was sure to find her at the Center, and when he was directed to the basket-weaving room and saw Alice working on a red-and-blue basket he couldn't help but step behind her and kiss her on the cheek.

"Hello, baby." He smiled at her. "You're not sore at me?"

"No." She stood up. "Girls," she said shyly to the group who was looking at them, "this is my brother Frank."

"Not your boy friend?" One of the little girls giggled.

Alice blushed. "He's my brother!"

"I'm going to the gym," Frank said hastily. "Call for me when you want to eat."

Frank took off his hat and jacket and carefully placed the gun inside one of the jacket sleeves. Then he rolled up the sleeves of his shirt, took a basketball from one of the racks, and went out on the court. He wished he were wearing sneakers so that he could do some dribbling. It had been a long time since he had played any ball.

Poised at the foul line, he aimed carefully for the basket and was pleased when his first shot went through without touching the rim. He missed the second and third shots and then took careful aim and watched the ball drop through the hoop again. It had been at least a year since he had shot any baskets, and the knack was not easy to regain. Rhythmically he dipped and swung his arms upward and watched the ball sail in a true arc to the backboard and into the basket. More often now he was ringing them, and he was pleased with himself.

"That's pretty good shooting, Frank," a voice behind him said.

Frank flipped the ball upward and then turned around. Without looking he knew the ball was going through the basket. "Thanks, Mr. Alberg," he said.

"My name's Stan."

"O.K.," Frank said without smiling.

Stan Alberg bounced the basketball. "I haven't seen you in the gym for almost a year."

"I've been busy," Frank said.

"Too busy to come here for a workout? Or maybe you're going to another gym?"

Frank smoothed his hair with his hands. "No. I'm just busy."

48

"Oh."

"Maybe I'll start coming around again," Frank said. "I think I could use a workout." He walked to the bench and buttoned his sleeves.

"Sure thing," Stan said with professional heartiness. "We're trying to get some teams up. Softball and handball, and later on basketball. We could use you, and it would do you a lot of good. Why don't you get some more of the Dukes to come down?"

Frank looked at him suspiciously. "How'd you know I'm a Duke?"

Stan sat down on the bench and sighed. "You can't keep that a secret, can you?"

"They're a swell bunch of guys."

"I know."

"You don't think much of us?"

Stan shrugged his shoulders. "Don't get me wrong, Frank," he said quietly. "I don't think much of gangs."

"Maybe it's because you never belonged to one."

"I did"—Stan stretched his legs and placed the basketball between them—"but I got out. You ought to ditch the Dukes while you can. Do you want me to walk away while you put on your jacket?" he asked suddenly. "I guess you've got one of those homemade pistols in the jacket and I'm in your way."

Frank stared at him. He didn't know what to say or do or how far he could trust Stan Alberg. Stan was tall and slender with narrow shoulders, but his body was lithe and supple as a well-strung bow. He wore thick-lensed glasses that were firmly supported by his prominent nose, under which grew a thin brown mustache. His cheekbones were high and added to the sardonic twist of his lips. Stanley Alberg looked like, walked like, spoke like a scholar and, what was most surprising, was a scholar. But for years he had been unable to secure a teaching job. The civil-service lists of New York City had been jammed full of young men of similar accomplishments who had eked out a meager existence by working in temporary positions as ticket agents at the ferry terminals, as proctors of civil-service examinations, and as delinquent-tax investigators. Now he was at the Jewish Community Center on Bristol Street and feeling that he was doing a worth-while job. Every juvenile he was able to interest in the gymnasium was someone who made his day a success. It was a tough job to go out and drag the boys off the street corners and make them want to meet in the Center gymnasium instead of the poolroom, make them want to meet in the Center clubrooms instead of the corner candy store, and make them want to go out and recruit their friends to join the athletic teams instead of the gangs.

The neighborhoods of Brownsville, East New York, and Ocean Hill were infested with gangs. The Pitkin Giants, the Amboy Dukes, the Sutter Kings, the Killers, the D-Rape Artists, the Zeros, the Enigmas, the Wildcats, the Patty Cakes were just a few of the gangs that fought, slugged, and terrorized the neighborhood. They fought for the sheer joy of bloodying and mauling one another, and no insult was so slight that it could not be used as an excuse for a mass riot and free-for-all. Every day and night Stanley was faced by new problems of organization, but there was the belief that he was doing something worth while, and each member he gained for one of his teams and clubs was a personal victory.

One of Stanley's great problems was money. He needed money to purchase the athletic equipment which had become increasingly scarce since 1942, and he had to operate on the niggardly prewar Center budget which governed athletic activities. He pleaded with the superintendent in charge of athletic and club work but was always palmed off with the same excuse: the Board of Directors was doing the best it could; people were not contributing to the Center because they could see nothing but the opportunity to purchase luxury items for which they had starved for years. That was why the Center had to get along on its inadequate budget and why the juvenile predatory gangs of Brownsville and Williamsburg and Harlem grew larger and more dangerous. It made Stanley sick with anger, and once or twice he thought of quitting the job at the Center, but Reba, his wife, had asked him to stay, and he knew she was right.

Now he watched Frank squirm as the kid looked at his jacket and wondered what to do about the gun.

"Go ahead," he repeated, "put on your jacket. I don't care either way."

Frank slipped his arm into the sleeve and dropped the pistol into his jacket pocket, where it sagged and bulged. "So you know about these." Frank laughed nervously. "I bet you think you're a smart guy."

"No"—Stan shook his head—"not so smart. But smart enough not to carry one of those."

"Aw, they're nothing."

"I know."

"I wouldn't use one."

"I hope not."

"Don't you believe me?"

"Sure."

"You don't. And what the hell am I talking to you for anyway? You guys make me sick. That's why we never come around here. You're always trying to make us reform. What the hell have I got to reform for? I haven't done anything!"

Stan took a buttonhook out of his pocket and tightened the laces of his basketball. "If you haven't done anything, Frank," he said, "then why are you giving me an argument?"

Frank sat on the bench and stared across the gym. "You're a pretty nice guy, Mr. Alberg, but you still give me a pain."

"Everyone's entitled to his opinion, Frank. Listen"—he turned to him—"you're not a dope. Why don't you get smartened up? Give me the gun."

Frank stood up and backed away from him. "No! And I'm warning you, don't rat to the cops if you want to stay healthy."

"You'll take me for a ride?"

Frank picked up his hat and books. "Don't think it's funny. I'm just telling you."

"I heard you. And any time you want to get rid of that gun you can come down here and I'll take it. That'll always be a good alibi for you."

"Thanks for nothing."

"You're welcome. When'll I see you around?"

"Never."

"Come back whenever you like." Stan ignored the reply. "And if you want to come over to the house some evening just let me know. We always have some good cake around."

Without answering him Frank went back to the weaving room for Alice. Walking along Bristol Street with her toward Pitkin Avenue and over to Davidson's Restaurant, he was silent. Mr. Alberg had disturbed him. Maybe he was right about the gun. Hell, he never used it, and the thought of using it made him shudder. He didn't even like the idea of using a knife on a guy, and when he thought of Crazy cutting the spick the night before, he—well, he didn't like the idea of being a Duke. And now he had another worry on his head, because Black Benny had told him in the morning that he'd better watch out for Crazy, for Crazy was the kind of a guy who didn't come right back at you. Crazy just saved it up for a long time, and when you were least expecting it, zingo, he would sneak up and get in his innings. But still he didn't need to carry the gun. If Crazy came at him, a milk bottle or a brick would be all he'd need to polish off the bastard. The sooner he ditched the gun, the better.

"I want to stop in the house for a minute, Alice," he said to her. "You wait downstairs for me."

"I'll come upstairs and wash my hands."

"All right." There was no point in making her suspicious. "But hurry up. I've got a date tonight."

"Can't you break it?" She looked back at him as they climbed the narrow tenement stairs. "I'm lonesome."

"Tomorrow night, baby. You wouldn't want me to give the girl a stand-up, would you? When you get older you'll know what I mean."

"Is she pretty?"

"Not as pretty as you'll be when you grow up. Come on, open the door."

While she was in the bathroom he hastily placed the gun in the box and stuffed it back in his drawer. Now he was relieved. But he wouldn't tell Benny or the other guys because they would think he was getting soft, and a guy who was soft didn't rate with the Dukes.

The girls were waiting for them on the corner as they coasted the car to the curb, and Frank's eyes were happy when he saw Betty again. For she was as pretty and exciting as she had been the day before, and when she sat next to him and he put his arm around her she moved close to him, and his hand rested at the open V of her yellow blouse. Her fingers were slim and cool, and he felt wise and strong as he grasped her hand and pressed it gently. The car raced along Kings Highway, and he tilted Betty's head back and kissed her, a long lingering kiss to which she responded as his hand slid into her blouse.

"Gee," he sighed, "you're swell."

"I like you too," she whispered to him. She stroked his hair and lifted her lips to him again.

The night breeze struck them as the open car sped along the road, and the music coming from the radio was dreamy and pleasant. Again he kissed her, and now he could feel her body tense as she clung close to him, and he gasped as she bit him on the lip. Now he kissed her endlessly, one kiss blending into the next, and it seemed to Frank as if they were sitting on a cool wind that was blowing them farther and farther into the darkness, off the earth, out of the world, into space, where they raced with the speed of excitement and the wild, passionate tumult of youth and heart and blood. He cupped her cheek in his hand and looked down at her closed eyes. Then gently he kissed her on the forehead, and as her lips parted he kissed her again, and the wind blew soft and cool, and they were swept along in the night.

The tires screeched as Benny swerved the car around the traffic circle, and Frank was jolted back to reality.

"Take it easy," he shouted to Benny. "You want to wreck us?"

Ann twisted around in her seat. "He's a good driver, Benny is. I like the way he drives."

"Slow up." Frank ignored her. "And don't turn around to give me an argument while you're driving, Benny. Come on," he ordered him, "slow up."

"Anything you say, sport." Benny eased his foot on the accelerator. "How about you driving and giving me a chance to work my points in the back seat?"

"You go on and drive." Ann giggled.

"I'd rather be loving you," Benny insisted, and stopped the car. "Come on"—he opened the car door and stepped out—"swap."

Frank worked the gearshift and was glad he was able to start the car without jerking. The gears ground noisily as he shifted rapidly into high, and Betty snuggled down in the seat and leaned her head against his shoulder.

"I'd put my arms around you, honey," he said to her, "but this isn't my car."

"You certainly can kiss," she said.

He laughed. "You're not half bad yourself."

"Do you like me?" she asked him.

"And how! You're really something, Betty. You're"—he faltered for words—"honest, I don't know how to say it."

"Just kiss me," she said to him. "That's all the saying I want."

"No more?" His lips brushed her face.

"Don't ask me," she said, "and watch where you're driving."

Benny was wrestling his date in the back seat, and Frank heard the rough exchange of lines that meant only one thing: Benny was going to lay Ann, but not before she had asked him what made him so fresh and who did he think he was and where did he get the idea that he could mess her up and did he think she was a pushover and if he didn't cut it out she was going to walk home and why was he in such a rush and couldn't he wait until they knew each other better and she didn't like doing it in a car and honest, she wasn't a teaser, and she'd prove it when they went back to his apartment that night. He was glad he was driving.

The moon came up hot and orange, and Frank stretched out on the Manhattan Beach jetty and cradled Betty in his arms. The black waves with their white froth broke gently across the narrow beach and swirled in among the rocks. Across the bay the revolving searchlights of Floyd Bennett Field stabbed the darkness in wide circles of light, and the red signal lamps on the small craft winked and bobbed with the movement of the waves. Frank stared up at the moon as it climbed higher into the sky and faded from orange to white, and then he closed his eyes and was at rest. Betty lay close to him on the rough blanket, her right arm across his chest, her breathing soft and relaxed. There was no need to speak, to say anything, for they both understood. And as they lay there Frank resolved that things would be cleaner with Betty, with sharp incisive lines and no ragged edges of telling the guys or even Benny how he had made out. Some guys like Crazy Sachs or even Mitch or Larry Tunafish wouldn't understand how he felt, but it wasn't any of their business. Sometimes they were too damn smart for their own good, with their hooting and jeering at everything which did not conform to their brutal, vicious, mean gang-world, and tomorrow when he had a chance he was going to break up his gun and start going to school regular.

Betty moved gently and kissed him. "What're you thinking about, honey?" she asked.

"You. Us."

"I'm glad," she sighed. "I like you a lot."

"I like you too." He kissed her. "And I don't want you dating other guys."

"I won't, Frank."

Somewhere in the darkness they could hear Benny and Ann laughing and scuffling, and Frank smiled at Betty. "I guess they're going at it in a big way," he said.

"Your friend doesn't waste any time," she agreed.

"Maybe." He pressed her shoulder. "I don't know. I like you"—he rolled over and looked down at her—"and I'm in no hurry. I feel different about you," he added. "Understand?"

She stroked his hair with both hands and kissed him. "Yes. Now let me lie in your arms again. It's nice."

Offshore the waves rolled onto the narrow beach with a smooth hissing of water, and the moon rode through the April night white and serene.

Frank drove the car back to Brownsville while Benny continued to maul Ann in the back seat as he bragged about what a tough mob the Dukes were, until Frank told him to shut up before he put his foot in his mouth.

"Here we are." Benny stood up as Frank pulled the emergency brake. "I live here." He waved at the tenement. "It's a dump, but I don't pay the rent."

"Shut up." Frank handed him the car keys.

Benny looked at him quickly. "All right. Come on, let's go."

Frank watched Ann smooth her skirt, and he hated the way she waited on the sidewalk for Benny to take her upstairs and the way the lipstick was smeared on her face. "Give me the keys." He held out his hand. "I'm taking Betty down the club."

"Why?" Benny asked him. "Sam won't cut into our party."

Ann tugged at Benny's sleeve. "Who's Sam?"

"My brother. This is his car."

"You giving me the keys?" Frank asked sharply.

"Sure." Benny laughed. "We're wasting time. Just bring the car back in a couple of hours. Say about three o'clock, so I can take Ann home."

"I will. Come on, Betty." He turned to her. "Get in."

They drove up Pitkin Avenue, and as the car stopped for a red light she asked him, "We going down your club?"

"No"—he looked straight ahead—"I'm taking you home. And don't say anything."

He kissed her briefly as they stood on the sidewalk before her house. "I'll call you tomorrow," he said to her. "I haven't got a phone, so I'll call you about four. Good night, Betty."

"Good night." She returned his kiss. Then she ran lightly up the steps of the porch, turned to wave at him, and was gone.

Chapter 4

Mr. Bannon looked sharply at Frank and Black Benny as they entered the noisy classroom and found it difficult to control the rage which burned within him with a heat that left him choking and mad. He watched them swagger to their seats while they kidded with the other boys in the official class about deciding to give the school a break and about the swell picture they had seen at the Paramount. Young smirking wiseacres, he would have enjoyed beating each one of them with a baseball bat.

Mr. Bannon slammed down on his desk with an eighteen-inch ruler and the class was stilled. He surveyed the hostile faces that stared at him, and he hated every one of them.

"You"—he motioned to Frank and Benny—"come up here. Hurry!" he said as they shuffled slowly toward him. "Move as if it were three o'clock and you were hotfooting it to the poolroom. Quiet!" He hit his desk again with the ruler and cut short the ripple of snickers. "Now," he said to them. "Where've you been?"

"I've been sick," Frank said.

"And you?" Mr. Bannon asked Benny.

Benny clutched his stomach and rolled his eyes. "Me too. I got the crut."

The room exploded with laughter, and Mr. Bannon gripped the ruler until the steel edge cut into the palm of his hand. He smashed down on his desk with the ruler, and the force of the blow snapped the wood in two. The class rocked with laughter as his face flushed, and Mr. Bannon wearily passed both hands across his forehead in a gesture that was becoming characteristic of his impotence.

"Hey, Teach'," one of the pupils in the back of the room yelled at him, "you're a regular Samson."

"Quiet!" He flung the broken halves of the ruler into the wastebasket. It was no use. All his pedagogy was no damned use. How in the hell could he keep his temper when these little bastards made his life so miserable? Why couldn't he haul off and clout that smirking Benny Semmel in the mouth? But no, he had to use all the damned instructional tools and psychological approaches that were successful in the textbooks and were never designed for his official class at the New Lots Vocational High School. How in the world was he going to cope with a classroom full of bastards who didn't give a damn about school or what they were learning or him? And they were keen and caustic, knew how to get under his skin with neat precision; and co-operation, being square, playing the game, were words and phrases to which they responded with Bronx cheers. If only he could keep his temper, but it was no longer possible. This class was also his first class in mechanical drawing, and there were two more classes of M.D., where he had to devote more time to keeping an eye on the equipment than instructing the classes; then lunch, at which he had to spend thirty minutes policing the lunchroom and breaking up fights, then two classes of elementary principles of aviation, and finally it was three o'clock, and he could slump at his desk and wonder how in the world he was going to get through another day.

"Quiet!" he shouted again.

Frank swung around to the class. "Hey, bums," he shouted, "don't you hear the teacher? He wants quiet! Understand? *Quiet!*" he screamed hoarsely.

"Quiet!" the class roared back at him.

"That's enough out of you, Goldfarb." Mr. Bannon's voice trembled.

"I was only trying to help," Frank said innocently.

"Sure, sport," Benny agreed, "he was only trying to help. I'd help, too, but I'm still sick." He clutched at his stomach again and stuck out his tongue. "If you were regular you'd let me go home. I'm liable to die right in the class."

"I wish you would." Mr. Bannon bit off each word.

Benny moved his head in mock surprise. "Don't you like me, Mr. Bannon? Hey, guys"—he turned toward the class —"'Teach' doesn't like me! Now I ask you, is that gratitude?"

"No, Lord"—the class swayed in unison—"that ain't gratitude!"

"Is that religion?" he went on.

"No, Lord"—they chanted and clapped their hands—"it ain't religion!"

The class stamped and sang and paid no attention to Mr. Bannon's shouted orders for quiet, and as they realized intuitively that he had lost control of the class the bedlam and uproar became more wild and violent, more rowdy and gross. He looked at them furiously and rushed out of the classroom and to the office of the assistant principal.

"Mr. Hayes"—Bannon burst into the office—"do you want my resignation? Do you?" he fairly screamed.

Mr. Hayes teetered back in his chair. "What's the trouble, Bannon?"

"Trouble!" Bannon acted as if he were ready to plunge into insanity. "That's an understatement! I've got a classful of congenital hoodlums and they're completely out of hand! If you don't come back with me right now and straighten them out I'm resigning as of now. And look, Mr. Hayes," he interrupted, and his hands trembled, "don't tell me that I'm not a good disciplinarian and that this is my own fault. I'm not the only teacher in the same boat and you know it. You just let me take a couple of healthy swings at my pupils and I'll show you discipline!"

"You know we can't do that."

"I know," Mr. Bannon subsided weakly, "I know, but are you coming with me"—his inflection hardened—"or do I resign?"

Mr. Hayes sighed and stood up. "I guess so, but this is setting a bad precedent."

"I don't care what it sets." Mr. Bannon opened the office door. "Come on."

They could hear the class singing and hooting as they approached the room at the end of the corridor, but as Mr. Hayes entered the room the impromptu spiritual petered out to a low defiant undertone of murmurs and whispers.

Mr. Hayes wasted no time. "All of you," he began, "are suspended from school until you bring at least one of your parents. And if you don't have them here by Friday afternoon, which gives you practically three school days to get them here, I'll declare every one of you a truant. Mr. Bannon, you'll send me a list of all the pupils in this class so that I can check it personally, and I want you to mark each boy whom you believe to be a serious disciplinary case. Now you're dismissed. And any of you found loitering in the halls or the schoolyard will be turned over to the police."

"You mean we all gotta bring up our mothers and fathers?" someone asked.

"Yes," Mr. Hayes said, "and by Friday afternoon, or I'll turn you over to the truant officer."

"But my mother and father work," another boy protested.

"Mine too," Frank said.

"And mine."

"And mine," Benny said. "They'll be sore."

"You should've thought of that." Mr. Hayes was inexorable. "Now take your things and leave the building."

The boys filed out of the room silently. They had never expected that Mr. Bannon, the son of a bitch, would go for the assistant principal.

"I'm thoroughly ashamed," Mr. Bannon broke the silence. "But I just couldn't handle them any more, Mr. Hayes."

Mr. Hayes walked to the window and watched the group pass out of the schoolyard into the street and break up into small excited clumps of boys. "I know," he finally said. "We've got a job. And sometimes, Bannon, I wonder if we're doing the right thing."

"My opinion is that we're not. These kids are restless and tough, and somewhere along the line we've missed the boat."

Mr. Hayes took his pipe from his pocket and rapped the bowl with his hand. "I guess you're right. But"—he shrugged his shoulders—"we'll see what happens when they bring their parents up. Get that list on my desk before you leave today."

"I'll do that, Mr. Hayes, thanks."

Frank and Black Benny walked aimlessly in the sun, unable to understand why their humor had backfired. Imagine Bannon getting so sore at them that he'd gone for Hayes, which proved to them conclusively that a teacher was always a rat.

"Hell"—Benny kicked a stone that lay in his path—"we didn't do anything we never done before. The clown doesn't have a sense of humor."

"We roughed him up plenty before," Frank agreed. "Gee, my old man is going to hit the ceiling."

"Must we tell them?"

"You heard what Hayes said. He'll turn us over to the

traunt officer if they don't come in by Friday afternoon. We're really caught with our pants down."

"And now. Say"—Benny paused before a small liquor store on Sutter Avenue—"I could use a drink. This sorta's taken the wind outa me."

"I don't want any." Frank began to walk on.

Benny took two dollar bills out of his wallet. "Wait. A couple of drinks'll give us some guts. I'll be right out."

Frank walked on to the corner, and soon Benny came up to him with a small wrapped package. "I got some Schenley's." He shook the bottle and it gurgled. "Let's go down to the club and drink it."

The clubroom was dim and cool in contrast to the heat of the day, and they felt better as they listened to the radio and swigged drinks out of the bottle. Frank smoked one of his reefers and gave one to Benny. They sat on separate sofas, drinking and inhaling the reefers, and soon they were floating in a world where everything was funny. The whole scene in the school was etched into the ceiling of the room, and they laughed as they saw and heard the class rocking and swaying in rhythm. It was only fun; they hadn't meant to be mean to Mr. Bannon; and, in fact, they had always considered him to be a regular guy. How, they asked each other, could he have gutted them so? Why, hell, they weren't any worse than any of the other guys in the school, and some of the official classes made a hell of a lot more racket than they did, and their teachers never got them suspended. That just went to show them what a louse Mr. Bannon was. Nothing he'd ever do would convince them that he was a regular guy.

"You know"—Benny wiped his lips—"I'll bet he doesn't realize what he's done. You know that he's holding up the national defense?"

Frank nodded solemnly in agreement. "That's right. What's more important, my mother packing ammunition or her coming to school because we kidded around a little bit? I'm askin' you, what's more important? You can tell me the truth, Benny; what's more important?"

"Bannon." Benny ignored Frank's questions and thought for a moment. "That's Irish. And the Irish aren't in the war. I bet he's a Fascist or German agent. He knows that

61

most the kids' folks are working in war plants, and that's how he goes around sabotaging the war effort, the son of a bitch."

"A first-class bastard." Frank broke his third reefer in two and threw a half to Benny. "What the hell does he care about the war? And why the hell isn't he in the Army?"

Benny sucked on the reefer. "I don't know." He held the bottle to the light. "All gone."

Frank staggered as he stood up. "I'm hungry. Let's go out to eat. Goddamn bastard Bannon. Why the hell isn't he in the Army? I wish I knew his draft board. I'd sure tell them a mouthful about his sabotaging the war effort. Tell me, Benny," he continued owlishly, "if Bannon ain't a bastard."

They rode back to Pitkin Avenue and were feeling pretty good as they passed through the revolving door into Davidson's. It was past one o'clock and the noon crowd had thinned out. The vivid picture of the class rocking in unison as they sang still made them laugh, and interspersed with their laughter were short periods of righteous outraged anger. Frank ordered two bacardis at the bar, then Benny ordered two more, and as they sat at their table eating Hungarian goulash and cursing Mr. Bannon, the assistant manager of the restaurant had to ask them to quiet down. Benny gave the assistant manager what he intended to be a tough look, but Benny was so drunk that he could not focus, and he grinned stupidly and placed a forefinger to his lips. The assistant manager laughed and walked away. He was too busy to bother with kids who were half tight.

"You know what?" Benny waved his fork.

"What?"

"I got a good idea."

"What?" Frank repeated.

"Let's go back to the school and have it out with Mr. Bannon. Let's tell him that if he does this to us he's a heel and we won't ever consider him a regular guy again."

Frank sipped his coffee. "You're crazy."

"No, I'm not," Benny insisted. "Come on. What the hell've we got to lose?"

"You're drunk."

"Don't you tell me I'm drunk, Frank. I don't like it."

Frank's lips twisted into a sneer. "So what'm I supposed to do, wilt?"

"Aw, forget it." Benny put out his hand and Frank shook it. "I'm telling you it's a good idea. We'll go talk to him and maybe he'll give us a break. Honest, I don't want to tell my old man or my mom. They'll be sore as hell, and maybe Sam won't lend me his car any more."

"It's after three o'clock," Frank said. "Maybe he's gone home."

"So if he's not there we haven't lost anything. Come on."

"I got to call Betty," Frank said.

"You'll call her after we get through. Come on."

The ride on the Pitkin Avenue bus cleared their heads, and when they got off at Pennsylvania Avenue they had mapped out what they were going to say. The schoolyard was deserted and the corridors of the building vacant as they trudged up the two flights to their home room.

Mr. Bannon sat at his desk, and they hesitated before they knocked at the door and entered. He looked at them for a moment and then returned to reading and correcting the drawings. Frank and Benny waited for him to acknowledge them, and as he continued to ignore them Benny coughed.

"And to what do I owe the honor of this visit?" Bannon asked sarcastically.

"We want you to give us a break," Frank began.

"A break?" He stared at them. "Why?"

"Well"—Frank hesitated—"because we didn't mean anything."

"Sure," Benny added, "we were only kidding. Honest."

Mr. Bannon walked to the window and looked down into the yard. His mouth twitched and his hands were cold. For more than a minute he stood with his back toward them, attempting to regain his composure. He hated them more now than he ever had.

"No." He finally turned around. "Mr. Hayes set the punishment. I had nothing to do with it. I'll have to ask you boys to leave this building and not return until you are accompanied by a parent."

"You know you're screwing up the war effort?" Benny asked him.

63

"I'm what?"

"That's what you're doing. My mother and father work in defense plants, and Frank's do too. And if they take a day off to come down here they're holding up the assembly line. And that's sabotage."

Mr. Bannon could not believe it. These damned kids in their sharp suits, obviously a little drunk, telling him he was a saboteur!

"And what's more," Benny went on, "why aren't you in the Army?"

"You little bastard!" The words shot out of Mr. Bannon's mouth. "Get out before I clout you one! Now get out!" He approached them with clenched fists. His face twitched convulsively.

Frank backed away, but Benny shifted into the boxing stance. "We don't want no trouble," Benny said, "but if you make a pass at me I'm going to slug you."

The rage and humiliation of weeks blinded Mr. Bannon. Instinctively he knew he was in error, that he should pack his brief case and go home, but he wanted to be a human, to be able to give expression to his resentment, to hurt these boys as they had hurt him. He decided to forget everything: his job, Mr. Hayes, his responsibility, the certain repercussions; he would welcome the publicity, for then he could speak out about what school conditions really were with the overcrowded classrooms full of boys who strained from nine in the morning until three in the afternoon to get away from the building and its educational controls. All this was a waste of time, for the educational authorities were attempting to control a war phenomenon with the static routines that had sufficed during peacetime. And no attempt was being made to cope with the situation. All talk and meetings and civic resolutions deploring youthful vandalism and vagrancy—and that was all.

"That's what I want." Mr. Bannon gritted his teeth. "I'm going to make a pass at you and you're going to try to slug me and then I'm going to beat the hell out of you."

"Get away from the desk," Frank warned Benny, "and we'll both work on him."

"Now you're talking," Benny exulted. "O.K., you Bannon bastard, you asked for it!" Benny rushed Mr. Bannon and attempted to kick him in the ankle, but Mr. Bannon's right fist caught him flush on the jaw and he reeled backward. Quickly Mr. Bannon swung around toward Frank and hit him a hard roundhouse slap across the mouth. Frank cowered as Mr. Bannon rained blows upon his head and shoulders, and then a short digging jab in the ribs made him groggy with pain.

Benny shook his head. That guy Bannon could really hit, and Frank was in trouble. For a moment he thought of cutting Mr. Bannon, but that was bad, and then he thought of his gun. Quickly he yanked it from his shoulder holster, grasped the barrel, and hit Mr. Bannon across the head with the butt. Mr. Bannon lifted his hands, and Frank hit him squarely in the throat. Spittle bubbled in the corners of Mr. Bannon's mouth, and he ducked and grabbed for Benny. There was only one thing he wanted to do now, and that was to kill the two of them. He wrestled with Benny for the gun while he tried to shake Frank off his back. Frank had one arm around his throat and was beating him with his right fist. Again he attempted to twist Benny's arm behind his back, and suddenly the barrel of the gun was pointed directly at his chest. He struggled to push the barrel away and he twisted on Benny's free arm. Benny screamed with pain and involuntarily pulled the trigger. There was a sharp muffled crack, and Mr. Bannon wavered, looked at them unbelievingly, then staggered forward to the desk, grasped the edge, collapsed, and died.

Benny wiped his flushed face and stared with wonder at the gun. For the first time he realized that the toy which he had made in the shop was a lethal weapon. The room was quiet except for their heavy breathing, and the silence screamed about them, engulfing them in the vortex of sudden death and murder.

Frank gulped and slapped Benny in the face. "What'd you do that for?"

Benny shook his head dumbly and continued to stare at the gun and the body. Blood soaking from the chest wound had discolored Mr. Bannon's shirt and jacket, and the stain grew larger and bright red.

Frank slapped him again. "You jerk," he hissed, "you've killed him! Coming here was your idea and you've killed him!"

Benny put the gun in the holster and gaped like an idiot at Frank. "What're we gonna do now?" he asked helplessly.

Frank shoved him toward the door and then stopped. Silently he opened the classroom door and looked into the corridor. It was empty. He pushed Benny ahead of him, shut the door, and they tiptoed to the stairs. Luck was still with them. As they passed the first floor they heard the janitor whistling as he swept the classrooms, and with the sweat streaming from their faces and necks they forced themselves to descend slowly and quietly. They walked rapidly to the main entrance of the school, opened the massive wooden door, and in ten steps were on the sidewalk and walking nonchalantly toward Atlantic Avenue. They were certain no one had seen them leave, but what about their entry into the school?

"We can't take any chances," Benny said as they doubled back toward Pitkin Avenue. "We'll have to blow."

Frank shivered. "You don't know what you done."

"Shut up." Benny poked him. "Shut up!"

"What're we gonna do now?"

"We'll have to blow."

"Where?"

"I don't know," Benny said slowly. "Someplace."

Panic welled in Frank and fear sucked at his throat. "We haven't any money. Why'd you do it? I stopped carrying my rod yesterday, and you had to go around carrying yours! I asked you yesterday and this morning to ditch it, but no, you had to be a hard guy! Now look at us!"

Benny stopped and grabbed Frank by the arm. "Listen," he gritted, "you better cut it out. We're in this together and we'll get away."

"Let's go down to the club." Frank felt as if he were going to puke. "Let's take a bus."

"We've got to walk there," Benny replied. "If we take a bus someone is liable to see us. We can't even take a cab. We've got to walk. Maybe we better walk apart. I'll cross the street and you follow me."

66

"Maybe we ought to go to the cops and tell them what happened."

"Listen, rat"—Benny's face paled—"one more word like that and I'll plug you too. They can only burn me once, and I'd just as soon knock you off to stay alive as not. Understand? Now you get across the street and I'll follow you. And you're walking right to the club."

"I'm no rat, Benny. But I'm scared."

"So'm I, sport. But we'll get out of this someway. Go ahead."

It was a two-mile walk to their clubroom, and at every step Frank heard the crack of the .22 and saw the stain on Bannon's chest grow larger and redder. And he hadn't called Betty, and now she'd think he'd washed her up. His stomach was taut with nausea and pain, and tears obscured his vision. He would have given anything to bring Mr. Bannon back, but he was dead, and they had killed him and they were murderers, not killers who got a couple of grand for dropping a guy and who had everything all fixed for a fast getaway, but just two stinkers who'd been fooling around with homemade rods and making believe they were hard guys.

Now Benny took charge of things. He took a pair of pliers from the toolbox they kept in the clubroom and tore away the wire that held the tube in the stock of his gun. Then he burned the stock and grip of the gun in the furnace and wrapped the firing-pin assembly, the tube, and the wire in a handkerchief, for he intended to dipose of the steel items at different places and at different times.

"We'll leave here when it gets dark," Benny said, "and we'll take Sam's car and drive it out as far as we can. You know, if we could get into Canada and into the woods the cops'd never get us."

"Mexico would be better," Frank suggested.

"And China best." Benny laughed.

"Look," Frank said, and then stopped as he chose his words carefully. "We ought to be careful about blowing. I'm pretty sure no one saw us leave the school, and if no one saw us go in, then we're pretty safe. How would anyone know that we—I mean you—knocked him off? And——"

"You were right the first time, Frank. We knocked him off. Understand? We!"

Frank saw Benny's face become darker and more menacing. Benny was right; they were both in it. "All right," Frank sighed, "we. But maybe we ought to hang around, act as if nothing had happened. Look at us, we don't look marked up."

Benny touched his face gingerly. "My jaw's a little swollen."

Frank leaned over and shook his head. "It's nothing. No one'll be able to tell by morning. And I look all right, don't I? Look, I'll go out and call up Betty and tell her to get Ann. It's only eight o'clock, and I guess she's still home. Then you'll get Sam's car and we'll take the girls out and get them home by twelve. Then we'll go home and tell our folks that we were bad in school and that one of them has to come up with us. We'll behave as if nothing happened, and who'll ever be the wiser?"

"You know," Benny reflected, "I think you got something there. I'll bet the evening papers are out now, and when you go out to call the babes, then you can find out if it's in the papers. If they don't know who done it, you're right, why should we blow?"

"Good." Frank stood up. "I'll be back in about ten minutes. Just hold tight."

"Get back in a hurry. And, Frank——"

"Yes?"

"Don't try to cross me up." Benny's voice was an iron gate that barred his escape.

The *Daily News* had the headline splashed across the first page.

H. S. Teacher Murdered in Classroom
No Clues to Killer

Frank whistled as he dialed Betty's number. No clues to the killer. Killer, not killers. No clues. No nothing. They were in the clear. But they'd have to be careful. Killer, not killers. In fact, he hadn't had anything to do with it. He hadn't carried a rod, and Mr. Bannon was giving him a beating when Benny stepped in and slugged him with the

68

gun butt. But he was there, and as long as he was there he was implicated. He was an accessory. It was as if he were a lookout while the other guys were sticking up a candy store and one of the guys shot and killed the owner of the store. Even the lookout got the chair. It had been Benny's idea to return to the school, and because of Benny he might burn. But the paper said killer. One.

He was glad when Betty answered the phone, and he smiled at the mouthpiece of the telephone as if she could see him.

"You know," he said, and he marveled that he spoke with such calmness, "when your mother and father work it isn't easy to take care of things. And I've got a kid sister, too, that needs watching after. So honest, babe, I'm sorry I didn't call you earlier. You'll meet me tonight? . . . Fine! And you can get Ann for Benny? . . . That's on the beam. Listen, we'll pick you up at the same place at about—let me see—say a quarter after nine? Good. Fine. I'll be seein' you. So long, honey."

Frank bought a *News* and read the murder story as he walked back to the club. The paper did not carry many details except that the teacher was bruised, as if he'd been in a fight, and that he had been killed by a .22 caliber bullet which had punctured the heart. There were no clues, and no one had seen anyone suspicious entering or leaving the building. And as he read he whistled more brightly.

He clasped his hands and waved them at Benny as he opened the clubroom door, and then he held a finger to his lips to stop Benny from asking any questions.

"Everything's fixed." He winked. "We've got a date tonight. Nine-fifteen. We'll have to hurry, guy, because I'm hungry."

"You mean it?" Benny whispered as they walked up the steps.

"Perfect," Frank replied. "I got a paper here which says they don't know who done it. Aren't you glad now we didn't take a powder?"

"And how! Christ, I feel a lot better, though I'm sorry for the poor bastard. But he got what was coming to him. He didn't have to clout us around."

"You're right about that," Frank agreed. "He said he

was gonna beat us up. But you gotta get rid of those parts. How're you gonna work it?"

"I'm putting the whole thing in plaster of paris, and we'll drop it off a bridge tonight."

"A very good idea." Frank slapped him on the back as they entered a delicatessen. "Let's get something to eat, and hurry, we haven't got too much time."

"You know," Benny said, "I'm not nervous any more."

"Me neither."

"Shake."

As they sat across the table from each other and bit into their hot pastrami club sandwiches they winked at each other. No clues. No nothing. The perfect setup.

Chapter 5

The Goldfarbs sat silently around the kitchen table, and occasionally Alice glanced at Frank. Frank ate stolidly, concentrating on the plate before him and attempting to be impervious to the hostility of his father and mother. They could have been working overtime this Thursday evening if he had not got into trouble. Now he had his picture in the paper and the police had told Mrs. Goldfarb that Frank was remanded to her custody and that he was not to leave New York.

Such a scandal. Not only hadn't he gone to school on Monday and Tuesday, when God only knew where he was, but Wednesday he had to be responsible for the riot in the classroom.

"Momser," his mother said bitterly, "you had to be a regular actor, a comedian. I think you're wasting your time when you should be in Hollywood making a fortune with your funny tricks."

"I've told you at least a hundred times that I'm sorry," Frank replied sullenly.

"Look"—she pointed at him with her fork—"he's sorry! So now maybe everything is supposed to be all right?"

"Let him eat," his father said. "I think he knows what he's done."

"I didn't do anything!" Frank stood up and then realized he was trembling. He sat down and toyed with the food on his plate. "Why can't you let me alone? I told you I'm sorry. Can I help it if somebody bumps off the teacher? If that didn't happen everything would've been all right."

"And what about the day's pay that I've lost anyway because I had to go to school because of your carrying on like an Indian? God knows you come from a good home where we give you everything you want. The least you can do is help. Do we send you to go to work"—his mother raised her hand to stop her husband from speaking—"like other parents? I see boys like you working in the factory and making fifty dollars a week with the overtime. Do we ask you to go to work? No! We want you to have an education so that you won't have to work like us. So with Benny Semmel you go around bumming!"

"Momma," Alice said timidly, "Frank didn't do anything bad. They were just fooling around."

"And what sort of care does he give his little sister?" His mother raised her eyes toward the ceiling and spoke to her personal deity. "Does he look after her like a good brother? No! Too busy being a regular lady *geher* with a haircut that looks like *kuss mir in tuchess* and pants that fit him like Turkish bloomers."

"Rashke!" her husband said. "Enough!"

"So"—she turned to her husband—"you don't like what I'm saying? I've got plenty to say to you! A fine father you are! Why couldn't you have been making a living like other men were before the war so that we shouldn't have to live in such a *hegdess* with bums and *bummerkess* all around us? If we were living in Crown Heights or East Flatbush we wouldn't have the trouble we have today!"

"There's no place to move," her husband replied, "and lots of good boys and girls live here." He reached across the corner of the table to stroke Alice's hair. "Children can be good all over."

"For every sensible thing he is always ready with his

71

philosophy." The edge in Mrs. Goldfarb's tone became more pronounced. "I know there's no place to move. Every day that I'm not working overtime I'm looking for a place to live. And instead of me coming home to rest my feet and my son here, my *nachess*"—she bowed to Frank with heavy sarcasm—"looking for an apartment, he is busy in the poolroom. Tell me, my darling son, my little gangster, have you already become the best player in the poolroom?"

Frank slammed his knife and fork on the table and rushed into his bedroom. Tears hung in the corners of his eyes, and he flung himself across the bed. The old lady was too damned much for him.

"Don't think you can get away from me, you momser." His mother opened the bedroom door and leaned across the foot of the bed. "I should slap your face so hard that you'd realize what you've done!"

"Please, Rashke"—his father stepped in as appeaser—"let him finish his supper."

"So who's stopping him? Get up," she said to Frank, "and finish your supper."

"I'm not hungry." His voice was muffled by the pillow.

Alice approached the bed and touched his arm. "Come eat, Frank."

"I'm not hungry." Tears made his voice quiver.

"Get up," his father said, "and come to the table. Rashke" —he turned to his wife—"you've said enough. Frank was foolish but not bad. So you're not to say any more."

Mrs. Goldfarb hesitated and then went back to the kitchen. "Tell him to come right back," she called, "before everything on his plate gets cold."

"Come, Frank"—his father shook him—"get up."

Frank washed his face and returned to the table. That was another thing he hated about the apartment, the bathroom being off the kitchen. As he sat at the table he wished he didn't have to eat. They thought he wasn't hungry because of their bawling out, but he wondered if they knew what it was like to have participated in the killing of a man and then to have gone out the same night with a date who expected him to neck her and say the things she wanted to hear. After he had taken her home and awakened his father and mother to tell them that one of them would have to go to school with him the next morning they were too sleepy to yell at him, and so he had got into bed with no more than a half dozen curses from his mother, who said she hoped he wouldn't live to wake up in the morning, but he couldn't sleep. The perimeter of the stain on Mr. Bannon's chest grew larger until it covered everything. And the next morning he had to hold himself as in a vise when he arrived at the school and saw the crowd and the police and was taken into the principal's office for questioning. If the detectives would've been tough and yelled at him like they did in the movies he wouldn't have been worried. But they were soft and easygoing. They asked the damnedest things, like they knew that he and Benny Semmel had been the leaders in the uproar, but they had checked and found that Benny and he had fairly good records at school, although their attendance had not been as good this term as it had in the past. Then the detectives asked them if they knew anyone who hated Mr. Bannon or ever had spoken about getting even with him. Then they asked him what he was studying and how many there were in his family and where he lived and where his mother and father worked and what he did with his time. While talking to them he felt as if he were wound up like a crossbow, for at any moment he expected them to start shooting questions at him, but they didn't. Then they told him that he wasn't to go on the hook any more and they expected him to be in school every day and he wasn't to leave New York without their permission.

After he left the principal's office Frank had to lean against the wall while he pulled himself together, and it seemed as if his mother's scolding and cursing came from a distance. Although he knew that she stood right next to him, her voice seemed to come through a fog and it did not bother him. The cops suspected nothing and would never find out who had knocked off Mr. Bannon. Not from him they wouldn't. But what about Benny? Benny was still waiting to be questioned, and he didn't know what Benny might do. If Benny were only smarter and not such a loudmouth. Look at the way he had started to tell the girls about the Dukes. And why hadn't the cops asked him about where he had been and where he had gone after the class had been dismissed by Mr. Hayes? He didn't know what to do about an alibi. Or maybe the best alibi was that they had gone from school to their clubroom to Davidson's and back to their club until they had called the girls, eaten in the delicatessen, and taken them out in Sam's car.

That was the first bad break: Benny didn't have a license. So what? Frank figured. Lots of guys drove without licenses, and the most that could happen would be another bawling out and then Sam would be fined. So it wasn't so bad, and they would be just a couple of irresponsible kids who had gone on the hook and driven a car without a license. The only thing was Benny. If he became rattled they were goners, but the murder rap would make Benny careful. Look at the way he had encased the metal parts of the gun in the plaster of paris and had dropped it off the bridge between Brooklyn and Jacob Riis Park in Rockaway. There wasn't an auto on the bridge when Frank had driven the car close to the rail, and Benny had heaved the package over so smoothly that the girls had seen nothing.

They had an alibi, and now they were going to go to school, and he was going to start hanging around the Center a little. He was going to stop drinking and smoking reefers, and Benny was going to do the same. They would never be caught, but the fear did not leave him, and that was why he could not eat.

"You know"—he kept his eyes on the plate as he spoke —"I'm sorry I caused you all this trouble, Mom. You too, Pop. Honest, it won't happen again."

"How can I believe you?" his mother wailed. "You stay out late and don't go to school and you're going to get into more trouble and disgrace us!"

"Rashke"—his father was exasperated—"please be good enough to stop. You're making things worse than they are."

"Still, Meyer," she said to her husband, "no one is asking you."

"That's why I'm telling you. You don't know when to stop."

"Let's all go to the movies after supper," Alice suggested.

Frank smiled and winked at her. "Sure," he said, "let's. We'll all feel better."

74

"I'm tired," his mother said. "You can go to the movies, but I've got to work tomorrow. I lost enough today," she reminded Frank. "Enough."

Frank approached his mother and forced himself to kiss her on the cheek. "I'm sorry, Mom, believe me."

She would never know how sorry, he thought.

Black Benny stood in front of the candy store on Amboy Street and wondered if he looked the same. Some of the boys had once said that as soon as you killed your first guy your appearance changed. He looked in the mirror of the gum-vending machine and didn't see any change, except that maybe his eyes were frightened. If only he were certain of Frank, for something about Frank made him uneasy. What it was he couldn't put his finger on, but maybe it was the moony, squeamish way of his, like when he didn't want to line up on a babe or the way he felt about this new babe Betty. The trouble with Frank was that he was always dreaming and out of the world. Like when he had tanked Crazy for kidding around with his kid sister. It was Frank who had insisted that they go to school yesterday. If they would've stayed out of school it was certain they wouldn't have knocked off Bannon.

They did it. No matter how Frank figured it, they did it. If Frank would've been able to give Mr. Bannon a battle, then Benny wouldn't have had to slug him with the gun butt and Bannon would be alive today. Bannon looked crazy when he was twisting his arm, as if he were trying to tear it right out of his shoulder. So what could he do? Bannon might have shot him, and he didn't mean to pull the trigger, only Bannon was ripping out his arm and the pain had been running in hot white flashes up through his arm until he just had to break loose from the son of a bitch. So now he was dead and the gun was destroyed and there weren't any clues, and still he didn't feel safe. If Mitch or Bull or Larry or Moishe or any of the other guys in the Dukes, except Crazy, had been in on it, he would've felt safe, but Frank was an unknown quantity, like the x in algebra. Sometimes it meant a lot and sometimes it was nothing; there was no way of solving the equation. Real hard guys, when they worried about a guy squealing or ratting, knocked off the guy who might get them in trouble, but he was never going to do that again. Why the hell hadn't he listened to Frank Tuesday night and got rid of his gun? Frank had wiped his fingerprints off his gun and dropped it down a sewer on their way to school Wednesday morning. But he had to be a hard guy, and now there was a feeling of pain in his chest whenever he thought of the look on Bannon's face before he died. It was driving him nuts.

The guys were leaving him alone because they knew he was feeling lousy, but now he wanted someone to talk to, and he went into the candy store and sat at a table with Larry Tunafish, Mitch, and Crazy.

"Where's Frank?" Larry asked him.

"I've been waiting for him," Benny replied.

"I guess he'll be around," Mitch said.

"He's a rat," Crazy said.

Benny's heart started to pound. "Why?"

"I don't know. He's just a rat. A regular rat."

"Shut your hole." Larry slapped Crazy across the back of the head. "You're always talking."

Benny tried to ask casually, "Is Frank a rat?" He wondered if the guys could hear his heart pounding.

"Are you becoming like Crazy too?" Larry laughed. "Don't listen to the jerk. Listen, Crazy"—he squirmed sideways in the booth—"I don't like to hear that kind of talk about one of our guys. Frank and Benny are in a jam and——"

"I'm in no jam!" Benny moved suddenly and tipped over his water glass. "You jerk," he said to Crazy, "now look what you made me do!"

"Me?"

"Yes, you!"

"Cut it out, guys," Mitch said. "Hey, Selma," he called to the girl behind the counter, "wipe up this table, will you?"

"In a minute," she called back.

"Everyone picks on me," Crazy went on. "All I've got to do is say something and everyone picks on me. Next time you guys want some steaks you know what you can do."

"No one's picking on you," Larry said to him. "But you can't go around talking like that about our guys. You don't like Frank; that's all right with me, but don't go

76

shouting your mouth off about him being a rat. He's got some good friends in the Dukes, ain't he, Benny?"

"You're damned right." Benny wished he were sure of it. "Frank is an all-right guy."

"I'm not saying anything any more." Crazy pursed his lips together. "See? I'm a dummy."

"You sure are," Mitch said kindly. "But we all like you."

"You know"—Larry sucked on his coke—"I wonder who did knock off your teacher, Benny."

"How the hell should I know!"

"Say," Larry said quickly, "what the hell is the matter with you?"

Benny drummed nervously with his fingers on the table. "Nothing."

"You in trouble?" Mitch asked him.

"No!"

"Listen," Larry said, "what's the matter? You're jumpy."

"I know," Benny agreed. "I must've eaten something."

"You want a reefer?" Crazy asked him.

"No, thanks."

"Then I'll smoke one." Crazy took a cigarette from his case.

"You're smoking too many of them," Larry said. "You're high now."

"I like them." Crazy sucked in his breath and exhaled. "Boy, I sure feel wonderful when I'm smokin'."

"He's becoming a regular hophead," Benny said.

Selma approached their booth, and they were silent as she wiped the table. As she turned around to walk away Crazy goosed her.

"You bastard!" She whirled about. "Someday I'll cut your fingers off for that!"

"You know you like it." Crazy leered at her.

"From you?" she sniffed. "Now I know you're crazy!"

Crazy stood up in the booth, but Mitch pulled him back to the seat.

"Go on, Selma," Mitch told her. "Don't mind him."

"Yeah," Crazy said to her, "go on. Beat it. Now I'm not gonna get you the present I promised."

"Stick your present up your you know what," Selma spit at him, and went back to the counter.

77

"What were you gonna get her?" Larry asked Crazy.

"Somethin' nice. A flask that fits over her bubs. I saw a nice one on Nassau Street that a guy in the store was gonna swap me for a roast. Now I won't get it for her."

"You're right," Mitch agreed, and looked meaningly at Larry and Benny, "she's not good enough for you."

"You're my friend." Crazy turned to him. "You're the only guy in our gang that I like."

"Don't you like us?" Larry asked him.

"Sure, but not like I like Mitch. Mitch, you know who I think I'm gonna make my new girl?"

"Who?"

"Fanny Kane."

"Her?" Black Benny laughed. "She's only about twelve. Crazy, you'll be saying good morning to a judge."

"You'd better stay away from her," Larry agreed.

"I like her," Crazy insisted stubbornly. "She's young but put together."

"Does she like you?" Mitch asked him.

"Sure she does. When I say hello to her she says hello to me."

"I guess she likes you then." Mitch winked at him. "You're just a sharp article with the women, Crazy."

"Come on, Benny, snap out of it," Larry said suddenly. "Say, I wanta ask you something."

"What?" Benny squirmed and wondered where Frank was. Maybe Crazy was right.

Larry leaned across the table and whispered, "Do you know who knocked off your teacher?"

Benny fought to keep himself seated. "No"—he shook his head slowly—"I don't."

"Then why in hell are you so nervous?" Larry asked him.

Benny bit his lips to keep from screaming and he picked up Mitch's water glass and drank because his lips were dry and thick. "Because I can't get it out of my mind that if Frank 'n' me hadn't horsed around that morning maybe Bannon would be alive today. He wasn't such a bad guy, and I don't know why anyone'd want to knock him off. Now Frank 'n' me got our pictures in the paper, and my old man would've given me a shellacking if Sam didn't stop him. And cops make me nervous."

"I don't like cops," Crazy said solemnly.

"If you don't stop cutting guys up like you did on Monday you're gonna see cops every day," Mitch warned him.

"And Frank was grilled today before I was, and I don't know what they asked him and I just gotta know, and the jerk isn't here or anyplace. I'd like to kick him right in the ass."

"Maybe his old man and lady are keeping him home," Larry suggested.

"Maybe," Mitch agreed.

"Well, he ought to get out someway," Benny insisted.

"He's a rat," Crazy said again.

"Shut up," Larry said.

"He's a rat," Crazy repeated. "A rat. A rat. A rat. Frank is a rat. Watch out for him, Benny. I'm warning you." There was mockery and cunning in Crazy's voice as he leaned across the table and whispered to Benny.

Benny looked at Crazy and said nothing.

Chapter 6

Frank sat next to Benny on the uncomfortable high-backed bench in the anteroom of the Liberty Avenue police station and traced the crack in the green paint from the baseboard to the ceiling. The crack went across the ceiling, but it was uncomfortable leaning back to see how far it went, and he shut his eyes and tried to recite the alphabet backward. He squirmed and was uncomfortable and wondered whether their alibi would stick. He saw no holes in it. For two hours now the detectives had been quizzing the boys in his official class, and the cops had brought in for questioning the boys who had been troublemakers in Mr. Bannon's other classes.

The boys slouched on the benches. Some rested their heads against the backs and balanced their hats on their foreheads and noses, pretending to be asleep and indifferent to the questioning, while others tried to read newspapers and magazines, smoked, or conversed in hushed voices. They hated cops impersonally and because cop-hating was the tough, right thing to do. If they walked along the streets and talked of innocent things they would instinctively break off the conversation as they passed a policeman or a scout car. Now they were waiting to be questioned and each one wanted to be tough, to tell the cops that he wasn't going to talk without his lawyer, even if they gave him a workout, and baffle the cops by his silence and hardness. Somewhere among them was the killer, and by sitting in close proximity to him they derived a vicarious thrill. They wouldn't tell the cops anything, and by being un-co-operative, vague, and ambiguous, they would be helping the guy who knocked off their teacher, sharing in the crime and putting one over on the cops, who were no good, who were always raiding their poolrooms and breaking up their crap games.

The door opened and one of the boys walked out. They looked at him and were disappointed, for he had not been beaten.

"You"—the policeman pointed to one of the boys at random—"come in."

They watched the boy swagger defiantly into the room, and then the door closed and again they relaxed to wait their turn.

Benny nudged Frank. "How much longer before they call us?"

Frank followed the crack to the ceiling before he replied: "I don't know."

"What d'ya think they'll ask us?"

"I don't know."

"Must we tell them about the car?"

Frank nodded affirmatively.

"Sam's sore already."

"We've got to tell them if they ask us. Now shut up."

"You're a hell of a guy," Benny whispered. "Going to the movies with your sister last night while I'm sweating it out on the corner with the guys."

"I had to do it. Stop worrying, Benny, and stop talking. You'll get us in a jam if you don't shut up. Relax."

Benny sighed, tipped his hat over his eyes, and slid down on the bench.

When the door opened again and the policeman ordered Frank and Benny to come in together there was an electric stir along the benches, an undercurrent of movement and quickened interest, for until now the boys had been interrogated individually, and taking the two of them together meant something.

"Sit down, boys." Detective Macon motioned to the chairs. He held out a pack of cigarettes. "Smoke?"

"No. Thanks," they said in unison.

Macon waved his match to extinguish the flame. "Sorry to keep you kids waiting, but things like this take time."

"Sure," Benny replied.

"Now let me see," Macon said. "Which one of you is Benjamin Semmel?"

Benny gulped. "I am."

"Then you're Frank Goldfarb?"

"Right."

"My name is Macon. Louis Macon. And I want you boys to feel that I'm a friend of yours. I know you don't believe that"—he laughed shortly—"and I guess you don't like dicks. But we aren't bad guys, and when you get to know me you'll know that I'm regular. Now"—Macon loosened his belt buckle—"I'll have to ask you some questions, and Miss Reid here"—he flicked his thumb toward the stenographer—"is going to take our conversation."

"Shoot," Frank said.

"Fine. Do you know who shot Mr. Bannon?"

"No," Frank replied.

"And you?" Macon turned to Benny.

Benny could feel his voice leaving him. "No."

"Did you shoot him, Frank?"

"No."

"Benjamin—say, do the guys call you that?"

"They call me Benny."

"That's what I thought. Did you shoot him, Benny?"

"No."

"That's what I thought. You kids don't look like killers."

Frank did not reply. The trap was too obvious. If this

81

was the way it was going to be they would have to step carefully if they expected to stay in the clear. For this dick was just playing dumb. He would have to be careful. Even though he had been getting the beating and Benny had shot Bannon, he would have to be careful. Careful for himself and careful for Benny. He knew that Benny was sore at him, but what could he do? He had to take care of himself, and the sooner he could cut himself loose from Benny, the better. Though any way he figured it he didn't see an out. He was stuck, and so long as he was stuck he had to be careful.

"What did you boys think of Bannon?" Macon threw out the question.

"He was all right," Benny said.

"Did you like him?"

"I guess we liked him as well as we liked any other teacher," Frank replied.

Macon ground his cigarette into the ash tray. "Which means you didn't like him."

"I didn't say that," Frank replied.

"You didn't," Macon admitted. "Did you like school?"

"I'd rather be working," Frank said.

"Me too," Benny chimed in.

"But my father and mother want me to stay in school, and Benny's do too. That's why we're here."

"Sure." Benny took a deep breath. "If we were working we wouldn't'a been cuttin' classes and horsing around and we wouldn't be sittin' here now."

"You mean if you were working you wouldn't be in trouble now?"

"Why are we in trouble?" Benny got his second wind. He wasn't frightened any more. "What've we done? We were clowning like the other guys. That's all."

Macon leaned back in his swivel chair and rocked. "I guess I was running ahead of myself," he admitted. "You mean if you kids had been working instead of going to school you wouldn't be a part of this investigation?"

"That's right," Benny said. "Believe me, Mr. Macon, I'm getting plenty from my old lady because of this."

"Your mom's found out about your going on the hook?" He laughed.

"You can say that again."

"Well," Macon said, "you deserve it. What did you kids do after you left school?"

"Who do you want to talk?" Benny asked Macon.

"No difference to me." He shrugged his shoulders.

"You tell him," Frank said to Benny.

Benny hesitated for effect. To begin talking immediately would show the dick that this had been rehearsed. All he had to do was tell the truth, but to make the dick drag some things out of him.

"Well," he began, "when we got out of the schoolyard we stood around for a couple of minutes and talked. Then me and Frank walked along Sutter Avenue and we went to our club——"

"You belong to a club?" Macon interrupted.

Frank nodded. "The Amboy Dukes. We got a clubroom in East Flatbush."

Macon lit another cigarette. "Nice place?"

"Sure is," Benny said.

"I may step around to see it someday."

"The guys'll love that," Frank said dryly.

Macon grinned as he puffed on the cigarette, and his face twisted into a grimace of mock pleasure. "I bet they will," he said. "Go on, Benny."

"Well, we went down to the club and played the victrola and then we went to Davidson's to eat. After one o'clock, wasn't it, Frank?"

Frank thought for a moment. "I guess so."

"Then what?" Macon prodded him.

"Then after we ate we walked around on Pitkin Avenue for a while looking in the windows and then we walked over to Lincoln Terrace Park and sat there. We were feeling pretty lousy about having to tell our folks about school."

"Your fathers and mothers work?" Macon asked them.

Frank and Benny nodded affirmatively.

"Go on."

"So we sat there, down in the dumps and feeling sorry for each other and cursing Mr. Bannon, though we're sorry we did that now."

"Sorry you did what?"

83

"Cursed him," Benny replied. "What else?"

"Go on."

"So then we called up our dates and told them we'd meet them about a quarter after nine, and we went to eat in Cohen's Delicatessen on Pitkin near Douglass. Then we met the girls about the time we said, and say, Mr. Macon——"

"Yes?"

"These girls are good kids and we don't want their names in the paper or things like that. So you won't get them in bad, will you?"

"No," Macon said. "Miss Reid"—he turned to the stenographer—"make a note that if we check the girls these boys were dating the reporters are not to be informed who they are."

"Yes, sir," she said.

"So that's okay. Now go on, Frank, you take up from there."

Frank cleared his throat. "Well, we went with the girls to Jacob Riis Park and sat in the parking lot and necked." Frank's face flushed and he looked embarrassed. "Gee," he went on, "the girls'd be sore if they knew what we were saying."

Macon winked at them. "Don't worry. Then what did you do?"

"We took the girls home about eleven-thirty. Then we went home and told our folks about their coming to school."

"When did you find out that Mr. Bannon had been killed?"

"The next day."

"You didn't see an evening paper?"

"No," Benny said.

"Frank?"

"No."

"Do you boys ever buy a newspaper?"

"Once in a while," Frank said.

"So you didn't even see the headlines Thursday morning?"

"I didn't," Frank said. "My mother was too busy bawling me out for me to do anything else."

"I didn't see a paper either," Benny said. "Honest."

"How did you boys get out to Jacob Riis Park?"

Now it was coming. "We got out there," Benny said vaguely.

"You said you were necking in the parking lot. Who was driving the car?"

Benny was silent.

"Come on," Macon said to Frank. "Who was driving the car?"

Frank looked at the floor.

"Were you boys in a stolen car?"

"What difference does it make whose car it was?" Benny asked.

"Honest"—Frank raised his right hand—"it wasn't stolen."

"Then why won't you tell me who the car belonged to or who was driving?"

"I was driving," Frank said suddenly.

"You?" Macon shuffled some papers on his desk. "You're not eighteen. You were driving without a permit?"

"Yes."

"I was driving too," Benny said. This was working just the way Frank said it would. Frank was an all-right guy who had something between his ears. If only he were more certain that he could trust him.

"And you're not eighteen either."

"I know."

"Oh," Macon said slowly, "now I get it. So who does the car belong to?"

"You won't get him in trouble?" Benny asked.

"I'm not making you kids any promises."

"Then I'm not gonna tell you," Benny said.

"Me neither," Frank said.

"You want me to turn you in for driving without a license?"

"You'll do it anyway," Frank replied. "We know what you said about you trying to be our friend was a lot of cr—— I mean——" He fumbled for a word.

"I know what you mean." Macon nodded. "Now you're trying to play on my sympathy. It won't do you any good unless you tell me the truth about everything I ask you.

Now I'm not going to waste any more time with you because I've got at least fifteen other kids out there that I've got to see, and I've got a home too. So if you're not going to tell me I'm just going to have you booked and locked up overnight until you do. So make up your minds, and you haven't even got two minutes to do it in."

Benny looked at Frank and Frank shrugged his shoulders.

"It was my brother's car," Benny said. "Oh boy"—he put the palm of his hand to his cheek—"now I'm gonna get it!"

"What's your brother's first name?"

"Samuel."

"And how'd you kids drive out to Jacob Riis?"

"Out Linden Boulevard to Rockaway Boulevard and then over to the park."

"Miss Reid"—Macon swung around in his chair—"check and see if a Samuel Semmel owns a car. What kind of a car is it?"

"A Dodge." Benny's voice was weak. "A blue convertible—1941."

"And check," Macon instructed Miss Reid, "whether anyone remembers seeing a '41 Dodge convertible driving out to Jacob Riis. Are you boys good drivers?" he asked them.

"My brother wouldn't have lent us the car if we weren't. Please," Benny pleaded, "don't get him in trouble. I'm in hot enough already, and Sam'll really fan me if I get him in trouble."

"I'll see," Macon said. "In the meantime I'm warning you not to do any more driving."

"I won't," Benny promised. "Honest."

Frank also raised his hand. "Me too."

"Now tell me the names of the girls."

"Must we?" Frank asked helplessly.

"Yes."

"Betty Rosen." Frank decided that he had to see Betty that night. Benny had to tell the cops they had gone to Jacob Riis by another route because there was always the chance that the cops might drag the channel for the gun. And suppose they decided to drag underneath the Flatbush Avenue Bridge? Frank shut his eyes to prevent Macon from observing the way they narrowed. It didn't look like the perfect setup any more.

"And yours?" Macon smiled as he questioned Benny.

"You promised not to give it to the reporters," Benny reminded him.

"I know. What's her name?"

"Ann Kleppner."

"Did you kids go right to your club after you left the school?"

"Aw, what the hell," Frank interjected, "you'll get it out of us anyway. We stopped off and bought a pint and we drank it down at the club."

"So you kids got high?"

"No," Frank went on, "we didn't get drunk."

"Regular drinkers." Macon rubbed his hands together. "And where'd you buy the bottle?"

"On Sutter near Junius."

"Check if there's a liquor store there," Macon said to Miss Reid.

"So you don't know who might've had a grudge against Mr. Bannon?"

Benny wrinkled his forehead and squinted. "I don't know. That Wednesday was the first time Mr. Bannon really got sore at us."

"What about Frank?" Macon asked him.

"I don't know."

"If you knew would you tell me?"

Frank and Benny were silent.

"You're through." Macon dismissed him. "You'll report back if we need you, and stay out of trouble."

"We've never been in trouble," Benny said.

"That's fine. Just stay out of it."

Frank and Benny stood on the steps of the station. It was almost six o'clock, and they wondered when the guys they'd left waiting in the station would get out. Frank wanted to get away, but Benny stuck to him, for although he tried to forget what Crazy had said about Frank he could not. He didn't dare. It wasn't a question now of feeling sorry for what he—no, they—had done. Now it meant keeping in the clear, and as they walked up Rockaway Avenue past the furniture stores with their elaborate displays of mahogany and walnut period furniture embellished, grained, and swirled to the saturation point of decoration, Benny wasn't going to take a chance. Not if he had to stick to Frank every minute of the day and night.

"That wasn't so bad," he began the conversation. "I said it wasn't so bad," he repeated when Frank did not answer.

"I know."

"What're you doin' tonight?"

"I'm stayin' home."

"How about seeing the girls? You know we didn't go out to Riis Park like we told that dick. And the babes better be tipped off."

Frank wished that Benny would be quiet, that he had never seen or been friends with Benny. All this talk and being careful of what he said and weighing each word so that there wasn't a chance of being tripped up was winding him up, making him want to scream and curse and kill Benny. And things were coming too easy. If only he could be sure that their alibi would stick. Maybe someone saw them get on the bus and ride back to the school, or go into the school, or come out of the school, or walk away from the school. Maybe there was someone who might suddenly remember having seen them near the school, for there was always the chance that a casual and even disinterested reader would recognize their pictures in the papers—then good-by to the perfect setup. Maybe someone saw them go over the Flatbush Avenue Bridge, and although he was certain that no one saw Benny throw the package into the channel, still he was not sure. And he knew that Benny no longer trusted him. Benny was a lousy actor and unable to conceal the fear and misgivings that consumed him. He was cold and metallic in the police station, but the calmness was engendered by a desperate determination to stay alive, and that frightened Frank. For he knew that Benny would not think twice about getting rid of him if he felt that Frank might crack, and walking along the avenue with a guy who had killed one man and might do him in thinned his blood and drained the color from his face.

"Why the hell don't you answer me?" Benny asked him angrily.

"I was thinking," Frank replied, "about what're we gonna tell the kids about our wanting them to tell the cops if they have to about our driving out to Rockaway a different way."

Benny dug his hands deeper into his jacket pockets. "You got something there."

"Maybe we ought to tell them they've got to trust us and not ask any questions," Frank suggested without hope.

"Don't be a sap!" Benny flung at him. "And another thing"—he pulled Frank close to one of the store windows —"can I trust you?"

"Let go of me," Frank said quietly.

"Answer me." Benny shook him. "Can I trust you?"

"You've got to," Frank said. "We can't help ourselves."

Benny laughed nervously and rubbed his face with his hands. "Geez, I'm jumpy. Come on, let's forget it. Let's call up the kids and tell them we'll meet them. We'll take them dancing tonight at Roseland and we'll figure out what to tell them. You wanta call Betty?"

Frank nodded. "You call. And tell them we'll meet them in front of the Fox. I'll meet you there too. About nine o'clock."

"Where you going?"

Frank stared at him. "Listen, Benny," he finally said, "let's get some things straight. You can't go tailing after me like a cop. I'm in this with you. I've got no out. The only way I get away is if you get away, and the way you don't trust me, I'm worried about you shooting off your big trap. You jerk, don't you realize that if we hang around together every minute somebody is gonna get wise? We've always been good friends, but not like this, with you hanging onto me and wondering where I am and what I'm doing. We gotta be natural, and if we aren't"—he shrugged his shoulders—"then we're up the creek. So I'll meet you in front of the Fox at nine, and let's stop acting like Siamese twins."

"Save the crap," Benny said abruptly. "I'll meet you at nine." Then he walked into the crowd and was gone.

Roseland was a riot of noise. On the stage in the center of the ballroom, Mad Monk and His Cats were beating it out as the hot blonde in the flame-red velvet gown swayed before the microphone and sang "Straighten Up and Fly Right." The dancers were locked in a tight swaying mass in front of the platform, while in the middle of the floor wildly gyrating couples whirled as the beat of the music increased in intensity. The revolving spotlights of sick green, red, and blue distorted and twisted the dancing shadows on the floor and walls and ceilings, and a blue pall of smoke drifted about the ballroom, fouling and contaminating the little fresh air that was left. With sweat running down their cheeks and their eyes and lips twisted in a rapt ecstatic grimace, the dancers spun through the intricate maddening routine of the lindy, pausing only as the band slackened its beat before passing the lead from the trumpet to the sax and then to Mad Monk, who pounded on the drums with a fury that made the dancers in front of the bandstand whistle and shriek. The sticks beat on the snare drum in two seemingly solid arcs while he pounded the bass wildly with the foot hammer. With a final rapid-driving tattoo, a whirring crash of the cymbals, and a shrill insane note from the trumpet, the number was over.

Now the whistling ceased as Monk signaled the musicians to get ready for the next number. Frank stood on the floor with flexed knees, waiting for the first bars of music. His collar was wet, and small beads of perspiration glowed on his forehead. He held Betty's left hand loosely and at the first crash of the cymbal sent her into a spin. Betty minced on her toes in a light tap step and twirled toward Frank, who passed her hand over his head and sent her into another spin. They glided together for a moment, moving rapidly from side to side with the swift beat of the music, and again they went into a half spin, with free arms flung out, before Betty whirled toward Frank. Now they broke again, and Betty clapped her hands as she swaggered saucily toward Frank. With her buttocks thrust back and her breasts high and jiggling as she moved her shoulders, she strutted toward Frank, and Frank felt the blood rush to his face. As she came close to him he kissed her swiftly and they whirled about rapidly, lost in the blue haze, the shifting lights, and the insistent beat and rhythm of the band. Now Mad Monk took the lead again. First he worked the drums with the brushes so that the taps were low and soft, and as the whirring of the brushes grew louder and more rapid he changed to drumsticks. Monk's body was bent low over the drums, and his tongue flicked out to lick his lips as he shifted from drum to tom-tom and back to drum. Now the cymbals crashed, and with a press of his feet Monk switched on the dim red light that glowed inside the bass. "Beat it! Beat it out!" the crowd milling around the bandstand shouted. "Beat it, Monk!" And Monk bared his teeth and grinned.

So fast that Frank knew it was only the marijuana that enabled him to keep up with the music, he led Betty through the maze of swift shuffling dance steps as his jacket began to soak through with perspiration. Betty danced with eyes half shut and lips parted. With a last violent surge of notes Monk smashed the cymbals and the dance was over, and from the milling mob on the floor there arose a short sigh as the orgasm of frenetic music expended itself. Frank and Betty swayed for a moment, and then Frank locked her in his arms and stood rocking on the dance floor.

"I'm beat, kid," he said to her.

"Me too." Her breath whistled.

Frank wiped the perspiration from his face with his hands and gave Betty his handkerchief. "Let's sit out the next one, Betty."

"Get me a coke," she said.

"When you cool off a little. That Monk is a killer."

"Solid."

"Some nights he's absolutely out of the world, and keeping up with him is like running a hundred yards in ten seconds over and over again."

Betty returned Frank's handkerchief and stretched her legs as she sat down. "Now get me the coke?" she asked him.

"Sure. I'll be right back."

Betty watched Frank thread his way through the crowd, and she waved as she saw Benny and Ann approaching her.

"Where's Frank?" Benny asked her.

"Getting me a coke."

Ann clutched Benny's arm and squeezed. "That's what I want, sug. I'm dying from thirst!"

Benny hurried toward the refreshment stand. No matter what Frank said, he didn't like to leave that guy alone for a minute.

"Frank," he shouted until he attracted his attention, "get two more bottles! I'll pay you back."

Frank nodded, turned again to the counter, and yelled to be waited on. Clutching the four bottles and straws, he shoved his way through the mob to Benny.

"Why the hell don't you get your own?" he said as he put Benny's coin in his pocket. "I only got two arms."

"Stop your beefing. You speak to Betty yet?"

"No."

"So what the hell're you waiting for? We seen you breaking your ass on the floor. What's more important, getting this thing fixed or dancing?"

"I'll talk to them now."

"Sure. That way it'll be better. I hope it works."

"It's got to," Frank said. "Everything we do is gotta work. We can't make any slips."

"You're not lying." Benny's voice was menacing and desperate.

They sipped the cokes as they sat in the crowded lounge and watched impatiently for a couple to leave who were necking in a dim corner which could accommodate four persons. Finally the couple came out of their clinch and Frank and Benny raced across the lounge to the corner.

"Now everybody get comfortable," Frank addressed the girls, " 'cause me and Benny wanta talk to you."

"Talk?" Ann scoffed. "You come here, Benny"—she stretched out her arms—"and we'll kiss and swap spits."

"Later." Benny rubbed his hand along her thigh. "But we wanna talk to you. Honest."

"About what?" Ann asked.

"Well"—Frank scratched his nose—"we want you kids to help us. It's this way. You know we're in that class where our official teacher got killed, and the cops've been grillin' us."

"Cops are bastards," Betty said.

"You're not tellin' us anything." Benny nodded.

"So the cops've been asking us all sorts of whacked-up questions about what we did on the day our teacher got plugged and everything," Frank continued. "And we had to tell them we were out with you."

Ann looked frightened. "You told them our names?"

"We had to," Benny said. "But they're not gonna bother you, and it'll never get in the papers. Didn't the dick promise it would never get into the papers?" He appealed to Frank.

Frank held up his right hand. "He swore, and you got nothin' to worry about because all the guys had to tell the dick where they were on Wednesday, and plenty of guys had dates. And if they had dates they'll want to check on the names of the babes to find out if the guys're lying."

"I shouldn't want them comin' to my house," Betty said slowly.

"Honest"—Benny tried to sound confident but failed—"you're not in no jam. We were with you Wednesday night, weren't we?"

"Yes." Ann nodded.

"So"—Benny flung out his hands—"we're telling the truth. The only thing is that we want you to do us one small favor."

"What?" Betty asked.

"You tell them, Frank," Benny said.

"It's really nothing at all. You see"—Frank held Betty's hand—"when they grilled us they shot the questions at us fast. We had to tell them what we did every minute of the day, and then the dick would go back and ask us the same questions later on to try and trip us up. One of the questions we was asked was how did we drive out to Jacob Riis, and they got us so screwed up for a minute that we said we drove out Rockaway Boulevard instead of over the Flatbush Avenue Bridge. Now we know we didn't go that way, but we couldn't say different."

Betty shook her head quizzically. "Why?"

"Because cops are funny," Benny replied. "Out of a little thing like that they can pin a rap on you, and we got twisted up and we don't want no trouble. Because some crazy bastard plugs our teacher is no reason for us to get into

93

trouble. You know we ain't got a license, and my brother is gonna be sore enough about the cops finding out that he lent us his car when we didn't have licenses without our worrying about the cops making it hotter for us because they got us balled up and we didn't tell them the right way on how we went out to Riis Park. Understand?"

"We're in trouble now for driving without licenses," Benny added for emphasis, "and we don't want to make things worse for us, especially when we didn't do anything. Boy"—he looked rueful—"we got plenty of trouble home without getting into any more."

"Sure we'll help," Ann said, "won't we, Betty?"

"Of course."

"Good." Frank squeezed Betty's hand. "Now everything's fine. Now if the cops question you, don't get rattled, and all you've gotta say if they ask you how we went out to Rockaway is that we went out Linden Boulevard and the way the busses go to Rockaway. Make believe you don't know the names of the streets."

Ann laughed. "We don't."

"That's better yet," Frank went on. "The only thing is this. If they ask you whether you went over a toll bridge, the answer is no."

"But think for a second before you say no," Benny added. "Don't get rattled or act like we made this up."

"We won't," Betty said. "Should we go back now and dance?"

"What time is it?" Ann asked.

Benny looked at his watch. "Almost twelve."

"Maybe we better go," Frank suggested. "You know we gotta be careful and stay outa trouble."

"One more dance," Betty pleaded. "You're a good dancer, Frank. Just one more dance."

Frank stood up and extended his hand. "Come on. You going on the floor?" he asked Ann and Benny.

Ann put her arms around Benny. "No, we'll sit here and muzzle. Pick us up when you're ready."

"Isn't she a character?" Benny asked admiringly, and kissed Ann while his free hand caressed her breast. "Don't hurry," he called after Frank and Betty. "I'm having a wonderful time."

94

Chapter 7

Crazy Sachs was feeling mean as he turned the corner from Pitkin into Amboy on Saturday evening after work. It really burned him to work a full day on Saturday when he didn't want the overtime. And when he had told the boss that since the summer was coming he was willing to do without the overtime, the boss had told him that he only employed men who wanted to make an extra buck when they had the chance. He wished he were smart enough to be a welder or a calker or to run a machine in an airplane factory, where maybe he could hitch a ride in a bomber or one of those fighter planes.

Crazy shifted the package he held in his hands and made a whirring noise like a propeller. He could see himself in the cockpit of a fighter, with the transparent canopy closed above him, wearing a padded helmet to which were attached the biggest goggles in the world. Now Crazy trotted slowly as he picked up speed, and he extended his right arm as he was ready to take off. As he cleared the field, with the exhaust of his plane spitting blue flame, he heard a sneering voice break into his consciousness.

"Look at the crazy thing," a housewife who was leaning out of the ground-floor tenement window called to her neighbor.

"Go to hell, ya bastard," Crazy yelled at her.

"Go on." The woman laughed at him. *"Meshugener!"*

"You should drop dead, you——" Crazy stopped himself. "You should drop dead, you hooer."

The woman stood up and held her kimono shut with one hand as she shook her other hand at Crazy. "Wait until my husband comes home! He'll give you for calling me names, you *meshugener paskudnack!"*

"Your husband!" Crazy spit in her direction and the

woman drew back instinctively. "Who's afraid of that *shmuck?* Just let him start something. Any time. He'll wind up with a broken head."

"I'll tell your mother what a fine boy you are!" the woman screamed at him.

Now he felt better. He always felt better when he was cursing someone or slugging it out with a guy. And the times he cut a spick or a nigger, those were the times when he really felt swell. Crazy turned around to laugh at the woman, who was still screaming that she was going to tell his mother what kind of a boy he was, and he looked in the gutter for a stone to throw at her. The woman ducked back in the room, and Crazy juggled the package of meat he carried. Three thick steaks, tenderloins, weighing more than three pounds each, rich with blood and yellow fat— Crazy saw them served rare with french-fried potatoes and potato salad. Maybe he was a dummy when it came to thinking, but he and his family ate better than most of the people on Amboy between Pitkin and East New York.

Crazy spit as he passed the tenement in which Frank lived. The guy really had his guts to slug him just because he was kidding around last Monday with his kid sister. He hadn't done anything. The kid was looking out of her window, and when she saw him he was only kidding around. What the hell would he want to bother with a skinny kid like Alice, who always looked scared and didn't even wear lipstick, when Fanny Kane always winked at him when he saw her sitting on the stoop? He hurried across the street to Fanny, who was sitting on a wooden bench rocking her baby brother's carriage. Crazy took off his cap, smoothed his long hair, and tried to think of something flip and smart to say. But his teeth seemed to stick together and his tongue became thick and immobile. Crazy waved his hand and stood nervously before Fanny.

"Hello," he stuttered.

"What've you got in the bag?" Fanny asked him.

"Steaks."

"Steaks!"

"Yeah. Three of them."

"Give me one."

"They ain't kosher."

"So what?" Fanny reached for the package, but Crazy held it behind his back. "Come on, give me a steak. My mom doesn't care if it isn't kosher. As long as it's good. Don't be a cheap skate."

"I'm not a cheap skate."

"Then give me a steak."

Crazy winked at her. "What'll you give me?"

Fanny looked at him boldly. "What d'ya want?"

Crazy looked about him to see whether anyone was approaching. "Meet me on my roof in a couple of minutes and I'll give you a steak."

Fanny shook her head and began to rock the carriage. "No."

"You're afraid," Crazy challenged her.

Fanny stretched her arms so that her sweater was taut and revealed the outline of her young breasts. Slowly and tantalizingly she twisted about, enjoying the look of hunger and longing in Crazy's eyes.

"Of you?" Fanny replied.

"Then meet me on the roof. I won't do nothing."

"I've got to mind the baby."

"Take him in or get some kid to watch him. You want a steak? Then come up on my roof and get it."

Crazy walked across the street, tossing the package in the air and whistling. He went up the steps of the stoop two at a time and kicked open the hall door. He was pretty sure that Fanny would meet him on the roof and he wasn't going to scare her. After all, she was his girl because she was going to meet him, and when a guy had a steady girl he didn't shove her around unless she were willing. Mitch believed him about Fanny, and Mitch was a good guy and smart and his best friend. Maybe he ought to give the steak to Mitch instead of Fanny, because what came first, a guy's best friend or his girl? The problem was too difficult for Crazy to solve and he dismissed it.

Crazy scratched on the door of his apartment and mewed like a cat. His mother opened the door, smiled at him, and welcomed him with a cry of pleasure as she held out her hands.

"*Nu, zindele,* what are you bringing home today?"

Crazy loved his mother. She was the only person who

was never cross with him. Even less cross than Mitch. "Steaks. Big ones," he said, and kissed her.

His mother sighed. "If they were only kosher."

"They're good, Momma. And they didn't cost me anything. Not even points."

"So give them here"—she pinched his cheek—"and we'll have one for supper tonight."

"With french fries and potato salad?"

"Only with french fries." She slapped at him playfully and he dodged the blow.

Crazy unwrapped the package and handed his mother the two largest steaks. "I'm keeping one," he said. "I promised it to a friend. I'll be right back."

"Hurry," his mother said. "You'll want to take a bath before eating, and supper'll be ready in a half-hour."

"I'll be back," Crazy promised.

Crazy ran down the stairs and entered Frank's hall and went up to the roof. He thumbed his nose at Frank's apartment door and wondered whether Fanny would be waiting for him. As he opened the door to the roof and saw her sitting on the ledge that divided the tenement roofs he felt like shouting and cursing to express his joy.

Crazy approached her shyly and gave her the steak. "See," he said, "I'm keeping my promise."

Fanny unwrapped the steak and stared at it. "What a beauty," she finally said. "Thanks."

"How about a kiss?"

"Sure," Fanny said. "Go ahead."

Hesitantly Crazy put his arms around Fanny and licked his lips before he kissed her. Fanny was the first girl he had kissed who was not a prostitute or a gang slut. Her lips were warm and soft, and she kissed him with the inexperience and simple ardor of a girl who was twelve years old. Her rouged lips were parted slightly and she did not protest as Crazy pressed her breasts with fumbling, awkward hands.

Crazy drew back, and there were tears in his eyes. "Gee, Fanny," he choked, "I'm nuts about you. I want you to be my girl."

"You're kidding." She laughed at him.

98

Crazy sniffed and for a moment he wanted to strangle her. "Can I kiss you again?" he asked her.

Fanny slipped her arms around his neck. "Sure."

Crazy felt as if he were rocketing to the moon. The clouds were pink, and he was dressed in white riding breeches and black patent-leather boots with a short red-sleeved shirt and a blue cape. He was a combination of Superman, Captain Marvel, and the Blue Beetle. These guys had girls, and even though they were always hanging around with cops, they sure could battle, and now he could identify himself with these heroes because he had a girl who smelled clean and held him as if she really liked him.

"I'm crazy about you," he said as he fought for words to express his emotion. "Real nuts about you. I think about you all the time and I even told the Dukes that you were my girl. I'll take you to the movies and rowing and to Coney Island and I'll show you a swell time, just as good, even better, than anybody else. So you just be my girl and everything is gonna be swell. And another thing, you mustn't let other guys kiss you."

"How could I"—Fanny stroked his cheeks—"when I'm gonna be your girl?"

"That's right," Crazy agreed. "I wanta take you out to-night."

"My mother won't let me go out with you."

"Why not?"

Fanny looked at him pityingly. "She thinks you're——" Fanny pointed her forefinger at her forehead and made a circular motion.

"That's what everyone thinks," Crazy admitted. "Maybe I'm not smart like other guys," he went on bitterly, "but I'm working, ain't I? I got just as much dough as they have. Look"—he took his wallet from his hip pocket and showed Fanny two ten-dollar bills and some miscellaneous other bills—"I can show you a good time like anybody else."

Fanny's eyes were greedy as she stared at the money. "I saw a sharp skirt in Adeline's on Pitkin Avenue. It's plaid and only five bucks."

"I'll buy it for you."

"When?"

"Monday night. Am I gonna see you tonight?"

"Look," she said to him. "I'll tell my mother that I'm going to my girl friend's house tonight and then I'll go to see my girl friend. I'll stay there till about nine o'clock and then I'll meet you. Where?"

"In front of the Pitkin? Where do you wanta go?"

"How about a Broadway show?"

"The movies?"

"Yeah."

"Sure." Crazy nodded happily. "I like the movies. We'll go see a war picture with plenty of fighting."

"I like love pictures."

"We'll see what's good," Crazy compromised. "So you'll meet me in front of the Pitkin about nine o'clock?"

Fanny jumped from the ledge and smoothed her skirt. "I'll be there."

Crazy pressed her to him and felt her young body, lush and supple, bend as he kissed and caressed her. "I'll be waiting," he said hoarsely, "nine o'clock."

Like a torpedo Crazy raced down the steps to his apartment. He plunged into the tub and lay under the water, holding his breath and making believe he was an American submarine and sinking Japs. Wroosh, wroosh, the torpedoes left their tubes and roared through the water to their target. Wham! They tore into Jap battleships, and the sponge and nailbrush went up in flames and the oil slick grew larger as the cake of soap dissolved in the water.

He stood up and wrapped the bath towel around him, as his mother called to him that supper was ready. "Hey, Mom"—he opened the door and called to her—"can I eat with the towel around me?"

"Get dressed," his father ordered him.

"You can come to the table in the towel," his mother said, and turned to her husband. "You let him alone and don't nag him. The boy looked tired when he came home."

"Tired!" his father sniffed. "If he went to sleep on time like a decent boy would do he wouldn't be so tired."

"Enough," his mother replied. "His life is not easy like

other people's. *Er ist ein Gott gestrafener,* afflicted by God. Let him alone and *genug."*

Mr. Sachs threw down his newspaper with exasperation. "Always genug! Do you know that people are complaining to me about the way he curses in the street and looks for fights?"

"Next time tell the *yentes* to let him alone," his wife replied fiercely. "You hear me? Alone!"

Crazy had buckled his belt around the bath towel and approached the table. "I look like a sheik," he said to his mother. "Don't I look like a sheik, Momma?"

His mother lifted a corner of the towel and wiped his back. "Like a regular prince. And for a prince and a sheik I've made a big dish of french fries."

"I wish I had potato salad too."

His father looked at him with disgust. "Do you know that there are other vegetables besides potatoes?"

"Sure," Crazy replied. "But I don't like them. That's a good one!" He pounded on the table with his knife and fork. "I was sharp then, Pop. Huh, Pop? Wasn't I, Pop?"

Mrs. Sachs placed the steak before her son. "Eat."

With his arms working like pistons and grunting as he chewed the meat with noisy smackings of his lips, Crazy shoveled the potatoes into his mouth as he drank glass after glass of bubbling seltzer. He belched loudly, sucked his teeth, and tore large chunks of bread from the half of the pound pumpernickel loaf which his mother had placed near his plate. He did not speak as he ate but looked at his mother with gratitude, pointed to the plate, and rubbed his stomach. His mother smiled at him encouragingly, and Crazy bent low over his plate and sopped up the steak juices with the pumpernickel. His father ate stolidly, deliberately staring at a fixed grease spot on the opposite wall to avoid looking at his son.

"I got a date tonight with my girl," Crazy said proudly.

His mother placed her hands in her lap. "You got a girl? Only one?"

"I could have lots of girls," he bragged.

"And why not?" his mother asked. "A son who can bring home such steaks would make any girl a good husband."

Crazy blushed. "I'm not gonna get married yet, Mom. Gee"—he thought for a moment—"I'm only seventeen. Huh, Mom, seventeen, isn't that right?"

"Who's the girl?" his father asked suddenly.

"You don't know her," Crazy replied.

"I don't believe you," his father said.

"I got a girl," Crazy insisted.

"And I don't believe," his father repeated.

"I have!"

"You haven't."

"I have! I'm telling you, I have! She's my girl!"

"You don't know what you're talking about." His father turned away from him.

Crazy trembled as he kicked back his chair and stood up. "You let me alone." His voice rose to an idiot scream. "I got a girl! My girl! She likes me and I gotta date with her. And don't you try to take her away from me or I'll——" Crazy looked about and snatched the seltzer bottle from the table.

His father stood up and stared at him. "You'll what?"

"Zindele"—his mother's voice stopped them—"what's going on here? You"—she pointed at her husband—"go downstairs! And maybe you shouldn't live to come back tonight! Go!"

Crazy slowly lowered the bottle to the table. "He's always picking on me," he said to his mother after his father left.

"But you shouldn't pick up things to your father."

"He hates me," Crazy said. "He hates me for nothing."

"He's your father," his mother insisted. "Here"—she went to the icebox—"I've got some fruit salad for you. Eat it and go get dressed for your girl."

Crazy opened the shallow closet in his room and looked at his three good suits. One was a blue chalk stripe, the second a gray chalk stripe, and the third a blue-purple tweed that looked like clashing cymbals. The tweed suit was the one he had bought himself. The other suits were chosen for him by Mitch, but he liked the tweed suit best.

Dressing was more difficult for Crazy than heaving sides of beef into the delivery truck or changing flat tires. He felt most at ease when he wore dungarees and denim shirts, but now that Fanny was his girl he was going to be as sharp as any of the guys in the Dukes. He placed his initialed tie chain across the tie and looked at himself in the mirror. The result was disappointing. The collar of his shirt appeared wilted and did not roll with the nonchalance with which Mitch's collars did. He fluffed the collar, but it did not help, and his tie hung awry and continued to shift under his collar. Crazy decided not to bother any more and slipped into his trousers.

The weather was warm and he decided not to wear his vest, and after looking at himself again in the mirror he decided that the knot in his tie was all right and he wanted Fanny to see his fancy initialed tie chain.

Carefully he lifted his pearl-gray hat with the blue Paisley ribbon which he had bought for the Passover holidays and which, remarkably enough, had only minor stains, and placed it upon his head. He tried tilting the hat at an angle, wearing it forward on his head, then pushed farther back, then straight on his head, then with the brim up in a nonchalant manner, then lowered on one side, but still the hat did not look at ease. In desperation he called his mother to help him, and she set the hat on his head as he had done originally, assured him he looked wonderful and handsome, and finally he was dressed.

As his mother left the room he shut the door, withdrew his knife from his pocket, and pressed the spring. The blade leaped into position, three and a half inches of thin stainless steel that shone as he twisted the handle. With a look of grim satisfaction he pushed the blade back into its socket and returned the weapon to his pocket.

"You have two handkerchiefs to blow your nose?" his mother asked him as he entered the kitchen.

"I'll get them now," Crazy said.

"You'll be a good boy?" His mother adjusted his tie.

"Sure, Mom."

"Don't spend your money on nothing. Where're you going?"

"To Broadway. We're going to the movies. I'm gonna see a war-fighting picture. I like those best."

"Oy," his mother said half to herself, "at least thank God they'll never take you in the Army."

103

"What?"

"Nothing."

Crazy felt his hip pocket to see whether he had his wallet. "Well, Momma, I'm going."

"Have a good time and be a good boy. And, zindele. Don't fight with anyone. And if the yentes on the block bother you, don't answer them."

"I'll do what you say, Momma. And, Momma——"

"Yes?"

"Tomorrow with the other steak, you'll make more french fries?"

"Yes."

"And can I go to the delicatessen and buy some potato salad?"

"Go." His mother pushed him toward the door. "Yes."

"Good-by, Momma." Crazy waved to his mother. "Good-by."

When he reached the sidewalk he remembered what his mother had said about fighting with people on the block, and he crossed the street. He was uncomfortable with his collar buttoned, but he wanted to look well for Fanny. The jeweler's clock on Pitkin Avenue was lit and the time was eight-thirty. Crazy crossed the avenue and entered the candy store.

"Selma," he said, "tell Mitch I won't be around tonight."

"Look at him," Selma smirked, "all dressed up."

"You like the way I look?" Crazy asked her eagerly.

"Well," Selma said, "I'd rather look like you than have my legs cut off."

Crazy scratched his ear. "What the hell're you talkin' about?"

"Nothing." Selma continued to rinse glasses. "I'll tell Mitch when I see him."

"Any of the other guys around?"

"Only Black Benny was here. He was looking for Frank."

"Who cares? Gimme a pack of Camels."

Selma took the cigarettes from the carton. "Give me the seventeen cents." She beckoned to him knowingly.

Crazy handed her the coins and Selma gave him the cigarettes. "You'll tell Mitch for me?"

104

"Yes."

Crazy pushed into the crowd along the avenue and walked toward Barrett. He crossed the street at Saratoga and had one of the bootblacks in front of the bank shine his shoes. There were too many people around to start an argument, so he paid the boy, and with his shoes gleaming he waited under the marquee of the Pitkin Theater. It was five minutes to nine. Fanny would be along any minute.

There wasn't anything doing around the Winthrop Billiard and Recreation Parlor, and the way Feivel kept talking to him made Frank nervous. For more than an hour, during the times when Feivel wasn't racking balls, taking cash, or selling behind the counter, he kept bothering Frank with all sorts of questions about who might have shot Mr. Bannon. And when Feivel wasn't bothering him the Tigers wanted to know what had happened and how it felt to be grilled by the cops and if he or anyone else in his class had seen the stiff. Frank answered them curtly, and soon everyone took the hint and left him alone except Feivel.

Feivel hoisted himself into one of the tall armchairs next to Frank and offered him a cigarette. "Take one," he said.

"I don't feel like smoking," Frank said.

Feivel placed the pack in his shirt pocket. " 'Sall right with me. You think they'll ever get the guys what done it?"

"I don't know." Frank wished he would go away.

"It must've been one of the kids in your class who did it."

"A regular defective," Frank sneered.

"Yeah." Feivel faced him. "Who else woulda done it?"

Frank stood up and put on his jacket. "I don't know. And I don't care. If you see Black Benny around tell him I went to the movies or something."

He did not want to go to the clubroom or back to the corner, and he did not want to see Benny. Betty had gone to a party in the Bronx with some other guy, and even though she had thought about breaking the date she had gone to the party, and he was alone and lonesome. If Betty liked him the way she said she did, he didn't see why she hadn't given this other guy a stand-up. Saturday night and nothing to do, unless he wanted to go to the club or hang around with Benny. While he had been hanging around the poolroom he had looked up Stan Alberg's telephone number, but he didn't have the nerve to call him, even though the guy had invited him over to the house.

Frank turned from Sutter into Howard Avenue and walked toward Pitkin. He wished it were summer and that school were over. Once the term ended, he felt certain the case would be just another unsolved murder on the police blotter, and interest would slacken and the case be forgotten. In June the boys in his official class would be promoted and dispersed to other classes; some would quit school and go to work, some would be drafted into the Army, and as the group would be separated the clues would become more obscure, and Frank would be safe so long as Benny was safe. So long as Benny was safe. That was a joker.

One thing was certain, Frank thought, he would have to stay out of trouble forever, and Benny would have to do the same. That morning when he had awakened he had lain in bed for almost an hour thinking of the rough break he had had. All the good things seemed to come naturally to some guys, while as soon as he had begun to get a little break, a little money and clothes, he had to be involved in a murder. Frank shuddered and was suddenly cold. So long as Benny was safe.

He saw the girl leaving the apartment house and turned again to see if he knew her. The slick chick who smiled at him and who was sharped up like a million was Fanny Kane, looking at least three years older than her twelve years, and wearing her high-heeled shoes with ease. Compared with her, his sister Alice was still sucking on a bottle. Fanny called to him and he stopped. As she approached he took in the slave bracelet she wore around her right ankle and noticed that her sheer stockings encased a pair of slender, graceful legs.

"You're really reet," he said as he guided her closer to the curb where they could speak without obstructing the sidewalk.

Fanny touched the belt of her dress. "Like it?"

106

Frank winked appraisingly. "Sure do. This is the first time I've really seen you."

"You never looked before."

"I know," Frank admitted. "Where you going?"

"I gotta date."

"How old's the guy?" Frank asked her. "Thirteen?"

"Yeah," Fanny said, "he's older than you. He's at least eighteen."

Frank laughed at her. "Stop dreaming."

"He is!"

"And he's dating you?"

Fanny started to walk away but stopped. "I got a date with Crazy Sachs," she said.

Frank thought rapidly. This might be another way of getting even with Crazy. And Betty too. All she did was talk about maybe giving the guy a stand-up, but she had gone to the party.

"I was only kidding you," Frank said. "You're all right, Fanny"—he placed his hand familiarly on her arm—"all right. A high-powered-looking babe. I sure wish I had a date with you tonight."

"You never asked me."

"So I'm asking you now. How about it?"

"You mean you want me to stand Crazy up?" Fanny asked him slowly.

"Sure, why not?"

"He gave me a steak."

"A steak." Frank chuckled. "So that's it."

"My mother doesn't know I'm going out with him," Fanny said.

"Crazy's a funny guy," Frank said. "He's liable to drag you into a cellar and pull your pants down."

"Don't you talk that way to me." Fanny stepped back. "You're fresh!"

"I'm different," Frank continued. "If I gave you some lovin' you'd really love it. You comin' with me?"

"Crazy'll be sore."

"So what? If he bothers you I'll bust him around."

"Where'll you take me?" Fanny wavered.

"Down to some guys' club. The Tigers. They've got some hot records. You dance?"

Fanny's eyes sparkled as she shook her shoulders. "And how!"

"So what're we waiting for?" Frank took her arm and they walked toward Sutter Avenue. "Let's go!"

Crazy looked at his shockproof, waterproof, radium-dialed wrist watch with the sweep second hand and computed the time. The large hand, which was the minute hand, was at number four, and the little hand, which was the hour hand, was a little past nine. Fanny was twenty minutes late. He was impatient for her to come, but if she wasn't there soon it would be too late for them to go to New York, and then he'd invite her down to the Dukes'. The guys would sure be surprised when he walked in with a date, and after he introduced his girl he'd give them the eye and they'd walk out and he'd have the place to himself. Some of the other guys might be around with dates, and about eleven o'clock only one blue light would be burning and the radio would be turned low and they'd all be muzzling. Thinking about it made him feel good. Fanny was sure to come along any minute now, and he'd tell her it was too late to go to New York.

The lights in the marquee were hot, and Crazy strolled to the haberdashery store next to the theater and admired the hand-painted silk ties in the window. They were five and ten dollars each. Next payday, he decided, he would buy two of the five-dollar ones. He would get the pink one with the large birds and the blue one with the race horse and the jockey. Fanny would like the ties. He withdrew his key chain and began to twirl it as he looked at the shoes in Dinny and Robbins. Not one pair on display had thicker soles than the shoes he wore. The salesman had told him that his shoes were very English. Did he make up to meet with Fanny in front of the Pitkin? Crazy bent his head and scowled as he sought to remember their conversation. He shook his head. The Pitkin was where he had said he would meet her.

Impatiently he looked at his watch again. The minute hand was just past five. Time was long and monotonous, and the display of shoes no longer interested him. Rapidly Crazy swung his key chain in swift circles while he wished that Fanny would hurry. Maybe, he thought, she was having trouble getting away from her friend. Some babes, the guys said, if they didn't have a date, didn't want their friends to have a date. Fanny's friend must be like that.

"Hey!" Crazy spun around as he heard Mitch's voice. "What're you doin' all zooted up?"

Crazy pumped Mitch's hand as if he had not seen him for many years. "I'm waiting for my date."

Mitch shook his head. "So why're you wearin' that circus zoot? I'm gonna have to burn it."

Crazy caressed the cloth of his jacket. "I like this suit, Mitch. It makes me feel happy. Them other suits you picked out for me are for old *kockers*."

"Who you got a date with?" Mitch changed the subject.

Crazy felt silly. "You know who."

"Stop being a character," Mitch said. "Who?"

"Fanny Kane."

Mitch whistled. "So you're dating her?"

"Gee." Crazy stopped swinging his key chain. "I kissed her on my roof tonight and she let me squeeze her bubs. She's my girl. She said she was my girl and she liked me and she wasn't going to go with anybody else because we're going steady."

"Fine," Mitch said patiently. "What time you meeting her?"

"Nine o'clock."

Mitch's expression was one of disgust. "Stupid," he said to Crazy, "you know it's almost ten?"

Crazy looked at his watch. "Two more minutes," he said defensively.

"You sure you made up to meet her here?"

"That's what I thought, but I could swear by anything that we made up in front of the Pitkin."

"Come on," Mitch said, "she's not gonna show up."

"Maybe she got held up somewhere," Crazy said.

"I wouldn't wait for Hedy Lamarr more than fifteen minutes," Mitch said. "Come on. We'll go down the club."

"No."

"Bull's bringing down Rosie Beanbags. You like her."

Crazy compressed his lips stubbornly. "I'm waitin' for my girl."

"How long you gonna wait?"

"Till she comes."

"All night?"

"She'll be here soon. Go away, Mitch." Crazy turned away from him.

"Rosie Beanbags," Mitch said cajolingly, "and we're gonna make her take all her clothes off."

"No!"

Mitch straightened Crazy's tie. "Hold it," he ordered him, "your tie's crooked."

Crazy stood quietly while Mitch undid his tie and reknotted it.

"Now"—Mitch patted the knot—"it looks better."

"Thanks," Crazy said. "I wish I could tie a tie like you can."

"I'll teach you," Mitch said. "Are you coming down the club?"

Crazy looked into the crowd. "No. I'm waitin'."

"Suit yourself." Mitch walked away.

The little hand was on ten and the big hand was past three. What could be keeping her? She had promised to meet him, and in Crazy's mind her promise was fixed and irrevocable, for he reasoned that if Fanny had not wanted to meet him she would not have made the appointment. When he told her he considered her his girl she had agreed. If only he knew where her friend lived. He crossed Pitkin Avenue and walked to Grafton Street and stopped. He didn't know where to go. While he was looking for her she might arrive in front of the theater, not see him there, and leave. He retraced his steps and stood under the marquee, bewildered and feeling the meanness, which was always a part of him, become more and more pronounced. Two girls passed by, and one of them bumped him and he swore at her. The girls hurried on, astonished and ashamed at the filth that Crazy heaped upon them. Pacing in front of the marquee made him angrier, and the blurred, monotonous voice of the doorman who repeated that no seats were available until the midnight show annoyed him. His right hand gripped the spring knife, and he would have enjoyed cutting and stabbing Fanny. It was easy for him to see her pleading

110

with him to leave her alone and the way her eyes blackened after he struck her. But why should he give her a pasting? Maybe she was sick or had been run over. Now he could see her in the hospital surrounded by tremendous wreaths of flowers he had bought for her. She would be lying in a white bed and smiling at him as she would tell him that she loved him and would be well soon and then he could take her rowing in Prospect Park and to the movies to see war pictures with lots of fighting. Fanny was still his girl. Something was keeping her, and he had to wait under the marquee until she came or until the messenger came and told him that she was in the hospital and calling for him.

At eleven o'clock Crazy became thirsty and went across the street to a candy store and bought a bottle of Pepsi-Cola. He drained the bottle quickly and went back to his station. Now the crowd became heavier as people left the theater and the doorman bawled that the midnight show would begin in an hour. Groups of people met under the marquee, laughing pleasantly as they waited for one of their group to purchase admission tickets to the theater. Crazy stared at them, trying to see Fanny in every slim pair of legs, every high pair of breasts, every laughing mouth. She would have to come soon; he couldn't wait much longer. The minutes ticked by methodically, and Crazy knew that soon he would begin to cry. The dream of bringing his girl to the club, introducing her, faded and became less distinct. Only his anger grew, and his rage was impotent and without direction. Confused and unhappy, he scanned the face of every girl who passed by, and still he did not see Fanny.

As he saw Mitch coming back up the avenue he wanted to run away, but then he might miss Fanny. He stood there, trying to be nonchalant and unconcerned, but Mitch saw instantly that Crazy was in one of his unpredictable and dangerous moods.

"I just left Bull Bronstein and Rosie Beanbags, and they were going to pick up a new friend of Rosie's," Mitch said casually. "So I told him that I was coming back to get you because you were waiting for me."

"I'm not waiting for you, Mitch."

111

"Oh." Mitch opened his mouth as if he were surprised. "I thought we made up that I'd come back here for you."

"Blow," Crazy said abruptly.

"You want me to beat it?" Mitch asked him.

Crazy turned away from him. "Yeah, blow."

"You sore at me?"

"No." Crazy grasped Mitch's sleeve. "I'm not sore at you. Where is she?" he asked desperately. "Why isn't Fanny here? I've been waitin' almost three hours!"

"She's not comin'," Mitch said kindly. "Come on, let's go down the club. We're gonna have us a time tonight. I'll buy a pint if you hurry, and we'll split it."

"Fanny." Crazy began to sob as he permitted Mitch to lead him. "Fanny. My girl."

Mitch nudged him. "Cut it out. You're a hard guy. Why're you acting like a kid?"

In the darkness of Barrett Street, Crazy sobbed and did not reply. The tie and closed collar choked him, and in his rage he tore the tie loose and ripped the collar button from his shirt. He threw the tie into the street, but Mitch picked it up and placed it in Crazy's jacket pocket. Walking and stumbling as if he were drunk, Crazy leaned against the iron railings before the tenements and cried violently, punching at the darkness as he called for Fanny. Mitch dragged him along, and when they reached Sutter Avenue Crazy refused to go any farther.

"I don't want to go down the club." He wiped his eyes. "I don't want nothing to do with no hooer tonight."

"That's all Fanny is. Get wise to yourself."

Crazy grabbed Mitch's shoulder and drew back his fist. "Don't you say that about my girl!"

"I'm sorry," Mitch said. "I'm just burned up because she stood you up."

"She didn't stand me up. She's been in an accident or maybe she's kidnaped. Or maybe her mother or her baby brother are sick and she had to stay home and mind them. That's what happened. Isn't that what happened?"

"Sure," Mitch agreed. "That's it. I'm a dope for not thinking of it. Her mother must be sick."

"Or maybe she was in an accident."

"I don't think so."

"How about some guys kidnapin' her?"

Mitch shook his head. "No. Her mother must be sick. Come on now"—he shook Crazy—"you don't want to go down the club. So let's go back to the candy store and I'll buy you the biggest frappé they got. I'll have Selma make you something special. And you know what, you jerk? In the ice cream I'll tell her to put french fries and potato salad."

"You're nuts." Crazy giggled with excitement. "Whoever heard of french fries and potato salad—— Say, I'll bet," he said earnestly, "it must be good. Ice cream is good and french fries and potato salad is good, so why can't they be good all together? Huh? Why not?"

"Could be," Mitch agreed. "Wipe your face and we'll go to the candy store."

Benny was sitting at the counter twisting straws into the figure of a doll. He followed Mitch and Crazy to a booth and continued to twist and pinch the straws into an awkward caricature of a figure with disproportionate arms and legs.

"What's eating you?" Mitch asked him. "I'm beginning to feel like a nurse."

"I can't find Frank."

"You go down the club?"

"Yes. He left a message for me in the Winthrop that he was going away, and I don't know where he went."

"Fanny's been in an accident," Crazy said.

"Stop it," Mitch said to him. "Crazy had a date with Fanny Kane," Mitch said to Benny, and warned him with a gesture not to comment, "and she didn't meet him. Someone must be sick in her family and she couldn't come. So what does our boy here do? He waits in front of the Pitkin for her for almost three hours. So"—he turned to Crazy—"she's not in no accident and she hasn't been kidnaped. Chrissake, you gotta stop reading so many of them joke books. You're becoming even whackier than you are."

"I dreamed last week I was Captain Marvel," Crazy said. "All I did was say 'Shazam' and I was changed into Captain Marvel. You know," he said earnestly, "I wish I could say

113

a word like 'Shazam' and change into a guy like Captain Marvel. Then I'd know what happened to Fanny."

Mitch looked at Benny with wonder and pity. "And you think you've got troubles. Selma," he called, "you wanna sell us some ice cream?"

Selma took their order and scuffed to the counter.

"And if you got chocolate sprinkles," Mitch called to her, "put them on Crazy's sundae. Put everything you got on it. I'm treating."

"I heard you the first time," Selma said crossly.

"Mitch said that he was gonna have Selma put french fries and potato salad in my frappé," Crazy said to Benny.

"It might be good," Benny said.

"Why didn't you stick around down the club?" Crazy asked him. "Bull was bringin' Rosie Beanbags down. Mitch wanted me to go, but I was waitin' for my girl."

Benny squashed the doll he made in his fist. "The guys told me she was coming down, but I was looking for Frank."

"So you couldn't find him, so what?" Mitch said. "I can't figure you guys out. You're supposed to meet someone and he doesn't show up. So you wait around for a while and then you blow. There's plenty of things to do. We coulda gone down the club and had ourselves a time or we coulda crashed a party or something. So instead you two guys are moping and you break up my Saturday. I'm disgusted."

Benny scooped the ice cream into his mouth. "I didn't ask your advice."

"So I'm telling you anyway," Mitch continued. "Hell, you 'n' Frank had a rough week in school. So suppose you think maybe his old man doesn't want him hanging around with us or something. Or maybe he's got a date."

"He's got no date," Benny said. "His babe and mine went to a party in the Bronx. The bitches."

"My girl didn't meet me either," Crazy added gravely.

"Figure it out, Benny." Mitch attempted to reason with Benny, whose face was a mirror of anger. "Frank told me that his folks want to move outa here and that he's gonna look for an apartment in East Flatbush."

"He didn't tell me," Benny said.

"So he didn't," Mitch said patiently. "Maybe he didn't

think of it or maybe—— Say, what the hell, Benny, must he tell you everything, like when he goes to the can too?"

"I tell Mitch everything," Crazy said, "and I don't tell him that. Do I, Mitch?"

"All right," Benny said. "Let's finish our frappés and stand on the corner. I don't feel like going home yet."

"You think maybe the guys are still down the club with Rosie?" Crazy licked the dish with his tongue.

"It's after one," Mitch said. "I don't think so. And I'm too tired to get laid now."

"Me too," Crazy said. "You think Fanny's brother or mother died?"

"I don't know." Mitch paid their bill. "Come on. Good night, Selma."

Pitkin Avenue was dark except for the street lights and the blinking traffic signals. Up toward Saratoga Avenue they could see the large neon sign in front of Davidson's Restaurant and the pearl light shining through the large plate-glass windows. Couples strolled slowly along the avenue, and occasionally the stillness would be broken by a sharp burst of laughter. In one of the chop suey joints the band was playing a waltz, and the sharp, yapping, staccato bark of the newsboy on Douglass and Pitkin calling the morning's headlines could be heard distinctly.

Mitch wanted to go home, but Crazy and Benny insisted that he stay with them.

"It's too early to go home," Benny said.

"I'm tired," Mitch insisted. "I've been taking care of Crazy all night." He looked at Crazy. "What a character! Look at that zoot."

"This is my best suit," Crazy insisted. "Fanny woulda liked me in this suit. Say"—he turned to Benny—"what's the matter with you?"

"Shut up," Benny said sharply. "I think I see Frank coming down Amboy Street. He's across the street there. Wait till he gets to the next street light."

They walked to the curb and waited. They saw two figures approach the street light, and as they passed beneath it they could see it was Frank with a girl.

"It's Frank all right," Mitch said. "Who's the babe with him?"

115

"Let's cross the street and see," Crazy suggested.

They crossed and waited on the corner for Frank to approach them, and when he was approximately twenty feet away Mitch grabbed Crazy and held him.

"It's Fanny!" Crazy choked and struggled to break free. "Fanny! She stood me up for that bastard!"

"Hold him, Benny," Mitch said as he tightened his grip on Crazy and Fanny shrank closer to Frank.

"You bastard!" Crazy cursed as his face became contorted and insane. "You little bitch! You stood me up for that bastard! Let me go!" He strove to get free from Mitch, who had twisted his arms behind his back while Benny held his shoulders. "I'll cut your hearts out for this!"

"Shut your mouth before I kick you in the teeth." Frank laughed at him. "Come on, Fanny," he said to her. "You see the kind of a guy you almost dated?"

"I'll kill you yet! I'll kill you! I swear by my mother that I'll kill you for this!"

"Beat it, Frank," Mitch said to him. "Crazy's in a bad way."

"I'm not afraid of him," Frank said. "Fanny's a good piece," he shouted tauntingly at Crazy. "Too damn good for you!"

Suddenly all the fight left Crazy and he went to pieces and began to sob again. Mitch talked to him soothingly, trying to make him believe that he was too nice a guy for Fanny and that he would find him a girl who would make Fanny look sick. Benny said nothing. Now he didn't know how he felt about Frank, for a guy who would take something away from Crazy was pretty much of a rat.

"Let's take him upstairs to his door," Benny suggested.

Crazy gulped. "I can go home alone."

"No," Mitch said. "We're taking you home."

Silently they walked along Amboy Street past the tenement in which Frank lived and up the steps of the next tenement. Benny waited downstairs while Mitch went up with Crazy. When Mitch came down they walked back to Pitkin Avenue.

"Frank better watch out," Mitch broke the silence. "Crazy's one guy I wouldn't want to hate me."

116

"I know," Benny agreed.

"Crazy's liable to kill him someday."

"I know," Benny said. Maybe Crazy would kill Frank. That would be the best way out for him.

Chapter 8

The hum of conversation ceased as Detective Lieutenant Macon walked into the conference room at the Liberty Avenue police station. There were approximately ten uniformed policemen and thirty-five detectives in the room, and they filed into the straight rows of seats as Detective Macon slid into his chair behind the desk on the raised platform. Behind him on the blackboards were two chalk drawings of the New Lots Vocational High School. One drawing was an aerial view of the ground plan of the school, showing the schoolyards and the entrances to the school. The other drawing was a floor plan of the second floor of the school.

"All right, men," Macon began the discussion, "you know why we're here. The mayor and police commissioner have given us orders to break this case or else. And"—he cleared his throat—"I don't want to think about that or else while pounding a beat in Staten Island."

Macon waited for the movement of laughter to subside before he continued. "Now what've we got? One tough high school and one murdered teacher and plenty of motives for killing him. The kids in his classes were tough—I know, I've talked to them—and he had a time keeping order. But so did the other teachers in the school. I've talked to them too. But this guy Bannon had trouble with his official class the day he got it, and since"—he referred to one of the cards he had on the desk—"there are thirty-seven students in the class, we only get thirty-seven first-class suspects."

117

Macon silenced the groan. "I know, it's tough. The mayor wants the killer. And we've got to find him. And we haven't much time. School lets out the end of June, and then we'll really be in a spot. So that's why"—Macon gestured with one hand—"the commissioner has assigned you men to the case. We've got to find the killer. Probably a kid that's been in here, that we talked to, and hasn't even got a record. We talked to about two hundred and fifty kids, and"—again he referred to his cards—"there were only fourteen who've been in a reformatory or before the juvenile court. So now you know what the newspapers know, and we'll go on from there."

"Can we ask questions?" one of the policemen asked Macon.

"Any time." Macon nodded. "Just get my attention. Now let's see." Macon stood up and went to the board. "The teacher was killed by one bullet, a .22. Our ballistics people say that there weren't any regular rifle marks on the slug, and so we know that it must've been fired by one of those homemade pistols. We fired some slugs with some of those pistols, and they looked like the bullet that killed Bannon. So we're pretty sure that he was killed by some kid. Nothing was taken out of his pockets and his clothing wasn't disturbed, so we're pretty sure that robbery wasn't the motive. Bannon had been in a fight. Before we go on, see if there's a reporter snooping around outside," Macon ordered one of the detectives in the last row of seats.

He waited until the detective opened the door, peered into the corridor, shook his head negatively, and sat down.

"Now we come to what the papers didn't have. Bannon had been in a fight, and we've got reason to believe that two kids are implicated in the murder instead of one. You see"—Macon paused for effect—"the autopsy showed that Bannon had been struck in the back of the head with some sort of weapon, maybe the gun. But the blow wasn't hard enough to knock him out. So he must've been fighting with someone else, from the bruises he had on his face, and maybe he was giving some other kid a licking. So we've got two kids to look for. Of course," he went on, "there's always the chance that it was one kid. But we don't think so."

118

"Did you find out what kids were friends?" one of the detectives asked.

"We did," Macon said, and took another card from the pile on the desk. "I'll write their names on the board and you can copy them."

When Macon had finished he turned to the group and said, "You all know that Benny Semmel and Frank Gold-farb were the direct causes of the riot in their official class. That makes them first-class suspects, except"—Macon paused for breath—"that their punishment wasn't any more drastic than that of the other boys. All the kids in the class have good alibis; some I've checked, and I'll tell you which ones, and they click.

"You see"—Macon sat on the edge of the desk—"what makes this so tough is that these kids aren't criminals yet, and we can't find holes in their alibis. I don't have to tell you what we're up against. They're getting wilder and tougher every day, and our jobs are going to get tougher. But to get back to these kids, they all did about the same thing. They hung around the school for a while. Then some went home, some went to the movies, some went to their clubrooms, and some went to the poolroom, to the park, or just walked around. That's what makes it tough. The kids with court records—well"—Macon pulled up his trouser leg—"we checked them too. We can't break their alibis."

"You sound plenty pessimistic, Lieutenant," one of the detectives said.

"I know," Macon agreed, "but we've got this to go on. I'm sure two kids knocked off Bannon. And I'm willing to go along on the premise that they were friends. First we'll concentrate on them"—he pointed to the grouped names on the board—"and then we'll work on the others. Now," he continued, "another thing. You see that a lot of these kids belong to clubs. All right. We're going to raid their clubs. Maybe we'll pick up something and maybe we won't. Maybe the ones that did it will've told the guys in their gang, and if we quiz them, we're liable to break them down. And then"—Macon raised his hand—"we're liable to pick up some kids in the clubs on other charges. Carrying concealed weapons, counterfeit ration coupons, stuff like that. If we hold them, the kids in the clubs are going to be sore at these kids." He pointed again to the names on the board. "And in that way somebody is liable to crack up. Remember, these kids try to look tough, and they hate cops and dicks"—Macon smiled as some of the men twisted their lips wryly—"but they're not old enough to know all the ropes. We'll get the killer or killers for that reason. We'll scare them, and that way we'll get them."

"Suppose we work on these suspects and nothing turns up?" a detective in the front row asked.

"Before we close this meeting," Macon said, "you'll have the names of everyone in Bannon's official class, his other classes, the clubs or gangs they belong to, and anything else we know. You've all seen the kind of guns these kids carry. We pick up at least a dozen every day all over the city. So if there aren't any more questions we'll go over the ground plan of the yards and the floor, and then we'll pass out mimeographed sheets with the names of Bannon's former students."

For more than an hour Macon led the discussion and oriented the assembled men in the physical features of the neighborhood, the location of the school, and possible entries to and exits from the school. He stressed again that there were no witnesses who saw or noticed anyone suspicious entering or leaving the school, and that this lack of witnesses complicated the case.

"So there it is," Macon concluded. "Now you know what we know. The first thing to do is to get after the gangs. Decide what you need and see Sergeant Fuller, who will keep a record of your activities and get anything you need. Good luck."

The four detectives, Gallagher, Leonard, Finch, and Wilner, who were assigned to check on Benny Semmel and Frank Goldfarb, read the files of both boys, quickly noted that they had been driving a car illegally and that they belonged to the Amboy Dukes.

"They hang out on Amboy near Pitkin," Wilner read from the report. "I know that corner. Pretty tough."

"Used to be a lot of trouble back there in '34 and '35," Gallagher agreed. "Some of the boys on that block were mobsters for Abe Reles and Buggsy Goldstein."

120

"I sure wish I wasn't on this case," Wilner said. "I don't like putting the rap on kids."

"Some kids if they knocked off their teacher." Leonard laughed and bit off the end of a cigar.

"Well," Gallagher said, "let's get started. Two of us'll go down their club with a wagon and pick up as many as we can, and you can pick the others up on the corner. Better take some cops with you. How about you coming with me, Finch?"

Finch nodded. "Suits me."

"We'll pick them up about ten o'clock tonight," Gallagher said.

"Wilner and me'll get those on the corner at ten," Leonard said. "Let's see"—Leonard reached for the report—"they hang out between Pitkin and Sutter on the east side of the street in front of a candy store. See you guys tonight. Come on, Moe," he said to Wilner, "let's get something to eat. We're working tonight."

Crazy Sachs and Bull Bronstein were the first ones to notice the patrol wagon coast to a stop in front of the candy store, and before they could run the police had run two squad cars onto the sidewalk on both sides of the store, completely blocking any attempt to escape. With quiet efficiency the police rounded up the Dukes who had vainly attempted to break through the cordon and ordered them into the patrol wagon. Five minutes later the squad cars backed off the sidewalk and accompanied the wagon back to the Liberty Avenue station.

"All right." A policeman opened the rear door of the wagon. "You gentlemen can unload."

"Ain'tcha got a plush carpet for us?" Larry Tunafish asked.

"Get out," the policeman said, "before you get a slap in the mouth."

"What you brung us in for?" Crazy wanted to know. "We ain't done nothin'."

"Come on," the policeman said impatiently, "get moving."

Muttering and grumbling, the Dukes entered the police station and filed into their assigned benches. They were

121

frightened, for although most of them knew they had not been implicated in any misdemeanor or felony, they were all armed, and a concealed-weapons charge could mean a stiff sentence.

"Don't answer any questions," Larry Tunafish whispered to Bull. "We can ask for lawyers. Pass the word."

Bull tried to wink confidently and whispered Larry's advice to Mitch. Mitch passed the word to Crazy, who sat next to him, and Crazy passed the message to the boy on his right. Soon they were all winking at one another, and Bull began to grin and twist about to wink at the other Dukes.

They turned in their seats as they heard the doors behind them open and saw more of the Dukes being ushered into the room.

"Hey," Crazy said, "they got all our guys! Don't say nothin' without seein' your lawyer!" he shouted to them.

"Shut up"—Detective Wilner approached him—"or you'll get a fanning."

"Don't mind him," Mitch interceded. "Crazy's a little nuts. He don't know what he's doing."

Wilner looked at Crazy and photographed him mentally. "All right," he said, "just keep him quiet."

"Get into those benches there," Finch ordered the Dukes who were entering the station, "and behave until we get to you. Who's the president of the Dukes?"

No one spoke.

"Maybe you didn't hear me," Finch said sarcastically. "Who's the leader?"

Larry stood up. "I am."

Gallagher counted rapidly. "We've got seventeen of you. Now, you," he said to Larry, "are all your guys here?"

Larry looked around, and Gallagher prodded him. "Don't take all night," he said.

"One guy's missing," Larry said.

"Who?" Gallagher asked him.

"Frank Goldfarb."

Wilner clicked his teeth. "Oh."

"What you got us here for?" Larry asked them. "We didn't do nothing."

"Who said you did?" Detective Leonard asked them. "We just want to ask you some questions."

"Suppose we don't talk?" Larry asked.

Leonard shrugged his shoulders. "We're not going to beat you up, if that's what you want us to say. But you'll talk. Step out here."

Larry did not move.

Wilner beckoned to him. "Step out! If you don't step out you're resisting an officer and I'll drag you out."

Larry stepped into the aisle.

"Now get up front," Wilner ordered him, "and put your hands over your head."

Larry walked sullenly to the front of the room and slowly raised his hands. He glowered as Detective Finch went through his pockets, removed his wallet, sun glasses, hand-kerchief, small change, cigarettes, and unsnapped his key chain. Finch ran his hands along Larry's body, feeling for a gun, and then turned Larry's hat inside out. Then, as if it were almost an afterthought, he raised Larry's trouser legs and from the sheath strapped about his right calf removed the hunting knife.

Finch straightened up and hefted the knife in his hand. "I suppose you use this to clean your fingernails?" he asked Larry. "I guess you can give yourself or some other guy quite a manicure with this? What do you work at?"

Larry did not look at him. "I'm a shipping clerk," he said.

Finch looked at the other detectives and the policemen. "Another one," he sighed. "I suppose you use this to cut cord and paper?"

"I do," Larry said.

"Maybe the judge will believe you," Leonard said with mock solemnity. "Kramer," he called to one of the police-men, "book him for carrying a concealed weapon and get ready to take him over to the line-up."

The Dukes were stunned, unable to believe what was happening. Forty-five minutes ago they were sitting around the club or hanging around the corner, and now they were in deep water. Each one was ordered to the front of the room and searched, and the collection of knives and blackjacks grew larger. Only Black Benny and Crazy were weaponless, and they were held on suspicion.

Gallagher called together the detectives and spoke quietly. "We got quite a haul, and you noticed that this kid they call Black Benny wasn't carrying anything?"

"So what?" Wilner said. "That Crazy kid was clean too."

"It's a hunch," Gallagher insisted as he shook a cigar at them. "I'll bet you guys a round of beers that if we get this other kid, Goldfarb"—he snapped his fingers—"we'll find nothing on him."

Leonard's mouth hung slack. "I think you got something there. But I'll bet you that round just to make it interesting."

"Good," Gallagher said. "How about you and Finch going out and picking up Goldfarb?"

"We'll bring him down to headquarters when we get him."

"Right. So get going. We're booking these kids and taking them down to the line-up. Kramer," he called to the policeman, "get these kids booked and take them back to the wagon. Then you better notify their parents to come down to court tomorrow morning and bail them out."

"Yes, sir," Kramer said, and motioned for the other policemen to help him.

With quiet efficiency that eliminated any attempts at nonsense the Dukes were individually booked for carrying concealed weapons, while Moishe Perlman had added to this charge the illegal possession of gasoline coupons that probably were counterfeit, and Bull Bronstein was charged with a narcotic violation in addition to carrying a large sailor knife. Black Benny and Crazy were booked on suspicion, and as they sat in the wagon and were driven to the line-up the Dukes did not speak to one another. For playing at being tough and putting one over on the cops was fun, but now they realized they were facing a real rap and that the bravado, the back-stiffening sneer, the cynical snarl which was supposed to intimidate the cops had not been noticed. Facing one another on the twin benches in the caged part of the patrol wagon, they were frightened boys who bit their lips to keep from crying.

Black Benny sat beside Crazy, who trembled and muttered incoherently to himself. Mitch sat on Crazy's right and kept a restraining hand on him. Benny rocked as the wagon sped toward police headquarters on Raymond Street and wondered why he wasn't lucky. Frank hadn't been around and thus had escaped the raid. In fact, he was hardly ever around. Frank kept telling him that it looked suspicious for them to be together so much, but he couldn't see it that way. Ever since last Saturday, when Frank had given Crazy the dirty deal, he hadn't been around the club, Selma's, or the poolroom. The only times Benny saw him were at school, and then he'd leave with some sort of whacky excuse about looking for an apartment for his family in East Flatbush.

It was plain as day to Benny that Frank was looking for an out, and he had to smile in the darkness as he reflected that Frank was in with him. Just as deep. Just as solid. He was fully implicated, and because he knew it he was avoiding him and the Dukes. Now they were all being booked, and Benny found little consolation that he had been weaponless when searched, for he was being booked with the others, and his parents would have to bail him out and they would give him plenty of hell.

Frank had to be lucky. Frank had to be the guy who was taking the beating, and if Benny would've known then what a rat he was he would've let Bannon give him the shellacking he deserved. Because he had tried to be a friend, a real Duke, he had shot and killed a guy for Frank, and now he was riding in the pie wagon while Frank was out somewhere horsing around with a babe.

Benny hated Frank. The gnawing hours of distrust and suspicion were now culminated in this newborn hatred, and Benny tried to think of some way of getting even. But he knew that he did not dare. He had to keep his nose clean and maybe if he would've been a smart guy he wouldn't have been hanging around with the Dukes. In a pinch he was as good as Frank—he knew that—but when it came to thinking things out long-range he fell down.

As he walked across the brilliantly lit stage ahead of Crazy and stood blinded by the battery of lights that shone upon him it didn't seem to be he whom the gruff strong voice was describing. Benjamin Semmel, known as Black

Benny, age sixteen; height: five-six; weight: 147; distinguishing features: dark complexion and blackheads; residing at 16A Amboy Street; attending New Lots Vocational High School; in the official class of the late Mr. Bannon; booked on suspicion for consorting with dangerous juvenile characters. Black Benny was known occasionally to drive automobiles without having an operator's permit.

"Anyone here recognize him?" the voice droned. "All right, step down. Next, Mitchell Wolf, known as Mitch, age seventeen——" The descriptions of the Dukes followed in rapid order, only halting as Crazy was dragged onto the stage by two policemen who held him as he screamed and cursed at the darkness beyond the lights.

Finally, still bewildered as they saw and heard themselves described as juvenile delinquents and not as mobsters, they were all off the stage and standing before the desk of the committing officer, who booked them before they were led away to their cells. As Benny waited to step before the desk he saw Frank being brought in by Leonard and Finch. Frank's father followed them, disheveled and pale with fright and worry. Now Benny was glad. At least Frank wasn't going to get away with it, for if they were going to sit in the can Frank would be keeping them company.

"Please." Frank's father held Leonard's sleeve. "What did you bring him here for? He was coming home when you stopped him, and what has he done?"

"We just want to question him," Leonard replied.

Mr. Goldfarb wrung his hands. "Then you'll let him go?"

"We can't tell you," Finch replied. "Take it easy, Mr. Goldfarb, we just want to ask your son some questions. If he hasn't done anything he'll be out of here in no time. You know these boys are your son's friends?"

Mr. Goldfarb looked at the Dukes. "Some of them I know." He nodded. "The Sachs boy and my son's friend there, Benny. One or two others."

"You know that we're holding every one of them for carrying a concealed weapon?" Leonard said. "Your son is hanging around with a fine crowd."

Mr. Goldfarb bowed his head. "There's nothing I can

126

say." His voice was hoarse and he swallowed. "Nothing I can say."

"You better sit over there," Finch said kindly. "We'll let you know soon what we're going to do with Frank."

Leonard approached Gallagher and they held a whispered consultation. Gallagher nodded and Leonard walked over to Black Benny and tapped him on the shoulder.

"Come on," he said, "we want to talk to you."

Benny saw Frank already seated at the table in the small room adjoining the court chamber. He tried to grin as Frank winked at him, but his smile froze and he turned away.

Gallagher pointed to a chair at the table. "Sit down, Benny. Now," he said as he sat down, "let's talk."

"About what?" Frank asked.

"Things," Gallagher said. "Where were you tonight, Goldfarb?"

"I was dating."

"Who?"

"Some kid on the block."

"Who?"

"Some kid."

"Stop stalling." Gallagher's voice sounded as if it were starched. "Who? What's her name?"

"Fanny Kane."

"That stinker!" Benny exploded and rose slightly from his chair. "That twelve-year-old jail bait!"

Frank's lips drew back. "Shut your trap!"

"No rough stuff," Gallagher interjected sharply. "So you were dating." He turned to Frank. "Leonard and Finch here"—he gestured to them—"tell me they searched you and didn't find a knife or other weapon on you."

"Why should you think you'd find me carrying something?" Frank asked angrily.

Gallagher shrugged. "That's what we want to know. You're a member of the Dukes. So's Benny here. We got out and picked up all your guys, and every one is carrying a knife or brass knuckles. All except that kid you guys call Crazy. So that's what's got us puzzled."

"What're you talking about?" Benny was glad he was seated, for he knew his legs could not support him.

127

"Because it's odd." Wilner leaned across the table and spoke with his face close to Benny's. "All you boys were hipped except you and Frank. What's the matter? Get scared after Mr. Bannon was knocked off?"

The color drained from Benny's face and he looked wildly at Frank. Frank's fingers were sticky and he felt as if the walls of the room were contracting and pressing upon him, squeezing him until there was no breath left in his body. They were trapped. It was all so simple. He saw Benny struggling to speak, to break the silence which stormed about them. Their innocence now only attested and emphasized their guilt. To be caught and trapped because they had not been guilty of a misdemeanor; it was too funny, even for the books.

"Struck dumb?" Gallagher's voice attenuated the silence.

"You're trying to pin a murder rap on us," Frank choked. He saw an out.

"We aren't trying to pin anything," Wilner said. "We're just curious why a couple of hard guys like you two weren't carrying your gats."

"We never owned gats!" Frank said.

"All right," Gallagher agreed, "knives and knuckles."

"We used to carry them," Frank began, and noticed that Benny's face was stiff with horror, "but we quit after Mr. Bannon was killed. You see"—he spoke rapidly to prevent Benny from interrupting him—"I carried a knife and Benny did too. But we never did anything with it. All the guys carried them. But after Mr. Bannon got killed we threw our knives into a garbage can because we knew we were in enough trouble already and we didn't want any more. Why can't you let us alone?" He began to cry. "We're in enough trouble already and you're never gonna let us alone just because we were fooling around that day! Now my father's out there and you're riding us when we didn't do anything." Frank bent over the table and sobbed.

Gallagher looked at Benny. "What've you got to say?"

Benny screwed up his face and began to cry. He didn't want to cry, but he had to. Now his mind was clear and ticking like a metronome. As much as he hated and feared Frank, he had to admit that Frank had saved them. With

128

every muscle and reflex he compelled himself to cry, and finally, as relief from the tension, the tears came voluntarily and he wept quietly and steadily.

Gallagher was disgusted and looked his annoyance. Finch and Leonard stared stolidly at the weeping boys. Wilner looked relieved.

"Snap out of it," Gallagher finally said. "You're going home."

Benny raised his head. "You're not booking us?"

"No."

"What about the other guys?"

"They're in."

"They're taking a rap because of us," Frank said. "They wouldn't have been in no trouble if it wasn't for us."

"You're a pretty smart kid," Gallagher said. "I guess your guys aren't going to like you much."

"Why can't you give them a break?" Frank pleaded. "I swear by my mother and father they never done anything. Suppose they were carrying knives and knucks? We never done nothing. Carrying a knife and knucks is like wearing peg pants and a sharp hat. It's like a part of a uniform," he reasoned desperately. "And most of the guys used their knives when they were working."

"Here we go again," Leonard snorted.

"Let 'em go," Benny begged. "The guys'll have it in for us."

"Maybe we could strike a deal," Gallagher suggested.

Frank was wary. "What?"

"Tell us who shot Bannon."

Frank looked at him as if he were insane. "We don't know," he said.

"Maybe Benny knows." Gallagher turned to him.

"I don't know either," Benny said rapidly. "You guys are really giving us a hosing. Why don't you let us alone? All of us? Let us alone!"

Gallagher opened the door. "Meeting's adjourned. Go on home and stay out of trouble."

"We stay out of it, but you put us right back in." Benny continued to cry, for he found safety in tears. "And you wonder why we don't like cops!"

Frank turned to Gallagher. "I want to wash."

"Me too," Benny said.

Leonard opened a door at the other end of the room. "In here. Make it snappy."

Frank shut the door behind them and started to speak, but Benny put his hand across his mouth and pointed to the walls. For a moment Frank looked startled, then he nodded and they washed silently. Their eyes were red and their faces drawn and peaked. Within them the terror and fear of discovery glowed like a red light of warning and danger, and it was with an effort that they left the washroom.

Frank stopped as he entered the outer chamber and saw Stan Alberg sitting with his father.

"Don't say nothing," he cautioned Benny. "I'll see you in school tomorrow. Hello, Pop." He attempted to be flippant as he spoke to his father. "The bastards let us go."

"What did they want?" his father asked him.

"Why we weren't carrying knives or guns or blackjacks," Benny answered. "I don't know what to do about guys like those cops. They're driving me nuts!"

"Let's get some coffee," Stan soothed him. "I got my car outside and we'll go to Fulton Street. Then I'll take you home and I'll square things with your folks, Benny."

"They're driving me nuts," Benny muttered.

"Don't worry," Stan reassured him. "I'll straighten things out."

Mr. Goldfarb opened the rear door of the automobile and stood with one foot on the running board. "What are we going to do?" he asked Stan. "All those boys locked up in jail. What're we going to do?"

Stan sighed as he slid into the driver's seat and pulled up his trousers at the knees. "I don't know, Mr. Goldfarb. This thing is way over my head. If the police raid all the gangs and clubs in Brownsville there won't be enough cells in the city to lock up all the kids they pick up for carrying concealed weapons and other things. They got two of your guys on other charges." He turned around to speak to Frank. "Counterfeit gasoline coupons and narcotics. Two very tough raps."

"God help us," Mr. Goldfarb whispered, and turned to his son. "First we were poor because we didn't have any

130

money, and now we're poor because there is no one home to look after you or the other boys. Frank"—he grasped his son's arm—"tell me you're not in trouble!"

"I'm not," Frank said roughly. "Stop bothering me."

Stan coasted to a stop before the White Tower. "Let him alone, Mr. Goldfarb. Get out, Benny."

Mr. Goldfarb entered the restaurant first, and Stan spoke to Frank. "Lucky thing you got rid of that gun. Benny too."

"Thanks," Frank whispered.

"You're a first-class suspect," Stan said, "and I've got a feeling you're not telling all you know. Remember, Frank, talking now might save you a lot of grief later on."

Frank sneered as he got onto the stool at the counter. Except for his red-rimmed eyes and the lines of weariness which furrowed his forehead, his gaze was cold and untroubled. The cops were dumb. Benny was dumb. The Dukes were dumb. All he had to do was think, and he could outsmart anyone. He was going to admit nothing, for they knew nothing, and what they did not know would never hurt him.

He twirled around on the swivel seat and softly, so that only Stan could hear him, he said, "Nobody's asking you for advice."

Chapter 9

For Frank the first of June meant only one more month of dread remained before the end of the school term. Frank associated the end of June with escape, but he now wondered if he could maintain a grip on himself and avoid discovery. Everything conspired against him, and as he walked with Betty along the path which followed the perimeter of the Prospect Park lake that first June night, her words made no impression upon him.

How could he rest and be at ease? Only six days after

they had bumped Bannon they had almost been trapped. Maybe, he thought, it might have been better to have been caught. Then this constant wariness and alertness which were sapping his strength and refusing him the relaxation of sleep would cease. Wherever he walked or rode or stopped he would see Gallagher, Leonard, Finch, or Wilner. When he went into Davidson's, Gallagher might be sitting there drinking coffee and would invite him to sit at his table. The talk would be aimless, so aimless that Frank would feel his jaws stiffen, his spine tingle, and his armpits wet with sweat, for he knew that this seeming lack of direction in Gallagher's conversation was aimed at catching him in a contradiction, a flaw in their alibis. One day as he entered Selma's with Benny they saw Wilner sitting at the counter noisily sucking a chocolate soda through a straw. They had wanted to back out of the doorway, but Wilner insisted upon buying them sodas and talking, and Wilner talked only about the murder and that it was the police theory that the murder had not been premeditated and that the boy would be certain to receive the mercy of the court if he confessed.

"Yes," Wilner had said, "maybe the kid that did it wants to confess, but maybe someone else is implicated in the killing and one guy can't confess because of the other guy. Tough." His straw rattled as he sucked upon it.

After he had left them Frank and Benny had sat silently in the booth, afraid to speak, unable to look at each other, for Wilner had sowed carefully in each of them a new seed of suspicion and distrust. Each feared the other would crack, and they sat silent, afraid to speak, for they could not trust their voices to be steady, as if they were unshaken by Wilner's suggestion of clemency.

Selma scooped the glasses off the table and leaned toward them. "That was a dick, wasn't it?" she asked them.

Benny nodded.

"I thought so," she said nervously. "Look, Benny, Frank, I hate to say this. But I think you better not come in here any more until this blows over. I got my customers to think of, and since the cops picked up you Dukes here, and now this dick—well, I don't like it. So maybe you better not come around for a while."

Frank stood up. "Come on," he said to Benny.

Gallagher, Leonard, Finch, and Wilner were everywhere: on Pitkin Avenue, in the Winthrop, near their school, strolling along their block, at Roseland, the Coney Island boardwalk, the Rugby Bowling Alleys. And always they would stop Frank and Benny, talk to them, ask the same questions over and over again, playing a sort of game whereby they seemingly deputized Frank and Benny and asked their opinion as to whether they thought Frank Alongo or Sam London or Socks Levy or Larry Riordan or Danny Abrams or Steve Cohen or Sam Abruzzi might have shot Mr. Bannon. Suddenly, and with terror, Frank realized they had eliminated practically every boy in their official class, and he warned Benny not to give his opinion any more.

And there was nowhere to go, for after the story broke in the newspapers about the Dukes being picked up by the police and all except three held on various charges, their landlord had made them move out of their basement clubrooms. In vicious desperation the Dukes had hacked and broken the walls of the basement rooms, stuffed the plumbing, ruined the floor by pouring melted tar onto the parquet, and had warned the landlord that his body would be found in a lot if he made a complaint. Now the Dukes were without a formal meeting place, and this, coupled with the fact that they were all out on bail and facing prosecution, made them turn on Frank and Benny as the direct cause of their present plight. Bluntly, with his lips purple with anger and his eyes glassy, Larry Tunafish had told them they were responsible for his facing a prison rap.

"Every dime I got in the bank," he told off Frank and Benny, "and plenty of my old man's, we had to give to a smart lawyer who thinks he can get me off. And it's all your fault. Aw, shut up!" He refused to let Benny speak. "You can tell the cops that you don't know who bumped off your teacher, but I got a hunch you know. And because you're keeping your holes shut I'm liable to get shoved in the can."

Frank looked at him with disbelief. "You want us to rat?"

"I don't know what I want!" Larry said. "Except to get

133

this rap off my neck. You know I can go to the Island for this rap?"

"You'll beat it," Benny said without believing his prediction.

"What's the use of talkin'?" Larry summed up the feelings of the Dukes: "You guys got us in bad with your goin' to school. School!" He spit in the street. "Look what it got us. A rap!"

Cut off from the Dukes, prohibited from entering Selma's, with the neighbors on their block looking at them with bold hostility, Frank and Benny were compelled to seek each other's company. After Detective Leonard had visited Ann Kleppner and Betty Rosen to check on Frank's and Benny's alibis, Ann would no longer date Benny. Betty continued to see Frank, but now there was no longer a smooth convertible for them to race around in, and walking with Betty in the park, Frank was silent and only dimly aware of her presence.

"You're not listening to me." Betty pressed Frank's arm and drew to a halt.

Frank put his arm around her shoulders. "I'm sorry, kid. I was thinking."

"Thinking so hard that you haven't even kissed me?"

Frank guided Betty from the path into a thicket of bushes that stood close to the rim of the lake and knelt to feel the grass. "It's dry, Betty"—he began to remove his jacket—"but we'll sit on this."

"That's a new suit," she protested.

"What the hell's the difference?" Frank lay on his back with his hands locked behind his head. "Come on, sit next to me."

Betty leaned across him, framed his face in her hands, and kissed him. "Feel better now?" she whispered.

His reply was to embrace her and to press his lips against her cheek as he held her close to him. "I wouldn't know what to do without you," he whispered. "I wouldn't know."

Again she kissed him and finally she relaxed and lay beside him with her arms locked tightly around him, feeling his body tense and electric against her as his free hand caressed the nape of her neck, her breasts, and her thighs.

"I love you, Frankie." Betty was hoarse with passion. "Love you more than anything!" She pressed close to him, eager and longing, possessed with the desire, magic, and promise of a June night.

He wanted to tell her more than that he loved her, but he could not. Through his memory raced distorted and rudimentary fragments of speeches and lines of poetry he had been compelled to read in his English classes and which he had never remembered. Across one corner of the moon hung a wisp of dark cloud, and the sky was lonesome without stars. The stillness carried to them the sound of the ripples softly striking the stone wall that girded the lake; the gentle warmth of June soothed him—and still he could not speak. For how could he tell her he was troubled, when an explanation would mean his death? It would have been a relief to tell someone, to share the secret with a trusted confidant, and Frank felt he could trust Betty, but to tell anyone would be the first fatal error, the first breach in the wall of anonymity that protected him, for to tell her of him meant revealing Benny's role in the tragedy—and he was afraid of Benny. No longer was Benny his friend, but someone bound to him by circumstances which enmeshed and entangled them both as they struggled, singly and together, to prevent their betrayal by a breach in their alibis and their distrust of each other.

That night at the White Tower when Stan Alberg had appealed to him in a brief moment to confess what he knew, if he knew anything, he had laughed mockingly at the well-intentioned advice, and now it was too late to turn back. Twenty-nine more days. He had to hold out. Frank kissed Betty's throat.

"Frank," she gasped, "what're you waiting for?"

"Here?"

"I'm dying for you." Her nails dug through his shirt. "We're alone. I never asked anyone before." She writhed in his arms with a desire she could no longer control.

Frank rolled over and looked down upon her as she lay with her hair flung back and her eyes half shut. He kissed her again, wildly, and pressed her to him. His hands trembled as he caressed her, and then there was no thought, but

135

only a series of sharp involuntary reflexes as he strained Betty to him, kissing and biting her lips. His breath whistled and he moaned with the violence of his passion.

Sighing, they relaxed and listened to the night sounds multiply about them while they watched the cloud efface the upper half of the moon. Betty lay on her side with her arms around Frank. Occasionally she kissed him, but he continued to stare above him, through the branches of the bushes which enclosed them.

"Frank," she said softly, "it's late."

He raised his left arm and looked at the illuminated dial of his watch. "Almost eleven. Once it wasn't late for me." His bitterness dulled the recent joy. "Now I've got to get in early and keep away from those damned dicks."

Betty sat erect and stroked Frank's hair. "Don't let them bother you," she attempted to console him. "It'll be all over soon. They're bound to get the one who did it."

Frank's grip on her arm tightened and relaxed immediately. He was glad it was dark so that she could not see the way his face twisted in agony as fright smashed him with its omnipresent fist. "What makes you say that?"

"Well, the cops are pretty good, and you never read in the papers about a murder not being solved."

"But they haven't any clues," Frank said.

Betty rubbed his nose with hers. "How do you know?"

Frank pushed her away roughly. "Stop it. Now you sound like that bastard Leonard. He's always popping up wherever I go. The bastard's driving me nuts!" Frank rolled over and lay with his face in his folded arms.

"I'm sorry I brought it up, hon." Betty spoke quietly. "Come on, you better take me home. Oh, Frank"—she embraced him as they stood up—"I like you more than anything."

"I like you too," Frank replied absently, brushed the loose grass from her skirt, and lifted his jacket from the grass. He snapped the jacket twice, brushed the back casually, and put it on. "Let's go."

Betty held his arm and walked so that their thighs brushed. "You're sure some guy at loving." Her laugh was shy yet bold. "What's the matter?" He had stopped, rigid with panic.

136

"That man ahead of us looks like one of the dicks," he whispered apprehensively. "Let's go back."

"No," she insisted. "You're seeing things. And even if he is, if you run away he'd think something's wrong. Come on." She dragged him along the path. "We'll walk fast and pass him. Maybe it isn't him."

Shaking, Frank permitted himself to be led. As they approached the man who was strolling ahead of them Frank saw it was neither one of the four detectives, and through the panic which still made his chest pound, he realized that he was seeing Gallagher, Leonard, Finch, and Wilner even when they were not present. He remembered the dream he had had in the middle of May, when the vividness of their presence had forced him awake and he had sat up in bed, shivering and trembling with terror. He had to snap out of it, for he knew his nerves were drawn, stretched to the point of snapping, and there were only twenty-nine days left. Twenty-nine days more of alertness, and then he could stretch his arms, yawn, lie in the sun on the beach, and be free.

"See," Betty said to him after they had passed the man, "it wasn't one of them. Was it?"

Frank offered her a cigarette from his pack. "No. Look, babe," he said to her, "it's late. Suppose I stick you in a cab and I'll take the trolley home?"

Before she could protest Frank whistled sharply at a passing cab, which stopped suddenly, ground gears as the driver shifted rapidly into reverse, and backed to the curb where they stood. Frank opened the door and Betty stepped inside the cab.

"How much to Sterling and Nostrand?" Frank asked the driver.

The driver looked disgusted. "About sixty cents."

Frank gave him a dollar. "Take this girl home. So long." He leaned through the open window and clasped Betty's hand. "I'll call you tomorrow. Between five and six."

Betty leaned forward and her lips brushed his. "Good night. Don't worry about anything."

Frank watched the cab swing into Flatbush Avenue and then entered the drugstore near the subway entrance. Why he wanted to know where Stan Alberg lived was something he could not explain. But in Stan Alberg he sensed a person who was willing and anxious to help him, and although the hope was a faint one, possibly Stan Alberg could suggest an escape from the secret that oppressed him. Frank felt no guilt, only a feeling of anger that he should have permitted Benny to get him into a jam that offered so few escape exits. In his mind there were many schemes: to throw the onus of suspicion on the few Negro boys in his official class; to send an anonymous letter to the police, telling them that Mr. Bannon was killed by a girl he had ruined; to somehow identify the dead teacher with a spy ring. And he had to reject every scheme because he could not fill in the necessary details to make the new angle appear logical and possible. His finger ran down the columns in the telephone directory and there it was, Stan Alberg's address and telephone number. He lived on Crown Street, and Crown Street was nice. Impressive elevator apartment houses and substantial one- and two-family semidetached brick homes with porches, window boxes, Venetian blinds, and two-car garages. As he read the address the idea which had lain within him for weeks, dormant and stifled, now became alive and insistent. Frank wanted to see where Stan Alberg lived. If it were earlier he probably would have called him, but now he wanted to see the house.

Crown Street between Albany and Troy. The apartment house stood tall and proud in its newness. Above the white Colonial front a large brass coach lamp shone on the house numbers. The panes of glass in the upper halves of the doors were colored and separated by lead strips. The white shutters stood out sharply against the bright blue trim of the apartment windows, and through the closed blinds Frank could see scattered patches of light.

He opened the apartment-house door so that he could see the lobby, and then it was too late, for the doorman, who had been drowsing in a wing chair, stood up and approached him.

"Looking for someone?" the doorman asked.

"Mr. Alberg." Frank wondered whether he was speaking distinctly.

The doorman looked at the banjo clock hanging over the Queen Anne sofa. "You know it's past twelve?"

138

"He'll see me." Frank didn't know what impelled him to say this. "What's his apartment number?"

The doorman pushed his visored cap back and scratched his forehead. "I'll bet he's asleep," he said, "and I can't let you in until I call up. Why don't you come back tomorrow about seven? He or Mrs. Alberg are usually home then."

Frank hesitated and put his hand on the doorknob. Then he changed his mind. "No. Call up. He's been expecting me around for a long time and he'll be sore if you don't call him. Go ahead. I'll take the blame."

Frank waited while the doorman plugged the switchboard. For about half a minute they could see the red light on the board winking and then it went out.

"Mr. Alberg"—the doorman's voice was full of apology —"you'll excuse me for waking you. There's someone here to see you and I told him to come back tomorrow, but he insisted on seeing you tonight. . . . What? . . . Just a moment, sir." He turned to Frank. "What's your name?"

"Frank. Frank Goldfarb."

"Mr. Frank Goldfarb," the doorman said. "All right, sir"—he nodded toward the mouthpiece of the telephone —"I'll send him right up."

The doorman snapped the plug out of the socket and turned to Frank. "Apartment 509. Take the elevator over there." He pointed. "Fifth floor—509."

"Thanks," Frank called over his shoulder, "509."

Covertly, because he knew the doorman was still watching him, he walked to the elevator as if he were accustomed to apartment houses with doormen and calling on people after midnight. The walls of the corridor were papered with a green and gray wallpaper depicting a woodland scene, too bucolic for anything but wallpaper, and the green patterned broadloom carpet was thick and luxurious underfoot. Frank pressed the elevator button and could hear the whir of gears, and then the elevator was at the lobby floor, and the door swung back silently. The elevator walls were of pickled pine, and for a moment Frank wished he had his knife so that he could cut something obscene into the wood. He had been looking for an apartment two or three times a week, but only when he consented to take Alice with him did he look earnestly. The only vacancy he had found was a shabby apartment over stores on Church Avenue near Utica, and the landlord, a thin, tall man with eyes so deep in his head that they looked like holes in the snow, asked a rental which was exorbitant. "I'm waiting." He shrugged his shoulders when Frank asked him if he did not think he was asking too much for the apartment. "Somebody'll be willing to pay." Some people had doormen and carpets in the lobby, while he had the dismal and reeky hallway on Amboy Street.

The elevator stopped with a slight jar, and Frank waited until the door slid back, then he pushed open the heavy safety door and stood for a moment deciding into which section of the corridor to turn.

A door opened and Frank heard Stan call to him, "Over here, Frank."

Stan was wearing a robe over his pajamas and stood holding the door open. His hair was tousled and his eyes were still heavy with sleep.

"Come in," he said.

Frank twisted his hat in his hands. "I'm sorry I'm disturbing you."

" 'Sall right." Stan shook his head and lit a lamp that stood on an end table in the parlor. "Sit down," he went on. "Drop your hat anywhere and take off your jacket if you want to. I'll be back in a minute. Going to wash my face so I won't look so punchy."

Frank placed his hat on the sofa, hesitated, and removed his jacket.

He squatted down to look at the titles of the books in the section of shelves nearest the sofa, but as he heard the bathroom door open he stood up guiltily and sat stiffly on the sofa.

"You usually go visiting at this hour?" Stan took a cigarette from the box on the coffee table and offered one to Frank.

Frank refused the cigarettes. "I don't know what made me come here, Mr. Alberg."

"Call me Stan."

"Stan."

140

"How about some coffee with me? Gee"—Stan shook his head—"I guess I can't take it any more."

"I'm making you a lot of bother."

"So what! If I said you weren't you wouldn't believe me and I wouldn't be telling the truth. But that doesn't tell me whether you want coffee or not."

"I guess so."

"Come into the kitchen while I put on the percolator."

Frank stood woodenly in the doorway and watched Stan turn the switch on the electric range and set the percolator over the hot wire coil.

"That's an electric range?" Frank asked him.

"Yes."

"I never saw one before."

"They're all right." Stan guided him back to the living room. "Now what's on your mind, as if I don't know."

"What do you know?"

"Enough that tells me you wouldn't be coming here after midnight if you didn't feel you were in a jam."

Frank grasped his knees to keep them from trembling. "I didn't do nothing."

Stan picked up the cigarette, looked at it, and ground it into the tray. "Maybe," he said laconically.

"Everyone's down on me."

"That's not hard to understand."

"You're not much help."

Stan wrinkled his forehead. "Help? Seems to me I offered you help more than once. What the hell do you expect me to do? Keep on offering it to you like free passes to the movies? You're in a spot, Frank. The cops are smart. Remember, Benny, Crazy, and you were the only ones who were found weaponless."

Frank did not look at him. "I threw away the gun the next day like you told me."

"Before or after your teacher was killed?"

Frank wearily rubbed his hands across his eyes. His voice was limp. "Before. Honest. Before."

"And Benny?"

"I told him to throw away his gun."

"Did he?"

141

"I think so."

Stan walked into the kitchen to look at the percolator. "Come in here," he called to Frank. "Coffee's almost ready, and we can talk better here. Anyway, Reba, my wife, is asleep, and I wouldn't want her to hear what we're talking about. She's all right and can be trusted, but this doesn't concern her."

"You're right."

Stan placed two cups and saucers on the table and took a small china cream pitcher from the refrigerator. "You use sugar?" he asked Frank.

"Not much."

Stan reached into one of the kitchen cabinets for the sugar bowl. "How about some crackers and jam? I think they'll be all right." He did not wait for Frank to reply and placed some crackers in a dish and took a jar of raspberry preserves from the refrigerator. "Here"—he slung a paper napkin at Frank—"sit down and we'll eat and talk. You drink more than one cup of coffee?"

Frank opened the napkin and placed it in his lap. It slipped and he tucked one end of it under his belt. "Sometimes."

"So do I." Stan adjusted the switch so that the coffee bubbled slowly. "Now"—he seated himself at the table—"dig in."

Frank knew that his table manners were clumsy and he watched Stan pour the cream into his coffee and wipe the spout of the pitcher with his spoon. He imitated Stan's motions and stirred his sugar slowly instead of in his usual wide-sweeping circles.

"Here." Stan placed some of the jam on Frank's plate and added some crackers. "There's more if you want it."

"Thanks. You're a good guy, Mr. Alberg—Stan."

"I could be better if you gave me a chance."

Frank did not reply.

"Come on"—Stan bit into a cracker—"cut the comedy. We've been sparring too damned long. You came up here for something."

"I don't know why I came."

"Who killed Mr. Bannon?"

142

Frank placed the cracker and jam back on his plate. "I don't know."

"You're not telling the truth," Stan insisted. "Look," he said, "let's be reasonable. I know that the detectives have been after you. I've seen them around the neighborhood. Two of them even came in to see me and they asked me about you and Benny."

Frank clutched the table. "What did they want to know?" His voice no longer belonged to him.

"The usual things. What I thought of you two and did I think you shot him."

Frank saw Stan through a mist. "What did you say?"

"I said I didn't think so. Don't worry." Stan anticipated Frank's question. "I didn't tell them you carried a gun."

"I threw it away the next morning. Honest."

"I believe you."

"I don't know when Benny did. But I know he threw his away too. You believe that?"

"Sure. You got scared."

Frank's cup rattled as he stood up suddenly. "Of what?"

Stan stirred his coffee idly. "I don't know. Something that brought you here after twelve o'clock at night."

"Maybe I better go."

"Sit down," Stan ordered him. "We're going to talk this out. Though you're going to tell me there's nothing to talk about. All right, I'm asking you again, why'd you come up here?"

Frank was silent. Slowly he spread jam over a cracker and did not answer.

"Come on," Stan insisted, "you're wasting time. Tell me what's bothering you and I'll try to help. Listen"—he tried another tack—"the cops picked up Fuderman and Socks Levy, the kids who belong to the Bristol Friends."

Frank shook his head. "I know them. The cops raided their club."

"I've had a talk with Julie Fuderman and Levy." Stan poured more coffee into his cup. "They're out on bail. Concealed weapons. And you know what else?"

"What?"

"They're not scared. They're sore about the cops bothering them, but they're not scared."

Frank looked at him. "And now I'm supposed to tell you that I'm scared?" he asked.

The coffee was hot and Stan blew at the liquid. "I think you are," he said. "What're you scared of?"

"Nothing."

"Don't yell." Stan placed his cup on his plate. "Then why'd you come here?"

"I——"

"Say it."

Frank's lips clamped together. It was so easy, so tempting, to tell Stan everything, and he felt that Stan would help him. But there was Benny. There were the Dukes. No matter how sore Larry Tunafish was, he really had not meant what he had said about wanting Frank to tell the cops what he knew so that they would leave him alone. If he confessed, Frank thought, to save another guy from taking the rap, that was different. But the cops had no one. Gallagher was in the dark and fishing. What Frank had was a case of nerves, the jitters. Too much thinking about weeks and days and hours and minutes, when all he had to do was to stop thinking about time and take it easy.

Now he had Betty, and she was wonderful. Better than any babe he had ever had before, and what was best, she loved him. She thought he was the greatest guy in the world, and she was good-looking, the kind of piece any one of the Dukes would give an arm for. Smooth, trim, really put together, and all his. And he had Fanny Kane, who thought it was wonderful that his name was in the papers. He hadn't laid her yet, but neither had anyone else. So there wasn't any rush, for he knew he could knock her off whenever he wanted to, and when he did he'd make sure Crazy would know it. It was easy. He would date every night, go to school in the morning and afternoon, then either look for an apartment or go to the Center or the movies, and it would be like coasting a car downhill——easy.

"Well?" Stan said sharply.

"Good jam." Frank sniggered, and Stan suddenly wanted to slap him. "I'm glad I'm eating it and not in it."

"So that's your attitude?"

"No attitude. I'm visiting you because I wanted to see where you lived."

"And I'm supposed to believe that?"

"Nobody's asking you to."

Stan picked up a cracker and crumpled it in his hand. "You know"—his smile was knowing—"you don't have to tell me anything, Frank. Remember the doorman downstairs?"

"What about him?"

"I know that Benny and you are being watched. You know it, too, and it's easy to see that it's getting you. Now suppose a cop or somebody was tailing you and they saw you come here after twelve tonight and they stop and talk to the doorman? He'll tell them you insisted upon seeing me. And they'll check and find out that I'm at the Center and they'll start putting things together and they'll surmise that you were scared and wanted to tell what you know or did——"

"I didn't do nothing!" Frank saw the walls of the kitchen shift and waver as if they were about to collapse upon him.

"So you didn't do anything," Stan went on remorselessly, smashing across the trenches of brazenness that surrounded and guarded Frank. "They'll question me and I'll tell them I don't know anything, because I don't, and I won't even tell them what I suspect!"

"What!" Frank whispered. His eyes were heavy and he placed a hand on the wall nearest him. It was stationary, but the other walls shimmied.

"What you think I suspect," Stan said.

"If the cops ask you anything you'll tell them that I came to you for advice because they were making my life so miserable."

Stan shook his head. "You haven't asked my advice."

"That's what you'll tell them," Frank hissed. "You'll tell them that my mother is making it tough for me and I feel that I didn't do anything. You'll tell them that I'm unhappy and sort of feel that I should be let alone, and that I wanted you to talk to the cops and to tell them to let me alone."

"I see."

"You better." Frank stood up and pressed his knuckles into the table. "I'm not taking nobody's rap! I threw my gun away! I swear."

"And Benny?"

145

"He threw his away, too, and the hell with Benny!" he blurted. It was out before he could stop it. "And don't ask me when." Frank anticipated the question. "All I know is that he did. I'm going now." He backed out of the kitchen. The walls were less active now.

Stan held Frank's jacket and handed him his hat. "Sorry you came so late. We could've had a longer visit."

"I'm sorry I bothered you," Frank said. "I'll be seeing you around the Center. Take it easy."

Stan held the door open. "Good night. Sleep well, if you can."

Frank waved, but concern and fear made the flippant gesture weak. "I will. Good night. Thanks for the coffee."

Chapter 10

For nights that seemed like years the Dukes had given Frank the freeze. At first he had been glad because he thought of this as a chance to break with the gang. But there was nowhere to go, he was sort of marked lousy, and Benny had kept closer to him than ever before. Benny, always Benny, with his talking and stupid scheming, until Frank thought he was going to go crazy if he didn't get rid of him. So when Larry Tunafish had called him into Selma's one Friday night he had tried to appear calm, but his heart was throbbing like a pump.

Selma nodded as he squeezed into a booth with Larry and Bull, and he knew it was all right for him to start hanging out there again. Then he saw Benny come in, and his stomach dropped as he wondered whether their secret had been discovered.

"We're waitin' for you," Bull said to Benny.

"I got your message just a little while ago. What's up?"

"Sit down." Larry moved over. "We're running a dance."

"A dance?" Frank and Benny echoed.

146

Larry reached into the bosom pocket of his jacket and removed a thick envelope, which he placed on the table. "Tickets," he explained. "We're running the dance two weeks from tomorrow night to raise dough for the Dukes. Yeah"—he looked squarely at Frank—"most of us guys need some dough. Not everyone's got a bank account. So we thought before the other clubs started to think about it we'd run a dance and raise some dough."

"We printed a thousand tickets," Bull interrupted.

"A thousand tickets?" Benny exclaimed. "Where you running this dance? Steeplechase?"

"A guy needs two tickets to get in with his date." Larry ignored Benny's question. "And tickets cost two-fifty apiece."

Frank's mouth hung slack. "You mean you're gonna get guys to shell out five bucks for a dance? Where we holding it?"

"The Tigers're lending us their clubroom, and they're all buying tickets to help us out. They're swell guys." Bull shook his head appreciatively. "So that means with more than twenty members we're getting rid of at least fifty tickets right there."

"But you must be nuts," Benny objected. "How the hell are you gonna squeeze a thousand people down there? Their club is no bigger than ours was. The son of a bitch," he swore as he thought of their ex-landlord.

Larry took two tickets out of the envelope and handed one to Frank and the other to Benny. "Very nice printing job," Larry said. "We got it for nothing. This dance is gonna be all profit. Look at the bottom of the ticket," he went on. "See what it says about not coming before ten o'clock? Some of the tickets say nine o'clock. Some ten, eleven, twelve, one, two, and three. And the tickets are on different-colored paper for the different times. And when a couple comes in they gotta pin their tickets on their suits and dresses where we can see them. We got a coupla real gorillas who're gonna stay at the door. And a guy with a ten o'clock ticket is only gonna get in between ten and one minute to eleven. Then we're gonna have a couple more hard guys circulating on the floor, and when they see that the place is getting crowded they'll go over to the people who've been dancing for about an hour and tell them that maybe they'd better cop a walk. So that way we keep the crowd changing and we won't have too much of a mob."

"Who're the hard guys?" Benny's voice was filled with admiration.

"Some guys from Flushing and Broadway," Bull said. "My cousin fixed it up. They're helping us out and all we're gonna do is fix them up with Rosie Beanbags and a couple of her friends. They're not taking a dime, and these guys are hard." He pounded a fist into the palm of his other hand.

Frank's forehead was furrowed as he computed for a moment. "So you're gonna make about twenty-five hundred, except for what you gotta pay the band."

Larry's smile was not pleasant. "Who's gonna pay what band?"

"Oh," Benny said.

"We're gonna run a checkroom," Bull informed them. "And everybody's gotta check, whether they got something or not."

"Checking is gonna be twenty-five cents apiece," Larry added. "Every dime we're taking in is gonna count."

"I hope it goes over," Frank said.

Larry stopped counting tickets. "It's gotta go over. I'm giving you thirty tickets. That's seventy-five dollars."

"Thirty tickets!"

"What's the matter, Frank?" Larry leaned across the table. "Not enough? Maybe you wanta take forty?"

"Stop horsing me around." Frank pushed his face forward and met Larry's stare. "I can ask questions. If I'm supposed to take thirty I'll take them. But don't practice being a hard guy on me."

"Cut it out," Bull said to them. "We got enough trouble already. You can get ridda thirty tickets, Frank, and it's for a good cause. Some of the guys're up against it. We're gonna divide the money according to who needs it most."

"I suppose I get thirty tickets?" Benny asked.

"Thirty for you." Bull nodded. "And how about your brother Sam? He knows plenty of guys and could get rid of some."

Benny whistled softly. "I don't know. Sam's sorer'n hell at me."

"Let me take the numbers of your tickets," Larry said to Frank. "You got a ten o'clock batch, so they should be easy to sell."

Bull counted off thirty tickets in one pile and fifteen in another. "This'll be your thirty," he said to Benny, "and take the fifteen for Sam. He's got to help out."

"You'll work fast," Larry said to them. "Try the stores, everybody. If they give you the two and a half and they don't take the ticket, you'll turn in the dough and still sell the ticket. And"—he glanced around the table—"I better not find out that anybody's sticking dough in his pocket."

Frank looked at the tickets which had been assigned to him, counted them, and placed them in his pocket. "Who gets the money?" he asked.

"Me or Bull," Larry replied.

"You know what Moishe is doing?" Bull interjected.

"What?" Benny asked.

"His rap is costing him plenty. So he went out and printed up raffle books to raffle off a pair of nylon stockings at fifty cents a chance to help a friend in need."

"A very good idea," Frank said. He wondered if he ought to take a couple of chances and fix it up with Moishe so that he would win and then he could give the nylons to Betty.

"But this is the pay-off." Bull laughed and Larry smiled. "Moishe is the friend in need, and the tickets don't say when the raffle is gonna be held or where, and who's got a pair of nylons?"

Benny roared. "That's solid!"

"But wait," Bull went on. "Crazy hears about this and decides that he's gonna raffle off twenty salamis for a friend in need. But he was gonna give the salamis. So he goes to that job printer on East New York near Rockaway and tells the printer he wants some books. The printer says all right and tells Crazy to design the slip. I don't have to tell you any more." He wiped his eyes.

"Nothing that jerk does strikes me funny," Frank said sourly.

"Anyway"—Bull ignored his comment—"he went back to Mitch and Mitch told him to give us the salamis and we'll auction them off at the dance. We oughta get at least fifty bucks that way."

"Selma," Benny called to her, "are we customers again?"

"I guess so," she replied.

"You want black and whites?" Benny asked the boys at the table.

"Sure," Bull answered for them.

"Four black and whites," Benny ordered. "I'm treating. Gee," he said to Larry and Bull, "I'm glad to be in business with you guys again."

"Me too," Frank said slowly.

"Cut out the crying towel," Larry said. "We'll drink the sodas and then we gotta get busy."

Frank found that selling the thirty tickets was not too difficult, for the Dukes had been the first to plan a dance, and when Frank told the prospective customer that the money was to be used to keep the Dukes out of prison they bought readily. Some boys who were reluctant to part with five dollars for two tickets had only to be reminded by Frank that there were many dark streets in Brownsville and guys occasionally were held up and had their suits taken off them—and more tickets were sold. Frank had sold one ticket that the purchaser had returned to him, and when he saw Fanny Kane sitting in front of his stoop he threw her the ticket, figuring that the kid might be good for some laughs at the dance.

"Take it," he said to her. "The dance's tonight and it's gonna be solid."

"For nothing?"

"Sure. I'm giving it to you."

"Who you taking, Frank?"

Frank paused before he entered the hall. "Not you. I got a date."

"Thanks, Frankie," Fanny called after him. "I'll be there tonight."

Frank opened his collar and loosened his tie as he climbed the steps. Everything was working out fine. Gallagher, Leonard, Finch, and Wilner were still hanging

150

around, but he had steeled himself to their presence. Only once had he been flippant when he had met Leonard and Wilner, and they had taken him to the Liberty Avenue station for questioning. For two hours they had questioned him without being able to shake his original story, and finally they had released him. Now he knew that it did not pay to be funny or friendly with cops. The only thing he regretted was visiting Stan Alberg that night, but Stan had kept quiet, and when Frank went to the Center, Stan never referred to his visit or their conversation.

Stan was waiting for Frank to reopen the subject, and Frank now felt sufficiently safe to bury the episode forever. The picture of Bannon lying on the classroom floor with the stain on his chest becoming larger was less distinct, and to Frank the shooting became an incident that was unfortunate, like getting a flat tire just when a couple of guys were starting on a hot date. Guys were being killed by the hundreds every day in Europe and the Pacific, and no one made any fuss about them; and if a guy believed in God, then it was fixed for Bannon to die that way, although Frank would have preferred that someone else had been chosen to make a stiff of him.

His father was just seating himself at the kitchen table when he opened the door of their apartment. "You're on time," his father said. "A miracle."

"I just came from East Flatbush," Frank lied. "I'm half dead with looking for a place. A guy told me about a basement apartment on Kings Highway near Ninety-sixth, but it was a bum steer. So I'm pooped."

"Sit down after you wash." Frank's mother was unimpressed. "We want to get done early because we're working tomorrow and we want to go to sleep early."

"Oh, Momma!" Alice ran into the kitchen from her bedroom. "Again? Working again?"

Her mother embraced her. "I'm sorry, *schondele*, but they want us to come in."

Alice clung to her mother's skirt. "You said you were going to take me somewhere tomorrow"—there was a treble in her childish voice—"and I was going to wear my new suit! I haven't worn it since *Pesach*."

151

Mrs. Goldfarb kissed her daughter and patted her hair. "What I earned from one Sunday's overtime was what bought you your pretty suit."

Mr. Goldfarb looked up from his newspaper. "Must you go in? Maybe you should stay home and take the children out tomorrow? To Radio City?"

Alice clapped her hands and trembled with excitement. "To the Music Hall, Momma! Take us. Take us! You said you were going to take me somewhere tomorrow, Momma! You said!"

Mrs. Goldfarb shook her head and glared with annoyance at her husband. "You with your ideas," she said to him. "You think I want to go to work tomorrow? Like I want a broken leg."

"Don't shout, Rashke," Mr. Goldfarb said. "I was only suggesting."

"I told the forelady I was coming in tomorrow. Why don't you stay home with the children?"

"Because my double time on Sunday," Mr. Goldfarb was patient, "is a lot more than yours."

Mrs. Goldfarb pushed Alice from her and adjusted the flame of one of the burners on the gas range. "Next you'll tell me you work harder than I do."

"Let's not fight. It's out of the question for me to stay home tomorrow."

"So I've got to stay home again alone tomorrow!" Alice burst into tears and ran into her bedroom. "I'm alone! Always alone!" they could hear her shouting.

Mr. Goldfarb looked at Frank. "Suppose I gave you five dollars," he began, "would you take Alice to the Music Hall tonight?"

"I can't, Pop," Frank said.

"Why not?" his mother asked him.

"I got a date tonight. Something special."

"Phui." His mother spit into the sink. "Dates with *junge stinkerkes* and *bummerkes* are something special. Better"—she waved the spoon with which she had been stirring the rice-and-milk soup—"you should be careful that you don't come home someday with a *krank* from one your special dates."

Mr. Goldfarb shut his paper with a snap. "What sort of

talk is this, Rashke? Do you know what you're saying?"

"Ask him, Meyer"—his wife pointed to Frank, whose face was red with embarrassment—"if he doesn't know what I mean. I read in the papers," she continued, "that they got a two-day cure for it now. At least we're lucky for that."

"Rashke!" Mr. Goldfarb stood up and took two steps toward his wife and stopped. "No more!" He turned to Frank. "You can't take your sister tonight to the Music Hall?"

"I'll take her tomorrow," Frank said. "I mean it. Honest"—he spoke to his mother's back—"I'd take Alice out tonight, but this is a date I can't get out of. And you shouldn't say things like that about this girl. She's a good kid."

"So I shouldn't say it." His mother shut off the gas. "Go get Alice and tell her I'll take her to the movies after supper if she helps me with the dishes."

Alice lay diagonally across her bed and refused to move when Frank asked her to come for supper. "Go away," she said to him. "I don't like you."

"Don't be that way, kid." Frank was distressed. "Mom's taking you to the movies tonight and I'm gonna show you a time tomorrow."

"You don't have to."

"But I want to. Honest."

"You don't."

"Look," Frank reasoned with her. "You'll say I don't and I'll say I do and we won't be getting anywhere. Come on in and eat supper like a good kid. Mom's got to get up early tomorrow."

Alice kept her face pressed into the bed. "She doesn't have to. She can work all the time. I don't care."

Frank pushed her. "Stop the acting."

"You can't take me anywhere," she continued unheedingly, "but you got enough time to take out Fanny Kane."

"Who told you that?" Frank hissed at her.

Alice sat up and wiped her eyes. "She did. And not so long ago you told me not to talk to her. All my friends know what she is. She lets boys feel her."

Frank raised his hand and approached the bed. "I'll rap you in the teeth if you talk that way and if you say any-

153

thing to them." He gestured toward the kitchen. "Come on. Get washed and tomorrow I'll show you a real time."

As they ate Alice spoke of her loneliness. She was tired of going to the Center and making raffia baskets, of eating her lunches and suppers in restaurants, of sitting alone in the lonely kitchen at night as she did her homework and attempted to read the books she withdrew from the library. At eleven the world still had its axis in her mother, father, and brother, and there was no counterbalance for their voluntary and involuntary neglect. A natural shyness and instinctive aversion kept her off the Brownsville streets, and she shrank from the noise and tumult of the afternoons and evenings which made Amboy Street reverberate with shouts and cries and curses. Alice lowered her eyes as she walked from the Center to the tenement in which she lived in order not to see the women holding infant girls over the curb while they urinated, not to see and hear the small boys who chased one another around baby carriages while they screamed vicious obscenities, not to see the dirt and refuse that lay in the streets and which everyone else took for granted. Each day as she climbed the steps of the tenement she said a silent prayer that they would someday find an apartment in East Flatbush where she could find joy in walking through the streets and not experience the fear, horror, and dread that seeped from the tenement walls onto the Brownsville sidewalks.

Mr. Goldfarb noisily sucked the last of his tea from his plate and moved his chair back from the table. "You go with Alice to the movies now," he said to his wife, "and I'll clean the dishes with Frank."

"You'll break more than you'll wash," his wife replied.

Mr. Goldfarb tried to smile. "Don't worry. I washed plenty of dishes. Where's the steel wool for the pots?"

"In the pan under the sink."

"So go. You've got money? And after the movies take Alice into a nice place and treat yourselves to good sodas."

"You come to the movies too, Meyer."

Mr. Goldfarb took an apron from the hook on the bathroom door. "Some other time. Go now and have a good time."

Frank wiped the dishes rapidly as his father handed

them to him and stacked them on the washtub. He had plenty of time before he met Betty in Dubrow's at ten o'clock. If he could have had his way he would not have gone to the dance, but he knew that the Dukes expected every member to be present. Ever since the guys had been arrested they were changed, especially Larry Tunafish. Now he bossed the Dukes and would not permit himself to be crossed in any decision he made, for he was obsessed with the idea of clearing every Duke. Thus Larry demanded a rigorous obedience from each Duke, and often Frank was tempted to tell Larry that he was dropping out of the gang, but he knew if he did this he would never be safe from Benny.

Too often he remembered that Benny had threatened to kill him if he endangered his freedom and security, and the threat worried him, kept cropping into his sleeping and waking, gave him no rest. Benny was desperate. No matter how often Frank reassured him that they were safe, the sight of Gallagher, Leonard, Finch, or Wilner would send Benny into a tailspin of violent fright. And after the detectives would leave them Benny would turn on Frank and accuse him of talking too much or too little, of being too flippant in the presence of the detectives, or suddenly acting as if he were in the possession of a great secret. Benny never repeated his threat to kill Frank if he had to, but the manner in which he would look at Frank before he would leave him made Frank's back turn to ice. Not for a moment did Frank doubt that Benny hated him, because Benny, in attempting to justify their crime, now considered him the reason for their being hunted, and once when Frank had mentioned that it had been Benny's idea that they return to the high school he had backed away as he sensed the murderous fury that obscured and extinguished reason within Benny.

"So how is it going in school?" His father spoke to him.

"Like it shouldn't happen to a dog," Frank replied.

His father handed him a soup bowl. "What's the matter?"

"Oh, I don't know. The place is driving me nuts. I want to transfer out of there next year. That is, if you won't let me quit."

155

"You're staying in school," his father said.

"What the hell I'm getting out of it, maybe you know. I don't."

"You'll get out what you put in."

"I'm not putting anything in."

Mr. Goldfarb stopped washing and turned to Frank. "Remember, I'm your father," he said quietly, "and I can still give you a good slap in the face."

Frank moved out of his father's range. "I was only kidding," he said hurriedly.

Mr. Goldfarb resumed his dishwashing. "Your kidding has got you into plenty of trouble already."

"For chrissakes"—Frank threw his dish towel on the washtub—"aren't you ever going to forget it?"

"It's not easy," his father said. "You keep reminding me, and people in my place who I hardly know ask me about it. Funny," he meditated, "if you would've made good marks in school nobody would even bother to ask me. But because they think my son is a gangster I've got plenty of people who are interested in my business."

"I'm not a gangster!"

"I hope not. But your friends?"

"They're all-right guys," Frank said hotly. "They just got a tough break."

"I don't know what's going to become of you." Mr. Goldfarb rubbed the steel wool hard along the inside of an aluminum pot. "I don't understand you. Not for years. Ever since you had to ask your uncle Hershell to buy you your bar mitzvah suit. Somehow"—he faced his son while he rinsed the pot under the warm water—"you've never forgiven me for that. No matter how you suffered, it was worse for me. You'll understand if you ever have children."

Frank was ashamed to look at his father. "I'm not sore at you," he said. "I'm just having a tough time, Pop. But once school is over, I'm going to change. You'll see."

"I'll finish," his father said. "Go get dressed for your date. Where you going?"

"To a little party," Frank said. "Nothing special."

He saw Betty sitting at a table as he passed through the revolving door of Dubrow's, and the old joy in seeing her

156

made his sullen face young and eager. Before each date with her he would wonder whether she was as pretty as he thought she was, and at each meeting he would know that his picture of her was accurate, that she was young, lovely, desirable, and his. Betty waved to him as she saw him enter the restaurant, and he nodded approvingly as he quickly noted the flowered jersey dress which accented her figure and the red velvet ribbon with which she had bound her hair. Betty wore high-heeled red wisps of sandals, and across her red fabric purse lay a pair of long red gloves.

"You look like a house afire," Frank greeted her. "Waiting long?"

"I don't think so." She smiled. "No one's tried to pick me up."

"That's a good way for you to tell time." Frank took her check. "You're gonna be a killer tonight. Want something?"

"Can we get a drink?"

"Not here."

"I'd like one before we go to the dance."

Frank stood up and pulled her chair back from the table. "I'll get you one."

As he walked before her he was proud of the stares and whistles Betty received from the wolves who sat at the tables. His eyes brightened and he half strutted after her, proud that real sharp guys who were lots older than he were eying Betty and even wishing they had her as a date. Her hips swayed slightly, a provocative promise of her grace and desirability, and Frank wished they did not have to go to the dance, even though he knew the guys would be rocking on their heels when they saw her. Betty held his arm as they entered the bar, and Frank felt himself grow in stature. She winked at him as they clinked glasses, and after they left the bar and were seated in the taxicab that was driving them to the dance she put her arms around him and kissed him slowly and sensually.

As they stepped out of the cab in front of the Tigers' clubroom Frank noted the four silent squat young men whom he had never seen before. Without speaking they examined his tickets and nodded for him to enter. There was no need for them to speak, for in their presence one

157

felt the electric spark of danger and violence, swift and savage, without pity or mercy, and only a fool would have disputed their suggestion or order. Certain and sure of their menace, they examined tickets and permitted the boys and girls to descend the clubroom steps.

Larry Tunafish stood at the checkroom counter behind which Bull Bronstein was checking hats and other miscellaneous articles.

"You're late," Bull said to him after he curtly acknowledged the introduction to Betty.

Frank took Betty's hand and led her into the clubroom. "So don't tell me the dance's been a flop," he called over his shoulder to Larry.

Bull looked at Larry and shook his head. "He's getting to be a regular wise guy."

"I know," Larry said with ominous patience. "And I'm not forgetting it."

Frank helped Betty thread their way through the crowd and the packed dance floor to the bandstand, where Frank looked around for someone he knew. He waved to Mitch, who leaned against the wall, and pushed over to him.

"I want you to meet my girl," he said to Mitch. "Betty, this is Mitch. Mitch is a Duke."

Mitch dropped his cigarette and crushed it underfoot. "Hello," he said appraisingly. "I'm glad to know you."

"Same here." Betty nodded.

"Where's the guys?" Frank asked Mitch.

"Circulating around. I'm waiting for my date. She's out to the powder room."

"How's the dance going?" Frank looked around for Benny, who was coming stag and who was sorer than hell because Betty was dating while Ann had blackballed him since the police questioned her.

"Pretty good," Mitch replied. "The crowd's sure coming. But they're leaving too. See that guy over there?" He pointed to a slight consumptive-looking boy about twenty who had a face as thin and deadly as the blade of an ax and whose double-breasted jacket was too large and too long for him. "He'll go into action soon as Larry tells him to."

"Who's he?" Betty asked.

158

Mitch replied respectfully, "A hard guy. From Bush-wick and Moore."

"Williamsburg," Frank explained to Betty.

"I saw him go into action about an hour ago," Mitch went on. "He sure cleaned up on a guy who was going to crash. Shimmy," Mitch called to the Williamsburger, "come over here."

Shimmy detached himself from the wall and walked slowly toward them. "What's the trouble?" he asked Mitch in a low-pitched voice that sounded like sharp slivers of ice.

"No trouble," Mitch explained. "I want you to meet another one of our guys. Shimmy Rosen, this is Frank Goldfarb, one of our guys. And this is his girl. Betty?" He turned to her.

"That's right," Betty said. "Hello."

"Frank can stay all night if he wants to," Mitch said to Shimmy.

"I'll remember. You want to dance?" he asked Betty.

Betty started to speak but stopped.

"Sure"—Mitch nudged Frank—"go ahead."

"You don't mind?" Shimmy said to Frank.

"No," Frank replied. "Go ahead."

Frank watched Betty move into the crowd with Shimmy and then he pushed Mitch. "What's the big idea?"

"These guys are helpin' us," Mitch explained. "We gotta show them a good time."

Frank's lower lip trembled. "So you show them a good time with your date."

"I am," Mitch replied calmly. "Shimmy's buddy is in the back room giving my date the business."

"I thought we were gonna have Rosie down with some of her friends?"

"They haven't come yet," Mitch said. "Stop your bawl-ing."

Frank grasped Mitch by the lapels of his jacket and pulled him forward. "Listen, guy," he said. "I think you're a pretty good guy even though you're a friend of Crazy's. But I'm tellin' you now that I'm in a lousy humor and I'll slug you."

"Get your hands off me, you bastard," Mitch said quiet-

159

ly. "You want to start a riot? The dance's gotta go over."

Frank released him and stepped back.

Mitch smoothed the lapels of his jacket and did not look at Frank as he spoke. "I'm not forgetting this, Frank. I'll take care of you some other time."

"Up your ass," Frank replied, and whirled around as he felt someone's hand on his sleeve. It was Benny.

"You come alone?" Benny asked him.

Frank's hands trembled as he took a cigarette out of the pack. "No. Betty's dancing with someone supposed to be a hard guy from Williamsburg."

"Looks like it's going over." Benny waved to a Duke who whirled by on the dance floor.

The band screamed to a stop, and Frank rushed into the dancers to find Betty. She was standing almost in the center of the floor, laughing at something Shimmy had said to her.

"I was bringing your date back to you." Shimmy's voice was so low that Frank had to strain to hear him.

"Thanks!" Frank said. "Come on"—he took Betty's arm —"let's go. It's hot and the dance stinks."

"But I like it," Betty protested. "And we just got here. You told me so much about the Dukes and now you want to go."

"Well, it's goddamned hot," Frank insisted.

"So let's go sit in a corner somewhere," Betty coaxed him. "Please."

"All right," Frank said sullenly. "I'll stay. But we'll go in about an hour."

The band began to play, and Betty did not reply but whirled toward Frank with her arms outstretched and Frank had to smile as her eyes invited him to dance. The band played, without rhythm or co-ordination, and the dancing became more unruly and violent. Frank and Betty saw Shimmy and two more of his gang on the floor quietly tapping couples and suggesting that they leave. Almost all the people left immediately, but one boy began to protest. As he pulled back his fist to slug one of Shimmy's friends Shimmy stepped forward and hit the boy a short open-handed slap across the jaw. The girl opened her mouth to scream, but another one of the Williamsburgers stepped

160

behind her and placed his hand over her mouth. The boy looked desperate and then he blanched as he saw the open knife in Shimmy's right hand. Without any further fight the couple permitted themselves to be led to the door, were given their hats, and left.

"That Shimmy's hard," Betty said.

"You like him?" Frank snapped at her.

"I didn't say I did," she retorted. "Gee, you're touchy tonight."

"Aw, shut up." Frank whirled her away from him.

Betty's eyes filled with tears. "What's the matter? I didn't say anything."

"Forget it." Frank led her off the floor. "I'm sorry, kid. I guess I'm a little jealous."

"But I don't like him," Betty insisted. "Let's stop it," she said. "We don't want to have our first fight, do we?"

At that moment Benny approached them, staggering slightly, and as he asked Betty if she would dance with him Frank turned his back on them in disgust. He sat on the arm of one of the easy chairs and reflected that the dance was not as he had expected it to be. There were other girls as pretty as Betty at the dance, and the boys were too excited by being at a racket which was being patronized by the hardest juvenile gangs in Brownsville and East New York to be concerned with a pretty face. Individually they were all interested in dating a girl who was attractive and stacked up like a million, but when the gang was dominant all girls were categorized as pieces, and Frank realized that he should have been proud to be in the company of fellows who belonged to the Bullets, the D-Rape Artists, the Powell Friends. But he was not.

Members of the Dukes and the Tigers greeted Frank, but his surly responses did not encourage them to stop and talk to him. The band continued to play, and the dancers paid no attention to it as the floor became crowded with small milling groups that obstructed the persons attempting to dance. Conversation degenerated to shrill cries and expostulations and shreds of laughter, and the cigarette haze floated like a murky cloud about the room.

Benny returned with Betty, and Frank knew immediately by her loose laugh that she had taken a stiff drink.

161

Benny patted his hip. "You want one?"

Frank's eyes were narrow slits. "I thought we were going on the wagon?"

"Ah"—Benny waved his hand—"tonight's different."

"With you it's always different. Give me the bottle." Frank held out his hand.

"You want a drink?"

"I'm going to empty it in the can."

Benny replaced the bottle in his pocket. "The hell you are."

"Come over here," Frank said to him. "Excuse us, Betty. Listen," he said to Benny as they stood in a corner of the room, "I'm warning you to ditch that bottle. The last time we got tight we got us in trouble, and now we gotta stay sharp if we don't want to wind up you know where."

Benny laughed foolishly. "I can hold my liquor."

"Sure, like you could hold an enema." Frank held out his hand. "Give me the bottle and let's cut the talk."

"Suppose I don't want to?" Benny clutched his hip pocket.

"Then you're on your own," Frank told him.

Benny blew his breath in Frank's face. "Whatever I do I'll never be on my own. You neither. I wish I were. I don't trust you, you bastard."

"Shut up!" Frank warned him.

"Don't tell me to shut up." Benny staggered a little. "I don't trust you. Crazy was right. He knew what he was talkin' about when he said you were a rat!"

Frank shook Benny, then slapped him and forced him to sit down on a folding chair. "You'd better cut it out." He shook him again. "Now I know you're drunk. If you don't give me the bottle I'm going to call Larry and Bull and we're gonna knock you cold."

Benny struggled to stand up, but Frank held him. "Let go of me," he began to shout. "Let go of me!"

Larry came over with Shimmy and Mitch.

"Benny's drunk," Frank explained to them, "and he's got a bottle."

"So let him have a good time if he's not bothering anyone," Shimmy suggested.

Frank released Benny and turned around. He approached Shimmy and stared directly into Shimmy's small fishlike eyes which did not blink. "Listen," he began, "the guys've been telling me you're a hard guy. Wait"—he raised his hand to prevent Shimmy from interrupting him—"maybe you are. But I'm a hard guy too. And I don't like you, and if you make a move for your shiv I'm going to beat the piss outa you."

Larry stepped between Frank and Shimmy. "Cut it out, boys," he pleaded. "We don't want no trouble."

Frank struggled to keep his head. He knew what Shimmy had that he lacked: the ability to present an outward appearance of calm at all times. No matter how Shimmy felt, whether he seethed with anger and rage, with the lust to stab or kill, his expressionless eyes and tightly compressed lips never betrayed him. Slugging a guy or laying a girl, Shimmy's countenance never changed, and now as he listened to Frank's threat he still kept his hands in the deep pockets of his double-breasted jacket, tensed, alerted for a sudden attack, but still master of himself.

"I'm not starting any trouble," Frank went on. "But I want him to stay away from my date. I just saw him over there talking to her, and now he's over here telling me what to do with Benny. Now you"—he turned to Benny again—"give me that bottle and make it snappy before we have a little accident."

"Give him the bottle," Larry ordered.

Benny withdrew the bottle from his pocket. "I'm just giving it to you because I don't want to start anything now." He glared at Frank.

Suddenly they heard Crazy's voice, pitched in the key that meant he was seeking trouble. "Don't give it to him, Benny," he said. "Give it to me and let's see if he can take it away from me."

"Shut up"—Larry turned to him—"and get the hell outa here. Mitch's been looking for you, so go find him. Come on, let's break this up."

With a great show of cordiality Larry grasped Shimmy's arm and led him toward the checkroom. He spoke earnestly to him, laughing and finally placing an arm around his shoulders in an effort to convince him that the flurry of words meant nothing.

"What's the matter?" Betty asked Frank as he rejoined her.

"Nothing. I saw you talking to that ape. Stay away from him if you want to stay healthy."

"He came over and talked to me," Betty said. "He didn't say anything or get wise."

"I know that kind of wolf," Frank told her. "He doesn't say anything, and the next thing you know you're flat on your back and wondering how the hell you got there."

"You want to go?" Betty asked him.

Frank looked around. "I think so," he replied. "Come on."

It was after eleven o'clock and the mob of new ticket holders was arriving, and the Dukes who were stag stood in a group near the door and greeted the boys and girls they knew. As Frank waited to get to the checkroom he saw Crazy push forward and jostle him.

"Stay away from me," Frank warned him.

Crazy hopped up and down, and Frank knew he was working himself into a rage.

"Who the hell asked you to come to our dance?" Crazy said to him.

Frank did not reply.

"Does your old man know you're down here? I heard about him being at the police station," Crazy went on while the other Dukes listened quietly. "Ya got your old man's permission to be down here?"

Frank shoved Crazy against two of the Dukes. "Keep my old man out of this, you lunatic bastard," Frank said.

"Your mother still buttoning your fly?" Crazy laughed and made a blowing noise with his lips.

"I'm remembering that." Frank tried to imitate Shimmy's impassivity.

"I'm remembering Fanny Kane," Crazy retorted.

Frank could not resist taunting him. "She's here. Why don't you get her?"

"I saw her," one of the Dukes answered Crazy's silent question. "She came in a little while ago."

"You better find her," Frank continued, and then he squared off as he saw the charging look in Crazy's eyes. "Come on, you crazy bastard," Frank dared him.

Bull ducked under the checkroom counter and came toward them. "Cut it out," he said.

"I'm not doin' nothin'," Crazy said. "Look at him." He pointed to Frank. "He's startin' the trouble."

"You're a crazy bastard," Frank repeated. "A no-good crazy bastard who was born crazy, is living crazy, and is going to die crazy."

Crazy spit at him. "Beat it. You're not one of the Dukes any more."

"Go to hell," Frank said.

"You're not one of us," Crazy went on, waving his arms and rolling his eyes. "You don't hang around with us any more. We don't even want you around. Do we, guys?" he asked the Dukes who stood around them.

The Dukes were silent, and Frank sensed their new and sudden hostility toward him.

"No"—he faced them—"I guess after tonight I'm not. Now I know where I stand with you guys."

"For cryin' out loud," Bull said, "don't you guys got anything else to do but start arguments? I'm breaking my ass in the checkroom and you guys are out here making trouble instead of keeping things going. You"—he pointed to Crazy —"you get in the checkroom with me."

"I want to find Mitch," Crazy said.

"Get in the checkroom"—Bull pushed him—"and leave Mitch alone. He's got a date."

"I want to see Fanny."

"Let him go, Bull," one of the stag Dukes said. "I'll help you."

Bull held Crazy by the arm and squeezed. "Listen to me," he cautioned him. "What's between you and Frank you can settle some other place. But you stay quiet. We'll need you later."

"For what?" Crazy asked eagerly.

"We're not paying the band," Bull said. "We'll need you."

Crazy rubbed his hands together and cackled. "We'll have trouble with them, huh? Boy, that's for me!"

"Don't say anything," Bull continued. "Now go find Fanny and stay out of trouble."

"I'll see you later." Crazy roughly bucked a dancing

couple out of his way and charged across the room to Fanny, who stood in front of the band with the arm of a D-Rape Artist around her shoulders. She moved in rhythm with the music, and the boy with her was making fast time. As he bent down to whisper something in her ear, Crazy snarled and tore Fanny loose from the embrace of the boy with whom she had been standing.

Fanny shrank away from Crazy. "Let me alone," she faltered.

Crazy walked toward her. "So I caught you at last," he said, and each word was a menace.

The saxophonist raised an arm to keep Fanny from falling over his music stand, and the D-Rape Artist looked around for some of his guys, and as one whizzed by on the dance floor he motioned to him for help.

"Let me alone," Fanny said.

"You stood me up," Crazy told her.

Fear paralyzed Fanny. "Let me alone," she repeated. She clutched the arm of the D-Rape Artist, who placed her behind him.

"Get away from my girl, Sam," Crazy said to Fanny's protector.

Sam's courage returned as he saw some members of his gang coming toward him. "For who?" He pushed Crazy.

"For me!" Crazy shouted at him. "She's my girl and she gave me a screwing!"

Sam turned to Fanny. "Are you his girl?"

Fanny trembled. "No."

"You bastard!" Crazy tried to get at her, but Sam and two of his friends blocked him. "You stood me up! Remember? Come outa there."

"Listen, Crazy"—Sam felt safe now as two more of his gang stood behind Crazy—"why don't you blow? This kid don't want no part of you."

With a smooth rapid motion Crazy drew his spring knife and simultaneously pressed the spring and shoved the knife against Sam's stomach. "One move outa you or your other crumbs and I'll have this in your guts," Crazy rasped. "Just one move."

"Don't do anything, Sam," one of the D-Rape Artists warned him. "I'm going to get Larry."

166

Crazy pressed the point of the knife against Sam and it made a little impression in the cloth of Sam's jacket. "In your guts," Crazy repeated. "You son of a bitch. You think I can't handle five guys like you? You think you're gonna fool around with my girl?"

"I was only kidding," Sam gasped, and tried to move away from the knife, but Crazy pressed the point into the pit of his stomach.

"Nobody kids around with me," Crazy told him, and Sam began to look sick. Crazy's reputation as a cutter and potential killer was well known in Brownsville. In one of his murderous rages Crazy was berserk, a street and gang fighter spoken of respectfully. Impervious to pain and blows, he would keep charging into the middle of any brawl, kicking and slugging with a fury and energy that was abnormal. Then—no one knew when—Crazy might draw his knife and begin slashing, and there were many who predicted that Crazy was going to be a big-time mobster if he lived long enough.

The crowd became more compact around Crazy, Sam, and Fanny, and the leader of the band signaled with his clarinet for the musicians to cease playing. There was a sudden cessation of noise as the word spread throughout the room that Crazy Sachs was going to give it to a guy.

Perspiration dampened Sam's face and his eyes were hunted and sick, for the knife pricked his jacket and he knew that any sudden movement he or his friends might make would be the impulse that would propel the knife into his stomach.

"Let's talk things over," Sam said to Crazy.

"You've said enough," Crazy said. "You got my girl."

"You've got me wrong," Sam protested, and quickly lowered his right hand, which he had raised to wipe his face, for Crazy had pricked him warningly. "I didn't know she was your babe."

The crowd gave as Larry and Mitch shoved their way toward Crazy and Sam.

"Crazy"—Mitch spoke quietly—"what do you think you're doing?"

"I'm going to give it to this bastard." Crazy continued to glare at Sam, and the killer look on Crazy's face made the crowd silent, for any sudden noise, sound, or movement meant that Crazy would sink the knife into Sam's stomach.

Sam's eyes were frantic with fear. His mouth twitched and he now kept his arms rigidly at his sides. Fanny shook with terror and cowered against the saxophonist's music stand. For a moment she held Frank's attention, but he shrugged his shoulders helplessly, and Frank's date held him tightly.

"Put the knife down," Mitch commanded Crazy.

"When I get good and ready," Crazy replied.

Mitch placed his hand lightly on Crazy's right arm. "Fanny wants to talk to you. Don't you, Fanny?"

Fanny nodded dumbly.

"I didn't mean nothing, honest," Sam said earnestly.

"You're breaking up the dance." Mitch tightened his grip on Crazy's sleeve. "Fanny wants to dance with you and," he whispered in Crazy's ear, "you can take her in the back and give it to her."

Slowly, almost imperceptibly, Crazy withdrew the knife. He looked questioningly at Mitch, and Mitch nodded affirmatively.

"Put it away," Mitch said. "You better take a powder," Mitch said to Sam, whose face was still pallid and streaked with perspiration.

Sam tugged at his tie and tried to catch his breath.

"Yeah, you better go," Larry agreed. "I'm sorry you got a shoving around"—he led the unprotesting Sam toward the checkroom—"but you tangled with a hard guy."

Mitch had ordered the band to start playing, and the musicians began to break down another number.

"Here's the key to the back room." Larry handed it to Mitch. "Give it back to me when you're through."

"Right," Mitch replied. "Come on," he said to Crazy, "let's go. You too," he said to Fanny.

"Where're you taking me?" she wept as Crazy pushed her ahead of him through the kitchen and cellar into a small bin which had been fitted up as a darkroom by some of the Tigers.

Mitch snapped the wall switch and shut the door before he spoke. "Crazy 'n' me want to talk to you."

168

"Let me alone!" she screamed, and was silenced by Crazy's slapping her in the face.

"You little bitch!" Crazy panted. "So you stood me up and thought you could get away with it!"

Fanny huddled in a corner and shielded herself from Crazy, who stood over her menacingly.

"I'm gonna leave you two alone," Mitch said to them. "And you," he said to Fanny, "you gave Crazy a raw deal and now you're gonna pay off."

"Let me alone!" she screamed and wept. "I never done it! I swear! My mother'll kill me when she finds out! I never done it!"

Mitch was unrelenting. "That's your story, stinker, and you're stuck with it. Don't give us that never-done-it stuff. It don't go with us."

Fanny clung to him. "I swear!" Her tears softened the mascara, and the hollows under her eyes became black. "I never done it! I never done it!"

Mitch pushed her from him. "So it's time you did. And Crazy's a good man to break you in. Gimme your knife," he said to Crazy.

Crazy tossed him the knife.

"You sure you haven't got another?" Mitch asked.

"No," Crazy said.

"O.K. Have a good time." Mitch opened the door, and as Fanny attempted to run out he punched her in the chest and knocked her to the cot. As he slammed the door behind him he could still hear Fanny screaming that she had never done it and begging Crazy to leave her alone. Before he entered the kitchen he stopped to listen and heard nothing. There was no danger of anyone hearing what was occurring in the darkroom. Mitch sighed. Taking care of Crazy was beginning to be a full-time job, and he had his own troubles. He had hardly danced once with his date and he had been so busy taking care of Shimmy and his guys that he wasn't having much of a time himself.

As Mitch re-entered the clubroom and heard the loud, high-pitched shrill laugh that started as a scream and ended as a sudden gasp, he knew that Rosie Beanbags had arrived. Rosie stood against the wall with two of her friends, and they were bantering the Dukes and anyone else who wanted

169

to join the fun. Rosie had jet-black hair which she wore in two thick braids that were fashioned into a halo on the top of her head. Her face was broad, with high cheekbones, and her eyebrows had been lengthened into two heavy lines which ended at the outer corners of her eyes. Her cheeks were heavily rouged to conceal the coarse and pitted texture of her skin, and the lipstick had been applied to her lips in a thick red cake. When Rosie laughed her heavy lips drew back to expose her gums, and her teeth were large and covered with tartar. Her breasts were tremendous, so large that they were a byword in the clubs and gangs of Brownsville and, as a sharp guy had once said, if a fellow were hit across the head with one of Rosie's knockers he'd be driven into the sidewalk up to his ankles. The low cut of Rosie's dress showed the heavy line between her breasts, and her high uplift brassière accented their size. Rosie's legs were heavy and covered with hair, and she wore a pair of French-heeled open-toed sandals with thick red soles studded with nailheads and straps that crossed her fat, stolid ankles. The nails of her toes were covered with silver polish, and the long nails of her hands were tinted a purplish black. Heavy bracelets decorated both wrists, and around her right ankle she wore a silver slave bracelet. Rosie's friends looked equally slutty, and as they stood in a group smoking their cigarettes and squinting at the boys through half-closed eyes Betty felt sick and overcome with revulsion.

"Aren't we going?" She nudged Frank.

"I changed my mind," he replied angrily. "Those guys want me to stay and I'm hangin' around."

"But we're not having a good time."

"I'm staying until it breaks up."

"Whatever you say." Betty shook her head as if she were unable to keep pace with the vagaries of his mood.

"Watch them," Frank said to Betty. "Rosie's a riot."

"I think she's disgusting."

Frank's reply was a sneer.

The boys rocked with laughter as Rosie heaved a bump at them.

"Come on, Rosie," one of the boys encouraged her, "you

musta heard some good dirty stories since I saw—I mean laid—you last."

The girls standing in the crowd began to slip away. Between them and Rosie and her two friends there was a clear and defined social gap—the difference between a girl who permitted a boy whom she liked to give her some loving and the girl who was common gang property. Rosie suggested cellars, vacant lots and roofs, obscene coarseness, and dirty bed sheets, and the girls who stood about her moved away, singly, in twos, ashamed that they should have been seen in such close proximity to this notorious gang whore.

"Yeah," one of the Dukes said as he nudged Shimmy and told him that now they'd see some fun, "give out with a story."

Rosie raised her hands, palms forward. "Sure," she yelled, "I got a good one!" She took a deep breath and began. Her story was pointless, without wit or humor, a dirty description of an impossible situation, related with a lewdness and vulgarity that made boys who had never before seen or heard of Rosie wince and despise her. And she was urged on by the loose laughter, the sudden dirty snorts of glee, the obscene delight which stimulated most of the crowd about her, until she came to the stupid climax of the story and in her thick throaty voice accented the dirty line. Then she laughed her shrill gasping laugh, and the crowd laughed with her.

"Rose," one fellow commented above the howls of laughter, "you're hotter than a two-dollar cornet."

Bull Bronstein approached her and slid his hand into the bosom of her dress. "Rosie," he said, "I wish I had them stuffed full of gold."

"You'd sure have something," she agreed, "but with Lilly here you'd starve to death."

"Oh yeah?" Lilly retorted. "It ain't knockers what count."

"So let's not waste any more time." Bull spoke quietly to Rosie. "We got some guys down here from Williamsburg who've been givin' us a hand all night. So how about fixin' them up?"

"Can't we later?" she replied. "We just got here and we wanta fool around first."

171

"You'll fool around later," Bull decided for her. "Larry, Jackie," he called the president of the Tigers, "Rosie and her babes are gonna entertain Shimmy and his guys in the back. You got some more cots?"

"The only cot we got is in the darkroom," Jackie apologized. "But we got some extra blankets."

"So we'll let one of the babes use the darkroom and Rosie and the other one'll use the kitchen. You'll have to keep people out of there," Bull said.

"Shimmy's guys can stand at the door," Larry said, "and I better go to the darkroom and get Crazy outa there with that stinker."

"Who's Crazy got in there?" Bull asked.

"You know. Fanny Kane."

Bull whistled. "That's jerky. Leaving him alone in there with her. He's liable to split her head. Get Mitch and get him outa there. All right, Rosie"—he turned to her—"let's get started."

"How many guys?"

"About eight and a coupla the Tigers. That's all. It won't take too long."

Rosie tried to look co-operative but failed. "Gee," she wailed, "we ain't been down no half-hour and you got us working."

Bull chucked her under the chin. "You know you love it. We're wastin' time."

The girls puffed nervously on their cigarettes as they stood in the kitchen, where the bright glare of the electric-light bulb in the open ceiling fixture caused everything to stand out in sharp abrupt lines. Jackie and Larry tossed the blankets onto the floor and made rough beds. Jackie knelt down and attempted to be funny by saying the beds were soft, but no one laughed.

The three girls stood transfixed when they saw Fanny stumble dully into the kitchen, her eyes puffed from crying and her lips swollen from the slaps across the mouth administered by Crazy. Her hair was disheveled and hung in loose strands about her head. Her stockings were in shreds, and the bodice of her dress was ripped to the waist. Haltingly she plodded to the sink, turned the cold-water

172

faucet, and dabbed futilely at her eyes and lips with her hands.

Rosie approached her and wet a handkerchief. "You poor kid," she whispered, "what'd they do to you?"

Fanny collapsed in Rosie's arms and began to sob, her shoulders shaking as the sobs choked her. She clenched her lips to keep from screaming, but then she could no longer endure the pain and shock, and her cries became wild and hysterical, racking her with their violence.

"I never done it before!" The words came out singly from her bruised lips. "I never done it before! I begged him to let me go! Never done it before. Never done it before. Never done it———"

"You sons of bitches!" Rosie faced them. "You no-good sons of bitches to do this to a kid!"

"Who's askin' you?" Crazy blustered.

Rosie removed one of her shoes and grasped it by the sole. "Come over and I'll show you, you son of a bitch!"

"She had it comin' to her," Larry said.

"Comin' to her?" Rosie looked at him with disbelief. "You mean she coulda done somethin' so bad that that son of a bitch had to rape this kid?"

"She stood up Crazy once," Larry explained.

"So who in the hell wouldn't stand up that crazy dope?" Lilly flung her cigarette into the sink, where it hissed sharply before it was extinguished. "Let me help you, Rosie," she said. "We oughta get some ice for the kid's lips."

"You guys are a bunch of dogs," Maybelle said. "No-good dogs."

Bull opened the kitchen door. "Get out, Crazy. You done enough for one night."

"Let's get this over with," Maybelle said to Rosie. "Get the guys," she said to Bull.

"Bring in Shimmy and his boys," Bull said to Jackie.

"How about my guys?" Jackie asked.

Rosie stopped washing Fanny's face. "Just the guys who're protecting this dance," she said to Bull. "No one else."

"Be regular," Jackie protested. "We didn't have nothin' to do with this."

Rosie's look was full of loathing. "Go on, you son of a bitch. We don't want no part of you or your bunch. Go on," she ordered Bull, "get them in and let's get going. We want to take this kid home."

Jackie looked at Bull, and Bull shrugged his shoulders.

"My dress," Fanny moaned suddenly through her swollen lips. "He tore my dress. I never done it before."

Maybelle gently stroked Fanny's hair. "Take it easy, baby," she said. "You're about my size and I'll fix you up with a dress. I got one something like you're wearing at home and I'll give it to you."

There was a knock on the kitchen door, and Bull opened it to admit Shimmy and the seven members of his gang.

"Gee," one of them whistled, "somebody's gotten a pasting."

"Let me take her outside," Lilly said, "and I'll find somebody to take care of her until we get done."

"I'll do it," Rosie said. "Come on, kid." She supported Fanny. "We'll have you outa here in no time."

The blare of notes, laughter, and confusion hit Rosie as she entered the steaming clubroom and looked around for someone she knew. She saw Betty and Frank sitting near the band, and Rosie led Fanny to them.

"Frank," she said, "I want you and your girl to take care of this kid. She's had a rough deal."

Betty stood up and gently seated Fanny. "Sure," she said. "What happened?"

"Some bastard just raped her," Rosie explained. "One of your guys," she said to Frank. "Crazy Sachs."

Frank held his throat and shut his eyes. "I'm through with them after tonight," he said half to himself.

"So'm I," Rosie said. "I don't like sons of bitches or guys who're friends of sons of bitches. We got some work in the back." Her laugh was contemptuous. "I'll be back soon."

Betty held Fanny's head on her shoulder. Frank nervously lit a cigarette, took a deep drag, and ground the cigarette underfoot.

"We'll go as soon as she gets back." He gestured toward the kitchen.

174

"Suits me." Betty closed Fanny's torn dress with one hand. "This is really some dance."

"I know." Frank lit another cigarette, looked at it distastefully, and threw it away. He saw Benny approaching him and wanted to ignore him, but he decided he had had enough nastiness to last him for the evening without another fight to climax everything.

"Someone's at the door to see you," Benny said. "You sold him two ten o'clock tickets and it's after twelve now and he first wants to get in."

Frank stood up. "Who is it?"

"Go see." Benny spun around and left him.

"I'll be right back," Frank said to Betty.

Since Shimmy and his gang were not on hand to urge the holders of eleven o'clock tickets to leave, the clubroom had become a milling jam of people, and the floor was so crowded that the dancing now consisted mainly of the dancers lifting their eyebrows in time to the music. Tediously Frank forced his way through the mob until he came to the checkroom.

"Frank"—Larry raised his hand over his head and urged him to hurry—"this guy says he couldn't get here before and wants to come in."

When Frank had sold two tickets to Stan Alberg he had never expected Stan to use them. Now Stan stood there smiling down at him, and beside him stood his wife.

"I couldn't get here before," Stan apologized. "I hope I'm not going to have to shell out another five bucks."

"Let him in," Frank said to Larry. "You know who he is. He's the gym teacher at the Center."

Larry nodded and ducked under the counter into the checkroom. "Check your things," he said. "Twenty-five cents each."

Stan picked fifty cents from the coins in his hand and gave them to Larry in exchange for the cardboard checking tags.

"Come in," Frank invited them. "I never thought you'd come."

"We didn't either," Reba replied, "but I changed Stan's mind."

"Where're you sitting?" Stan coughed. "This place could stand some ventilation."

"Over there." Frank pointed and bit his lip. Fanny was sitting with Betty.

"Thanks for inviting us to join you," Stan said sarcastically. "We'll follow you."

Frank looked back and saw Larry watching them. Now it didn't seem like such a good idea, but at the time it was an easy way to get rid of two tickets. But really it didn't make any difference because after tonight he was through with the Dukes.

Fanny was still huddled in Betty's arms, and Stan and Reba were silent, waiting for an introduction and an explanation.

"Fanny had a little trouble," Frank began lamely. "This is my girl, Betty. Mr. and Mrs. Alberg."

"I'm glad to know you," Reba said. "Can I help you?" she asked Betty.

Fanny shivered and Betty pressed her closer. "No," she said, "not unless you got some pins with you. Her dress is ripped."

Reba rummaged through her purse. "Just when you want them you can't find them. Here"—she dug deeper into her purse—"I have some. I bought them for one of my neighbors who has a baby and I never gave them to her. Let me help you." She knelt and took a pin from the card.

"It's all right, Fanny," Betty said to her. "This lady wants to help."

Fanny kept her hands over her face, but even in the semidarkness Reba could see the swollen eyes and lips. But what astonished and upset her, made her want to strike out at the tough-faced boys and girls about her who accepted the sight of a beaten girl as a normal occurrence, was the apparent youth of the girl. Deftly she opened the pins and caught both sides of the torn dress and clipped them together.

"Stan"—she stood up—"I think we ought to take this girl home with us."

"Some girls are going to take care of her," Frank said.

"I think we oughta leave without them," Betty said sharply.

"Too late." Frank glanced toward the kitchen door, which had opened. "Here they come."

Rosie shoved through the mob to them, her face set and grim. "All right," she said to Betty, "how's she been?"

"Crying," Betty said.

"The bastards'll get paid back for that, don't worry," Rosie said bitterly. "You ready to go?" she said to Lilly and Maybelle.

"We're ready," Maybelle replied. "Let's get the hell outa here."

"Where are you taking her?" Stan asked.

Rosie turned on him. "Who the hell wants to know?"

"Hold your water," Frank warned. "This guy 'n' his wife are my friends and they wanta help her."

"So why're they lookin' at us that way?" Rosie asked. "We ain't poison."

"I'm sorry," Stan apologized.

"Ah," Rosie grimaced, "guys like you make me sick. Don't say anythin' "—she stopped him—"I know what you're thinkin'. And you and your wife know what to do if you don't like us."

"Jesus," Frank exploded, "is everyone going nuts? Listen, you"—he grasped Rosie's arm and held her as she struggled to get loose—"Fanny's hurt and you wanta help her. All right. These people'll take her home and straighten her out, won't you?" he appealed to Stan. "You got any place to take her except another club?" he asked Rosie.

Lilly looked at her friends. "We don't know. You were gonna get her a dress, weren't you, Miriam?"

"The name's Maybelle."

"I'm sorry, Maybelle. I just forgot. I'm all excited."

"Yeah," Maybelle replied. "If we'll only get started I'll go home now and get it. You'll give me your address, mister?" she asked Stan.

Stan took out a notebook and fountain pen. "I'll write it down for you. Crown Street," he said as he wrote, "near Albany. You know how to get there?"

"Sure." Maybelle squinted at the name and address. "You come with me, Lilly. We'll be there in about an hour."

"Get our things," Betty said to Frank. "You have anything checked?" she asked Fanny.

Fanny reached into her bosom and shook her head. "I lost the check," she whispered. "It was nothin'. Only my lipstick and a dime in a blue change purse."

"I'll try and get it for you," Frank said. "You coming, Stan?"

Stan nodded, and they wormed through the mob. Shimmy and his gang were again busy weeding out the dancers who had stayed beyond their allotted time. The press around the checkroom added to the confusion, and they could hear Larry and Bull cursing at people and telling them to take it easy.

Frank held out his hand. "Gimme your checks and I'll get our things."

"Think you'll manage?" Stan smiled. "That's like the rush hour in the subway."

"I will," Frank said. "Larry!" he shouted. "Let me through, you jerks!" He charged into the mob and shoved people to the right and left of him. "Larry, I'm comin' through." Frank ducked under the counter and leaned against the wall to catch his breath. "Wow," he breathed heavily, "how the hell're you guys standin' it?"

"Whadd'ya want?" Bull asked him as he shoved a hat across the counter. "Two bits!" he yelled to the boy who took the hat.

"I paid you once," the boy said.

"Then scram," Bull said, "you're blockin' traffic."

Frank juggled the checks. "How about giving me my stuff and Fanny Kane's? She lost her check. She said it was a little blue pocketbook."

"I want you to hang around." Larry took the checks from him. "You ain't done nothin' but take it easy all night except when you were fightin' with Mitch, Shimmy, Benny, and Crazy. You must think you're a hard character"—he gave Betty's purse to Frank—"but you're taking on an awful load."

"You guys bother me."

"We can't figure you out," Larry went on. "You usta be a

178

nice guy and now you just go around fightin' with Benny and Crazy. I still think you and Benny got somethin' worrying you, but if you don't wanta talk about it, that's all right with me."

"I'm waiting for our stuff," Frank interrupted him.

"I'm gettin' your things," Larry said. "But you're staying here. We got some work for you."

"I was takin' Fanny over to Mr. Alberg's."

"So you won't. Why the hell are you getting mixed up in that? You know"—Larry paused—"if you wouldn't've given Crazy a lousing that time the kid wouldn'ta been hurt now. How's she look?"

"Like I'd like Crazy to look. Are you kidding about me hangin' around?"

"If he is, I'm not," Bull answered. "You gotta help us. I hardly been outa this room all night."

"They're waiting for me," Frank protested. "Stan Alberg, his wife, and everyone."

"That's another thing." Bull matched two checks and threw a hat to Larry. "What was the idea of selling tickets to him?"

"Why shouldn't I?"

"Because he's down at that lousy Center, and all they do down there is go to the cops so they can sponsor clubs together. And I don't like the way he looks. And I don't like cops."

"Maybe he doesn't like the way you look."

Bull was reaching for another hat but paused. "Listen, wise guy"—he shoved Frank against the wall—"you watch what you're saying or I'll start busting you around. You've been shootin' your mouth off all night, and I'm one guy who knows that he can kick the crap outa you. Now you're staying. If they wanta wait for you it's all right, or you can meet them when the dance is over. But you're staying."

Frank remembered Shimmy and the way he controlled himself, and instead of yelling at them that after tonight he was through with the Dukes he remained silent until he felt that neither by word nor action would he betray to Bull and Larry how he felt. Two weeks ago he had been glad that the Dukes apparently were willing to reinstate him as

179

a member in good standing, but now he was determined to break with them. After what had happened this night he knew he could drop them gracefully, leave them without regret. The only thing they would say about him would be that he was a rat, but it did not worry him.

When he spoke his voice was composed and nonchalant. "All right, guys," he said, "I'll give them their stuff and I'll be back in a coupla minutes."

Larry took a small blue purse from a corner of one of the shelves and handed it to Frank. "Is this Fanny's?" he asked him.

Frank opened the purse and nodded. "She said she only had a lipstick and a dime." He collected the hats and purses and asked Larry to raise the counter. "Help me get through here," he said.

Larry forced a path through the crowd, and Frank repeated that he would return in a minute.

Shimmy and his boys were slowly losing their control over the crowd. The Dukes had sold tickets to clubs and gangs who prided themselves on not backing down for anyone, and against one wall of the room the Thatford Giants had isolated two of Shimmy's gang and were slapping them around. Shimmy struggled to break through the ring of Giants but stopped when one of the Giants, a six-foot boy with a broken nose and a scar that extended from his left temple to the chin, brandished an iron poker in his hand and invited Shimmy to step forward and have his head split open.

"You want me to plug him?" one of the squat gangsters asked Shimmy.

Shimmy shook his head. "They'll murder us if you do. Why don't you cut it out?" he asked the Giant. "We don't want no trouble."

"We're not shellin' out no two and a half bucks to hang around here for an hour," the Giant said. "We don't take that crap from no one, least from a stinker like you. Who'd you ever kill?" The Giant swung the poker threateningly. "I never seen your picture in no post office."

Frank grinned as he heard the Giant telling off Shimmy.

"Here"—he gave Stan his hat and Reba's purse—"you go ahead and I'll try and get away soon."

"You're not coming?" Betty asked him.

"I gotta stay," he apologized. "We're liable to have trouble and I gotta hang around."

Rosie snatched Fanny's purse from his hand. "He's like the rest of them sons of bitches. He must be hangin' around because they're gonna line up some other babes."

"Watch your mouth!" Frank warned her.

"Son of a bitch!" Rosie turned away from him to help Fanny.

Frank appealed to Stan. "I gotta stay if I don't wanta get in trouble," he explained. "I'll try to get away as soon as I can, but if I'm not over your place by"—he looked at his watch—"it's almost one, say three o'clock, then you'll call a cab for Betty?" He took out his wallet and began to remove some bills.

Stan pushed the bills aside. "I'll drive her home. My doorman is going to go crazy when he sees you." He had to laugh.

"I'm packin' these guys in," Frank said. "Honest," he insisted as he noticed Stan's quizzical smile. "After what they done tonight I see that I'd be a dummy to hang on. I gotta pack them in. For my own sake."

"Then maybe we'll see you later." Stan did not care to continue the conversation. "Looks like somebody is being worked on." He motioned to the knot of Thatford Giants surrounding Shimmy's boys.

"We'll have to break that up," Frank said. "I'll see you later, Betty." He kissed her. "You're not sore?"

"No."

"Help me with her," Rosie said to Betty.

Frank watched Stan push ahead while Rosie and Betty supported Fanny between them. This was definitely no good. He crossed to the other side of the room where the Giant was still inviting Shimmy to step forward so he could fracture his skull.

"Hey, Meyer," he called to the Giant, "how about breakin' it up? You're spoiling the dance."

"When I get good and ready to."

"Come on." Frank approached him. "We don't want the cops here. You gave them a shellacking already," he said softly. "So let the bastards go. Later, if you want to, get them outside and beat the crap outa them. You're screwing things up." He raised his voice.

"We're not leaving." Meyer looked down at him.

"So stick around," Frank said cajolingly, "and we'll put you to work. Just let them alone."

"Hey, guys," Meyer shouted, "we're stayin'. Let the jerks go."

The Thatford Giants shoved Shimmy's boys into the center of the dance floor. Their right hands went to their hip pockets, but Shimmy shook his head negatively.

Meyer grabbed Shimmy by the back of the collar and twisted. "You tell your guys that if they do that again they'll be found tomorrow on an empty lot in Canarsie."

"Let go," Shimmy said quietly. "I want to talk to you. I think me 'n' you can get together."

Meyer pushed Shimmy away and laughed. "Who the hell cares about getting together with a rat like you? G'wan, blow, before I beat your brains out."

Shimmy said nothing and placed a restraining hand on the arm of one of his boys. He looked steadily at Meyer, memorizing each of his features, for Meyer was marked to die, and soon, a day, two days, a week, a month, but soon Meyer's body would be found in a vacant lot in Canarsie or floating in the river. The eyes in Shimmy's head shone like bright sparks and he smiled, for he would still be alive when Meyer's head would be blown off his shoulders. There was no alternative; no lesser punishment would appease Shimmy; he was going to prove to other would-be hard guys that shoving Shimmy around was a quick way of inviting death. And as Meyer stood there brandishing the poker, cursing and full of fight, he did not know that soon his parents and sister would be sitting *shive* for him.

Moishe Perlman had joined Larry and Bull in the checkroom, and when Frank ducked under the counter there was little room for him.

"I ain't had a chance to talk to you all night," he addressed Moishe. "It's crowded here. You get out and I'll help. I just broke up an argument between Meyer Oxenburg and your buddy Shimmy," he said to Bull. "Shimmy was gonna get his head busted."

"I'll be ready for the cleaners by the time tonight's over," Bull cursed.

"Should I get out?" Moishe asked Larry.

"Go ahead," Larry said. "Try and keep things from getting outa hand."

"What about raffling the salamis?" Moishe asked him.

Larry leaned across the counter, pushed someone in the face, and peered into the smoke-fogged room. "We'll forget it and take the salamis home."

For an hour Frank helped Larry and Bull check and return hats, purses, and other articles. Crazy ducked under the counter and stood in a corner, ostensibly arranging the checked articles in neat piles, but actually rifling the purses of money and other articles which he fancied. He placed the loot in a cigar box, and Frank, Bull, and Larry maneuvered in front of Crazy to keep him from view of the crowd.

Frank looked at his watch. It was a little past two and he wondered if he was going to get to Stan's apartment that night. Betty had become angrier as the evening had progressed, and the whole affair had turned out to be a bust. No longer was there any semblance of order at the dance, only a cacophonous jumble of noise, shrieks, yells, shouts, curses, and confusion against the background of a band to which no one listened. The president of the Tigers had informed Larry that it would be best to close the dance, as their landlord had stormed into the clubroom threatening to call the police and dispossess them.

"Wind it up," Jackie begged Larry, "before you get us in a jam."

"Sure," Bull said. "We can close up now. It's a little past two."

"Whadd'ya say?" Larry asked Frank.

"You askin' me?" Frank said. "Sure. Close it up."

"Get Shimmy," Larry said to Bull, "and tell him to start cleaning the place out and tell our guys to help him. Crazy"—he turned around—"get some of the boys outside and tell them not to let anyone else in. Then you come back."

Bull and Crazy ducked under the counter, and Larry

cupped his hands to his mouth and shouted into the room that the dance was over and that everyone was to get his or her belongings from the checkroom and leave. Bull spoke to the band leader, and soon the strains of "Auld Lang Syne," so syncopated and garbled that there was little of the original melody and lilt left, informed the dancers that they were to scram. Crazy, Mitch, Whitey Levine, and five other Dukes plunged past the entrance into the street to prevent anyone from entering the clubroom. Bull opened a path for himself by pulling people out of his way and rejoined Larry in the checkroom.

"The band wants to get paid," he panted.

"Let's get these people outa here," Larry replied, "and then we'll take care of them. Are they wise?"

Bull grabbed checks and stacked hats and purses on the counter. "I don't think so. Maybe we oughta pay them."

"Shut up," Larry said. "Don't tell me what we maybe oughta do."

Crazy returned for a last ransacking of the few purses that remained in the checkroom, and Frank wished he did not have to stay in the same little room with him. Crazy upset him, made him ill. He remembered the way Fanny Kane had looked and that she was only twelve, one year older than Alice, even though she was lots older in looks and experience. He knew that what he wanted to do more than anything else that night was to put Crazy out of commission. But it was best to ignore Crazy and to fade out of the Dukes. Then the break would be clean, and if Larry or Bull asked him why he didn't come around any more he could say that it would have meant a violent battle with Crazy and he wanted to avoid it if he could.

There were only a few people left before the checkroom, and Bull placed the remaining articles on the counter and told the guests to pick out their belongings. One girl began to yell that her purse was missing and that she was not leaving until she was compensated for its loss.

"Get going," Larry said. "We don't know if you had a bag."

The girl thrust her check forward. "Don't give me that!" she shouted. "I got my check! You jerks lost my purse and I want it!"

"Take it easy," Bull said. "You'll strain your knockers."

"Who the hell're you talkin' to?" The girl's lips were contorted with anger. "Get up my purse or pay me for it."

The girl's escort jiggled her elbow. "Come on, Lucy," he said. "They'll give you nothin'."

Lucy shook off her escort's arm. "Stop being so yellow," she said, "and tell these apes to pay me for my bag."

"Sure"—Crazy grimaced at them—"you tell us to pay you, bud, and we'll pay you off in the dark."

Larry wanted to get rid of her. "How much was the bag worth?"

"Five bucks. And I had a buck in change in there and a new dollar-and-a-quarter lipstick and a good compact and I only bought it about a week ago and——"

"So here's three bucks"—Larry held out three dollar bills—"and we'll call it even. Don't open your mouth," he warned her, "or all you'll get is loose teeth. Now take the three bucks and blow. We wanta close up."

"Yeah, blow," Crazy said. "I'd-a given you nothin'. Oh, wait." He reached into a cardboard carton and withdrew a salami. "Here's a *wurst* for you. Don't say we never gave you nothin'."

"Slam the door on your way out," Frank suggested.

Larry took the handkerchief from his breast pocket and wiped his forehead. "Boy"—he fanned himself—"whadda night. We sure worked for our dough."

"But we got it," Bull said. "How much we get, Larry?"

Larry added some figures on the whitewashed wall of the checkroom. "Start counting what Crazy put in the cigar box," he said to Frank.

"Girls are cheap," Crazy complained. "Only one babe had more than a buck. Some of them had nothin'."

"Bull"—Larry was still adding—"what did we make on checkin'?"

"Don't you snitch anything else in that box," Crazy warned Frank. "The other stuff is mine."

"You can shove this junk," Frank replied. "I wouldn't have any of it. Crazy collected a little over thirty-one bucks," he said to Larry.

Larry winked approvingly at Crazy. "Good work. Say,"

he asked him, "how'd that Fanny kid get down here? Did you sell her a ticket?"

"I gave her one," Frank answered. "I had one left and I thought I'd give it to the kid. Don't worry," he forestalled their question, "I paid for it. Though I'm sorry I gave it to her, seeing as what happened."

Crazy's eyes began to glitter angrily. "Who told her to fight like she did? She got what was comin' to her, and you will too!" he threatened Frank.

Frank looked him over from head to foot. "Jerk."

"Almost two hundred bucks," Bull finished counting. "Geez, this change is heavy."

"We sold all the tickets," Larry said, "plus we got some extras. Twenty-five hundred and fifty bucks. Not bad."

There was awe in Bull's voice. "Almost twenty-eight hundred bucks! We sure did it!"

"You think with all that dough that we oughta stick the band for a lousy fifty bucks?" Frank suggested.

Bull nodded in agreement with Frank and waited for Larry to speak.

Larry hesitated.

"Give them a stiff," Crazy said. "You want me to throw 'em out?"

"Don't listen to him, Larry," Frank said. "It isn't worth it. We got enough dough, and this way we're windin' up the dance like square guys."

Crazy lunged at Frank, but Bull stepped between them. "You don't wanna fight for the Dukes!" Flecks of spittle bubbled from the corners of Crazy's mouth. "You're a yellow bastard! You don't wanna fight for the Dukes! Don't give the band nothin'," he pleaded with Larry.

"Am I president?" Larry asked sternly.

Crazy relaxed and hung his head. "Yeah," he whispered.

"So cut it out. Go find Mitch and go home with him."

"All right, Larry. I'm doin' it for you. Only for you."

Larry laughed and embraced Crazy. "What a nut you are," he said. "You're sure the world's prize screwball. Go on"—he shoved him gently—"find Mitch and go home with him. And listen," he said seriously, "maybe you better watch out that Fanny don't go to the cops. You shouldn't've done it."

186

"You can say that again," Frank said.

"If you're goin' up this guy's house, Frank, you'll see the kid and tell her to keep her mouth shut."

"For him?" Frank pointed to Crazy.

Larry stepped up to Frank. "For us," he said with emphasis. "You know what a rape rap'll mean to the Dukes? Bull"—he turned to him—"take fifty bucks and give it to the band. Crazy, I thought I told you to beat it. Get Mitch and go home."

"I'm goin'." Crazy raised the counter and held it for Bull. "So long. Say, can I have one of my wursts?"

"Take one," Larry said. "So long. Wait a minute," he said to Frank after Bull left to pay the band. "I wanta talk to you."

"I wanta call up Alberg and tell him I'm comin'," Frank said. "It's almost three o'clock, and I gotta go to Ninety-eighth Street for a phone."

"I'm going with you," Larry replied. "But what I gotta say is only goin' to take a minute. What do you and Benny know about your teacher being knocked off?" he asked suddenly.

Frank recoiled. "Nothing."

"Walk away," Larry ordered one of the Dukes who approached the checkroom, "we're talkin' private." Then he turned to Frank. "Stop kidding me." Larry spoke in a low voice. "I saw it tonight when I heard you 'n' Benny had a fight. He called you a rat, didn't he? Now I get it why he was always lookin' for you and he'd be jumpy as hell when you weren't around. Now I know why you don't smoke reefers no more, don't hardly take a drink, don't carry no knife, don't——" He stopped suddenly and pointed a forefinger at Frank, who cringed against the wall, his face the color of paste. "You 'n' Benny done it! You knocked off your teacher!" His voice trickled to a wisp of sound.

Frank felt the desire to vomit leave him. "You're getting to be like Crazy," he said. He felt better as he spoke.

"You guys knocked him off," Larry repeated. "Who shot him? What did you do with the gat?"

Frank opened his mouth and gulped. "You're trying to frame me!" He glared. "Me 'n' Benny. We didn't do nothing! You wanta go to Alberg's house you can go alone! A

187

fine bunch of guys you are! Let me outa here!" He lifted the counter. "I'm getting Benny and telling him what you said."

"Benny's drunk," Larry informed him. "He's laying on a blanket in the kitchen."

"So I'm gonna take him home," Frank replied. "The next thing I know, if I leave him here you'll be sweating him."

"Sure," Larry agreed. "Take him home. But remember, Frank"—he paused to pass Frank his hat—"that Benny's worrying and drinking because he thinks you're gonna give him away. And when a guy's drinking he ain't much good. So you better get him home and go over to see him tomorrow and tell him that he don't have to worry. That's what you better do. And another thing, you don't have to worry about us. You're a Duke and we're Dukes. You play square with the boys and you got nothin' to worry about. Understand?"

Each word Larry uttered was like the stroke of a bell, booming, decisive, and final. Frank ran his hands nervously around the welted edge of his summer-weight felt hat. There was no quitting the Dukes now. At least not until the end of June.

Chapter 11

As the bus rumbled to another uneven stop Frank's stomach rose and he felt as if he were going to puke. Why Alice doted on these damned Fifth Avenue bus rides was beyond him, but he had promised to take the kid out and now he was stuck.

"Let's get off at the next stop," he said, "and walk a couple of blocks. I feel lousy."

"I'm sorry." Alice grasped his hand. "Sure. I like to walk on Fifth Avenue."

As they descended from the bus and the nausea left him he remembered that he was glad Alice had awakened him at seven-thirty. He had not slept well, as he had reconstructed the dance in his overtired and taxed mind and seen every scene in its true tawdriness. If only he could have taken Betty home, left the dance before he had seen Fanny's battered face, before he had given Larry the opportunity to tear open his secret and Benny's, before he had seen the look of resignation on Stan Alberg's face as Stan realized how strong his allegiance to the Dukes was. How could he explain that he was caged, that Benny's drunkenness was as dangerous as a runaway automobile without brakes, that his only safety lay in ostensibly staying away from Benny while he remained close enough to him to keep Benny from doing something dangerous or rash, something that would bring disaster to them?

"Frank," Alice began hesitantly, "you got something on your mind?"

His head snapped back. "Why?"

Alice fidgeted with her hat and small leather shoulder bag. "I don't know. You look so worried. You know what I heard this morning when I went to the grocery?"

"What?"

"Mrs. Kaplan was telling the grocery lady and some other ladies that Fanny Kane came home early in the morning all beaten up. Mr. Alberg from the Center took her home, and Mrs. Kaplan who lives in her house said that she could hear Mrs. Kane screaming that she was going to kill Fanny for staying out late and becoming a bum." Alice hesitated at the last word.

"So what the hell do I care?" Frank asked her.

"Nothing," Alice continued slowly, "only she told my girl friend Gladys yesterday that she was going to the dance your club was having."

Alice winced as Frank squeezed her upper arm. "You talk too much and hear too much," he told her. "You just stay away from Fanny if you know what's good for you."

"She told Gladys and me that you gave her the ticket," Alice persisted. "She even told me once that you took her out. You didn't do anything to her yesterday?"

"No! Shut up!"

"Who did it?" she asked him.

"Shut up!" Frank ignored her question and clutched

189

at his stomach. "Stop asking me so many damn-fool questions!"

He had the worst luck. He had not realized the implications of Crazy's attack upon Fanny. If the kid squealed and her mother and father went to the police it meant that Crazy and the rest of the Dukes would be in trouble again. But he had nothing to do with the attack; still he was there, and it was so damned important that he stay out of trouble. He only hoped Fanny would keep her mouth shut. Anyway, he'd have to tell Larry and Bull what had happened and let them figure this one. He could tell them that Stan Alberg wouldn't help them. He knew that without seeing Stan. And anyway, it was Crazy's rap.

Alice held his hand and glanced at Frank. She knew that the news about Fanny Kane had disturbed him, although she believed he had known the night before what had happened. And she was worried about Crazy. Frank hated Crazy and Crazy hated her brother, and people said that Crazy was liable to do anything. She shuddered.

Frank felt her tremble. "What's the matter, baby?" He looked at her.

"I got a chill," she apologized. "It's nothing. Look at the gardens!" she exclaimed as they entered the promenade from Fifth Avenue. "They're beautiful!"

Frank pointed to a square of cardboard at the end of a stick. "Read the little signs. They tell the names of the flowers and"—he bent forward—"their Latin names."

Alice sat on a wooden bench and stared at the azalea shrubs, whose red blossoms were like a vivid splash of flame against the short thick grass. Surrounding the azaleas like an antique gold frame that has become mottled and foxed were rows of jonquils and tulips, with their yellow, red, and purple-black blossoms swaying in the light breeze. At the outer border of the plots the clumps of velvet-petaled pansies, with startling blues, purples, and yellows, added the final thrust of extravagant color to the formal flower arrangement.

Frank smiled and tugged at his sister's arm. "I'll take you to the Botanical Gardens next week." Her childish and trusting face with frank brown eyes that were suddenly happy as he spoke to her made him want to cry. He felt like a rat, a heel. If he had given her more attention he wouldn't have had so much time for Black Benny and the Dukes—but there was no use thinking about it.

"Hurry up," he said again. "We want to make the show and we want to get out before it's too late. You gotta eat. I never noticed how thin you were."

Alice stood up and smoothed her skirt. "I could sit here and not go to the movie. I eat plenty."

Frank paused as Alice leaned over the parapet to see the people eating and drinking under the awnings.

"They eat like that in French restaurants in Paris," he informed her. "It's kinda nice."

"I don't want to go to the movies," Alice insisted. "Please."

Frank looked at her. "All right," he said. "Suit yourself."

For almost an hour Alice sat on a bench in the promenade staring at the flowers as if she wanted to impress forever in her mind their colors, their grace of line, their beauty and unconscious loveliness. And as she sat there, darting shy glances at the people who strolled past them, reaching suddenly forward with a quick yet timid motion to touch the bright face of a pansy, and breathing the wonder and excitement of the stone fountain whose white spumes of spray hung as a fine irisation in the sun, the hour was a magic time.

Frank pushed a strand of hair back from Alice's forehead. "Come on, baby," he said, "let's get something to eat."

Reluctantly she permitted herself to be led back to Fifth Avenue. "I could still stay," she said.

"I believe you." Frank nodded. "Now look, we gotta eat. I'm taking you to a swell place to eat. Wait till you see it. Nothing like what we got in Brownsville."

The sun was joyous over Fifth Avenue, and Frank permitted Alice to gape and goggle at the store windows. Each window held something of interest for her, and Lord and Taylor, Franklin Simon, Best and Company, stores whose names she had read in the newspaper advertisements, suddenly were real to her, and she was not disappointed. The season depicted in the windows was summer, and the mannequins portrayed the average citizen and

191

his family, clad in expensive cottons, tending their victory garden and flower beds. An excited terrier stood near the master of the house, dumbly protesting as his master dug up a bone. Another window depicted a carefree, light-hearted group picnicking on a terrace, and their set faces were fixed in an eternal smile. Their shorts, culottes, garden hats with wide-sweeping brims, slack sets were witnesses that the outdoor life still was fashionable. There were windows depicting gay, carefree, bright people at the beach, at the country club, strolling to the badminton courts. There were windows featuring the correct dress for the junior miss, and Alice covertly glanced at the suit which her mother had purchased for her in Klein's better store, and the suit now appeared drab and uninteresting, without charm or smartness.

Alice turned to Frank. "Do people live like this and dress like this?" Unconsciously envy had crept into her voice.

Frank nodded affirmatively.

"Will we?"

Frank shrugged his shoulders. He did not want to hurt his sister.

"Where do people live who have outdoor fireplaces in their back yards?" she asked.

"Around," he said vaguely. "Not around Pitkin Avenue," he added.

"Let's go home," she said suddenly. "I don't want to see any more."

Frank looked at a street sign. "We're almost at Thirty-fourth Street. I wanta show you the Empire State, and it's after one and I'm hungry."

Alice walked along, looking neither to her right nor left, concentrating upon the Empire State Building, whose steel and granite, bright in the afternoon sun, surged from the earth and dwarfed the buildings around it. She tilted her head back as her gaze went upward.

"I can't count no more," she gave up. "It's too big."

"We'll go up to the top someday," Frank said. "I never been on the top, and they say you can see for almost a hundred miles. Come on, baby." He led her toward Long-champs Restaurant. "I'm starved."

192

"In there?" Alice asked unbelievingly. "It must cost a lot."

"Pop gave me five bucks." Frank guided her through the restaurant doors into the sudden air-conditioned coolness. "Two," he said to the smiling hostess.

The hostess led them to a table, and after Alice was seated Frank awkwardly pushed her chair toward the table.

"Shall I take off my hat?" she whispered.

"You don't have to." He stood up. "I want to hang mine."

He watched Alice scan the menu and shook his head. Funny how the kid had reacted to what she had seen. Then he remembered there were no reasons for her to respond differently. Alice's vision of wealth had been Uncle Hershell's home, but Uncle Hershell was a sloppy little man who received his infrequent guests in a shaker sweater with gaping elbows and old carpet slippers. The furniture in Uncle Hershell's house was hideous and massive, with intricately carved walnut frames and stolid legs, built to last forever and to withstand all attempts at beautification. Uncle Hershell's back yard consisted of a sickly sycamore and a number of untidy hedges, and nowhere was there evidence of a dining terrace, an outdoor fireplace, or a badminton court. But to Alice, Uncle Hershell had represented wealth, until today, when suddenly, without warning or preparation, in a sudden sunburst of color, she had seen the true glories that money could purchase, and her initial enthusiasms had now been replaced by the first twinges of envy and sadness. He had felt the same way as Alice, years ago, when with some of the boys on the block he had been taken to a charity summer camp for two weeks and had known the joy of trees, flowers, grass, running streams, hills, and forest trails. He had to smile as he remembered how he had clung to his cot on the last day of his stay, refusing to leave, biting the hand of one of the counselors, and finally, how he had been pried loose and forcibly placed in the camp truck. He had tried to leap off the tailboard, but the counselors were prepared for him; and, weeping and sobbing, he had made the return journey to Brooklyn, and when his parents met him at the welfare office he had greeted them with a kicking and swearing because they were not farmers.

"I'll order for you," Frank said to Alice as he saw her continued hesitation. "Bring her a fruit cup," he said to the waiter, "a tuna-fish sandwich on toast, lettuce and tomato salad. She'll have something to drink and her dessert later. Me"—he pondered the menu—"I'll have a fruit cup on the roast-beef dinner. Mashed potatoes and squash, salad, and I'll take my drink and dessert with hers. All right what I ordered for you?" he asked Alice.

"Yes," she said softly.

Frank nodded to the waiter and picked up his water glass. The outside of the glass was frosted, and he drank slowly, enjoying the coldness of the iced water.

Alice was worried. "You sure you have enough money?" she asked anxiously.

"Plenty," he reassured her.

She gestured to the silver placed before her. "It's so fancy here. I don't know what to do."

"No one's watching you. Just keep one hand in your lap and eat slowly, and don't put your elbows on the table."

Alice glanced about her and saw the men and women chatting and eating with ease. At a near-by table a man and woman sat with their two children, and Alice saw that the girl was about her age, but this girl cut her meat and used her salad fork with confidence.

The waiter placed the fruit cocktails before them, and Frank smiled encouragingly at Alice as she hesitantly dipped her spoon into the cup.

"Snap out of it," he whispered. "We're as good as the jerks in here. Start eating."

Alice nodded and ate timidly, taking such tiny bites of her sandwich that the taste of the tuna was barely discernible and neglecting her salad because she was afraid to cut the slices of tomato. With relief she heard Frank order milk for her, but she insisted upon choosing her own dessert.

"I'll have chocolate pudding," she said to the waiter, and then she dropped her glance and sat stiffly with her hands folded in her lap.

The family at the near-by table were too engrossed in one another to notice anyone else, and Alice tried to imitate the self-possession of the girl. She smiled at Frank and nodded appreciatively at the smooth taste of the pudding,

194

and Frank winked at her as he cut his slab of apple pie which was decorated with a golden strip of cheese.

Frank sighed expansively. "That was good; I sure was hungry. I'll finish the cigarette and we'll go."

"I hope you've enough money."

"More than enough."

He motioned to the waiter, who approached with the check. Frank glanced at the check and withdrew some bills from his wallet.

"Keep the change," he instructed the waiter.

He nodded slightly as the waiter thanked him, and inhaled deeply on the cigarette. He wished it were a reefer. It might have been better if he had continued to smoke them, continued to act as he did before—it happened. Then Larry would not have guessed what was bothering Black Benny and him. But he hadn't admitted anything, though what Larry said was true. Benny drinking and losing control of himself was bad for them. He would have to see Benny after he took Alice home and have it out with him. Today was the eighteenth. There were only two more weeks of school. They could hold on for that much longer. Even Gallagher and the other bastards didn't seem to be bothering them so much, but suppose they came around somewhere and found Benny drunk and they started to pump him and the dope shot off his mouth? Benny didn't trust him, but at least he knew how to keep his lips buttoned. Frank ground his cigarette into the ash tray, stood up, and walked around the table to Alice. "Let's go," he said.

Alice opened her purse and looked at herself in the mirror.

Frank pulled her chair back. "You look fine. When're you gonna start using make-up?"

Alice laughed shyly. "I don't know."

"You don't need it." Frank removed his hat from the clothes tree.

"I don't want to wear it for a long time."

"You don't need it," Frank repeated. "So you had a good time?" he asked her as they walked toward the Lexington Avenue subway. "Well," he replied to her nod, "I'll take you out again soon. To the Botanical Gardens or someplace."

As they walked along Pitkin Avenue from Saratoga to Amboy, Alice narrowed her eyes so that she saw nothing but the sidewalk before her. She turned the corner into Amboy, and the contrast with Fifth Avenue was more startling than she had imagined it would be. She did not expect to see the well-groomed and handsome men and women strolling leisurely in the sun, nor uniformed chauffeurs in gleaming and polished limousines, but she had not realized how drab the tenements were. She remembered the apartment houses with their impressive canopies and casement windows, their clean brick and stone vaulting pridefully toward the washed blue of the sky. Here there were only ugliness and the sour smell of boiling wash and the wretchedness which everyone on the block accepted.

Suddenly she felt older than Frank, wiser, more certain, more settled. She saw her brother as he was: too sharp and slick in appearance, with an expression furtive and too old for his face and eyes. He was not the sixteen of the boys and girls whom she had seen eating in Longchamps and strolling along Riverside Drive and Fifth Avenue. She realized that normal boyhood had never been a part of Frank. He had grown up too suddenly, and the mold of the slum tenements and the years of public charity had cast Frank true to form: sullen, suspicious, bitter, cruel, uncaring as to what had happened to Fanny Kane, who was twelve, and only a year older than she.

The first thing she noticed as she opened the kitchen door was that her mother had spread their good linen tablecloth across the kitchen table. Then she saw Stan Alberg sitting with her father near the open kitchen windows. The good tablecloth usually meant a party, but one glance at her mother's seething, angry face and she knew that the tablecloth was only in use to impress Mr. Alberg. Frank immediately sensed the troubled silence and he mumbled a greeting and went into his bedroom to prepare himself for the storm which he knew was coming. It was only four o'clock, which meant that his parents had come home early, and he knew that their early home-coming had something to do with Fanny Kane. He was getting tired of these week-end battles, with their curses and accusations and threats of punishment, these battles when his parents

196

raved and stormed at him for not devoting more time to Alice, not keeping their flat looking tidy, not studying and paying closer attention to his schoolwork. Between Frank and his mother and father there seldom passed a cheerful or happy word. All their conversations were sharp, violent, hateful, as they tore and clawed at one another's wounds and deficiencies, and only when they spoke to Alice did their voices become less strident and harsh.

Frank heard his father's chair scrape as he stood up and walked toward his bedroom.

"Come in, Frank," his father said patiently. "We got something to talk about."

"What the hell did I do now?" he began to shout.

"Ssh." His father motioned toward the kitchen. "The windows are open. Come in and say hello to Mr. Alberg."

"I'm coming. I just want to put away my hat."

Frank's mother was busy boiling water as he entered the kitchen. Anger had flushed her face and clamped her mouth into a tight twisted line. Alice stood near her mother, nervously tapping with one foot as she waited for the outburst that was sure to come.

"So," Frank addressed them, "what've I done now? Let's get it over with."

"Bum, *momser!*" his mother shouted. "Do you know what's happened to Fanny Kane?"

Frank turned to Stan. "You squealer!" he sneered. "You and your goddamned sticking your nose where it doesn't belong." Frank spoke rapidly. "Who asked you to butt in?"

"Bum!" his mother screamed at him. "Do you know what that *meshugener* did? Sure you knew, because it happened by that bunch of bums that you go with!" His mother strode toward him and Frank retreated. "Must I never know peace? Or rest? Must I spend my days in working and my nights in worrying about you? Do you know, you *zulick*, what they done last night? They ruined the girl!"

Shrieking, Mrs. Goldfarb cornered Frank against a wall and began to strike violently at him with both hands, but Frank covered his face with his hands and managed to catch most of the blows on his arms.

"Let me alone," he began to shout. "I didn't do it! I was trying to take care of her! Ask him." He pointed to Stan, and as he lowered his guard his mother smashed him across the cheek and the nose. Involuntarily he drew back his fist to strike her, but he stopped, and at that moment Mr. Goldfarb dragged his wife to a chair and Frank ran into the bathroom and slammed the door.

No one spoke, and the only sounds were the boiling of the water and the heavy, raspy breathing of Mrs. Goldfarb. Alice stood rooted near the sink, writhing with shame, sick that Mr. Alberg had been a witness to her mother's fury.

"More troubles than anyone." Mrs. Goldfarb held her hands to her head and rocked in the chair. "Working and slaving for my children," she singsonged, "working and slaving for my children, and no rest and no peace. Today I have to have Mrs. Kane come to my shop like a crazy woman and start to pull my hair. Without a badge she got in," she said to Stan. "Rushed by the guards and finds out where I'm working and comes in and begins to pull my hair and to curse me. Curse me"—her voice broke and she tugged at her straggly hair—"me who's been her friend for more than ten years. Cursed me and pulled my hair because of him." She pointed to the bathroom, and her voice became hoarse and scratchy. "He had to give her a ticket and now she's ruined! Made dirty by a bum! Ruined, ruined for life." Mrs. Goldfarb began to cry slowly, as if it would take many hours for her grief to spend itself, and they watched her, unable to speak, to say anything that would comfort her.

With a screech the whistle in the spout of the teapot began to shrill, and Mrs. Goldfarb was galvanized into action. She wiped her eyes with her apron, poked futilely at her hair, and motioned for Alice to turn off the gas burner.

"You see, Mr. Alberg"—Frank's father turned to him— "a woman can be so excited she don't know what she's doing, but once the water for the tea is boiled, she forgets all her troubles." Mr. Goldfarb shook his head after he asked Stan to sit at the table. "These are bad times," he said. "The war."

Alice gave Stan a napkin and he thanked her. "I know," Stan agreed, "plenty of work and nothing else."

"What shall I do?" Mrs. Goldfarb appealed to him as she

extended her hands in a gesture of futility. "I don't have to be ashamed in front of you; you lived in Brownsville, hah? So," she went on as Stan nodded affirmatively, "you know what we had here. The dirt and the relief and the gangsters for so long, so long. Now we work, but we had bad times for a long time." Mrs. Goldfarb struggled to express herself. "So did our neighbors all around us. Now we're working, but our children seem to be getting the wrong things out of our working."

"Where are we making our mistake?" Mr. Goldfarb asked Stan.

Stan dipped the spoon into the sugar bowl. "I don't know. I don't know where to begin. I seem to be getting nowhere. People are expecting too much from us and from teachers in general. Everyone yells juvenile delinquency and expects us to find the remedy for all the evils, but we have to have more than yelling."

"Stop your goddamn preachin'." Frank opened the bathroom door and re-entered the kitchen. "We don't need it around here."

"Shut up, you bum!" his mother shouted.

"That's all right," Stan said. "Let him talk."

Frank closed the open kitchen window. "The neighbors already heard plenty. We sure give them an earful," he said to Stan.

"Please, Frank," Alice pleaded with him, "don't make Momma angry."

"Once," Mr. Goldfarb apologized, "I could better understand what you said. Years ago I took an interest in politics and things that were supposed to better the world, but that was before the bad times."

"You could've always worked"—his wife pointed at him with a stubby finger—"only you were for unions. Now you got your union," she continued, "and you're working, and him"—she pointed to Frank—"is doing God knows what and is disgracing us. Everyone knows that he gave Fanny the ticket to go to his dance and——"

"Mrs. Goldfarb," Stan interrupted her, "that wasn't Frank's fault. If the Sachs boy was after her he would've——" He stopped as he saw Alice listening with

199

too much interest. "Well, it would've happened sometime."

Mrs. Goldfarb noticed Stan's halt. "Alice," she said to her daughter, "go downstairs."

"I can stay," Alice protested. "I know what you're talking about."

Mrs. Goldfarb clutched her head and began to rock again. "What am I going to do? I was sixteen, believe me, Mr. Alberg, sixteen, before I knew that boys were different from girls. And now look, my daughter, a baby, sits here and tells me that she knows what we're talking about. How do you know?" She grasped Alice's wrist and twisted. "How do you know such things? Tell me! How do you know?"

Mr. Goldfarb rapped on the table with his spoon. "Stop it and let her alone and stop being such a fool. Sixteen," he snorted. "Maybe you were brought up in a convent?"

"I was brought up in a home where there was always enough to eat," she flung at him. "You hear me? Enough to eat! My father, *olav hasholem,* took care of his family so that they were dressed and fed and had a decent roof over their heads. Maybe he wasn't so smart as you," she spat scornfully at her husband, "but all his children were decent. Decent! Even my brother Hershell that you talk so much about, he's decent! His children are decent! Not like him"—she pointed to Frank—"who is now a God knows what!"

"Aw, for chrissake," Frank interrupted her tirade. "Shut up! What happened?" he asked Stan. "My old lady keeps on yellin' and I don't know what the hell she wants from me. What happened?"

Stan shrugged his shoulders. "Not much to tell. You know most of it. After you didn't show up last night I took Fanny home. The girls brought her a dress and some new stockings and we cleaned her up as best we could. But her face was bruised and we couldn't do anything about that, and of course you know what happened. So I took her home, and when I got there her mother and father were waiting for her on the stoop, and her father wanted to clout me because he thought I'd kept her out." Stan smiled. "Being the good Samaritan can be dangerous. I told them Fanny had been in a little trouble and we all went upstairs, and when they saw her in the light, her mother blew a fuse.

That started Fanny off again, and she told them what Crazy had done to her. Mr. Kane grabbed a bread knife and was going across the street and kill Crazy."

"I don't like to say this," Mr. Goldfarb interjected, "but he deserves it."

"I got the knife away from him," Stan continued, "and I stayed there until morning."

"They call the cops?" Frank asked cautiously.

"No. They're ashamed."

"But Mr. Kane went over to Mr. Sachs this morning," Mr. Goldfarb went on, "and Mr. Sachs beat Crazy with a razor strop until he fainted."

"He should've killed him, the outcast." Mrs. Goldfarb's cheeks were wet. "Some friends you have." She turned again to Frank. "Some friends! Spoilers of small girls. You bum!" She suddenly lunged again at Frank. "God-forsaken bum!" She struck at him again.

Frank backed away from her. "Let me alone," he panted. "Stop shovin' me around or you'll be sorry."

"Bum!" his mother shrieked. "God-forsaken bum! Threatening your mother!"

"I'm getting outa here!" Frank shouted. "You can't shove me around like nothin'. I'm gonna beat it."

"Go!" His mother pointed to the door, and her face was a fury. "Go! Bum! Like the Shapiro boys and Abe Reles and the Kaplan boy who killed the policeman, you'll be like them!"

"Rashke," her husband pleaded.

"Bum!" Her shriek was a continuous torment. "Gangster!"

Frank opened the front door. "The hell with you!"

Suddenly his mother threw a glass at him and it shattered against the jamb of the door. "Bum! Now a bum! Later a gangster. Then a murderer! What else can you become?"

Frank paled as Stan caught his eye. In Frank's face there was graved a new terror, a fear that was new to him and which turned his blood to ice, made his legs tremble with a sudden chill as his mother cursed him.

"Become a murderer!" His mother tore at her hair as Alice futilely attempted to restrain her. "My children old before their time because you"—she turned to her husband—"couldn't provide for them!"

"Rashke," her husband pleaded, "please, please! Not before him." He pointed to Stan.

"Before the world, before everyone!" his wife shrieked as if she were demented. "No hope, no future, no nothing, with my son growing up with bums and becoming a bum, a gangster, a murderer!"

Each of his mother's words was like the blow of a whip across Frank's back, but as she continued to shriek "murderer" at him in ever-mounting spirals of hysteria it was as if the lashes were tipped with lead. He could feel nausea gorging him and he clenched his hands, bit his lips, as he attempted to blot out the shrill screaming of his mother's voice.

Stan watched Frank retreat before the violence of his mother's anger and curses, but he did not intervene. It was too late to help Frank, for Frank was beyond the help that he could offer and give.

Now there was nothing left but to wait, wait until the weary drama stumbled to its end, and Frank would either escape or be trapped, and Stan no longer had confidence in Frank's ability to escape. At one time, yes, but now he saw fully and clearly that Frank was not smart or wise or strong enough to avoid situations that tended to enmesh and corrupt him, and suddenly Stan was tired, tired as he knew that he no longer could, would, or cared to help Frank, even though he believed that Frank was neither good nor bad, nor a sensitive complicated mechanism of mental contradictions. Frank was only a boy who had the normal urges of youth, but these urges had been perverted until he had become delinquent. Now Stan was certain that Frank would die young, for his death by violence was certain and inescapable.

"I'm not to blame because I gave her the ticket!" Frank slammed the door shut and faced his mother. "Why blame me if that stinker got in a jam? It was her fault."

"That's not true," Stan said.

Frank's face was bloodless. "Keep outa this," he warned Stan.

"Bum!" his mother screamed again.

"I'm going!" Frank shouted. "Go to hell!"

"Gangster!"

"Go to hell!"

"Murderer!"

Frank wrenched open the door and hurled himself down the steps.

In the kitchen the steam rose lazily from the teakettle and Mr. Goldfarb stared at Stan, who could say nothing, and the only discernible sounds were the harsh breathing of Mrs. Goldfarb and the childish weeping of Alice, who sat huddled in her chair at the kitchen table, sobbing and wanting to die.

Chapter 12

Detective Lieutenant Macon spat at the headline of the *Daily News,* tore the offending paper in two, and threw the halves into his wastebasket. He just couldn't seem to get a decent break in this damn Bannon case. He looked at Gallagher and Wilner, whose faces were fat pictures of gloom.

"We never get a break," Macon said. "Not one single break. How the hell did this get into the paper?" He pointed to the wastebasket.

Wilner shrugged his shoulders. "How do I know? We kept it quiet. After all, it was only a hunch."

"But a good hunch," Gallagher said to him. "You called your shot, Bert."

"That's right," Macon agreed. "You suggested that we try dragging those Rockaway channels because maybe Benny and Frank got rid of the gun there."

Wilner nodded sadly. "So I was right."

"And how," Macon continued. "The second try with the dredge at the Flatbush Avenue Bridge and up comes this plaster-of-paris block with some gun parts. They sure are slick kids."

"So I still don't know how the *News* got it," Gallagher cursed. "They're slick kids and there aren't any fingerprints on the block or the gun parts, and now I'll bet a hundred to one that we got the right kids. But they'll see it in the paper, and when we pick them up now they'll have another good alibi. Damn it!" Gallagher removed his hat and crushed it. "It burns me up."

"It would've been a beauty," Macon said, "if we could've sprung the gun parts on them. Well," he sighed, "I better send out a call to pick them up."

Frank shivered as he sat in the Winthrop and read and reread the scream headline in the *News*. They had found the gun parts. Now they had the weapon, at least part of it, and how certain could he be that there weren't any of Benny's fingerprints or, for that matter, his on the plaster block or the gun barrel? He could no longer be certain of anything, for who would have dreamed that the cops would find the gun after so many weeks? It was Wednesday, the twenty-eighth of June. Two more days and the term would have come to its official end. Now the cops had the gun, had fished it out of the channel underneath the Flatbush Avenue Bridge.

Frank sat erect and electric in the chair. That meant the cops had doubted them and had decided to drag the Rockaway channels. Now they had the proof. Frank felt himself going limp, and his heart and pulses began to pound violently, beating and thumping with fright. They were caught. Trapped. Benny, the smart apple who made him go on the hook, made him go back to the school to talk to Mr. Bannon, *made him a murderer,* made him think that the cops would never find the gun! If they had thrown the gun into a sewer they would be safe now, but no, Benny had to know it all. Now the cops had the gun and they had told Lieutenant Macon that they had been necking in the Jacob Riis parking lot the night of the murder, and it wouldn't be long now before the cops would have them again, sweating them until they confessed, and after they confessed there would be the trial and the chair. Frank sprang out of the tall chair with the arms. The resemblance was too close.

204

"Let's see your paper," Feivel called to him. "I hear they found the rod what knocked off your teacher."

Frank handed him the paper. "Keep it," he said.

"Hey," Feivel called after him, "I'll give it right back. Where you goin'?"

Frank closed the poolroom door behind him without replying. What was he going to do? For certain the cops would be out looking for them now. He had to get out of town. Alone. Without Benny, the bastard who knew so much that he was in a jam now that was going to burn them. If only he were certain that there weren't any fingerprints on the plaster or the gun. But then cold reason showed him that even the lack of fingerprints was not a defense. They were suspect, and the police, if they had to, would painstakingly check every store in Brooklyn in order to find out whether he or Benny ever had purchased plaster of paris, and then they would be through. Even at that very moment as he was walking along Remsen Avenue the cops might be at his home or Benny's searching for a container of plaster of paris.

Frank moaned in anguish. He was through, done for. He would die in the electric chair, moaning as he was dragged along the corridor to the death chamber. All his nerve, poise, reason had left him. He stumbled along Remsen Avenue, unseeing, his face white and drawn. There wasn't an out for him. Nothing. At any moment he expected to feel a firm hand on his shoulder, a hand which would be the first instrument that would take him to his death.

And as he thought of death the desire to live became stronger, more dominant and insistent, and Frank began to reason again. Things were bad for him and for Benny. He shut his eyes to eliminate Benny. Benny no longer belonged in his thinking. Benny didn't count any longer. Only he, Frank Goldfarb, mattered. He had to figure his way out of this jam, not Benny's. The bastard. The drunken bastard. Two more days and it would have been Friday and June thirtieth, the last day of the term, the last day of the month, the last day of the nightmare. July would have meant escape. But why should he wait three days to escape? Why escape only in July? Why not now?

The sudden buoyance left him as he looked in his wallet.

205

Three dollars. Seventy-two cents in his jacket pocket. At home he had a little more than twenty dollars tucked away in the bottom of his bureau drawer. He had to have the money. He had to have some clothes. He had to have the reefers. The reefers would pep him up, give him the courage and guts he needed. As he smoked them he would think of being tough and not being afraid of anything, and the mood would be carried over and exaggerated so that nothing would faze him. He had to get home for his money, clothes, and cigarettes. He had to get the twenty dollars so that he could buy a gun, for he was determined to go out fighting, shooting, killing. With the gun he could stick up a poolroom or lunch wagon and maybe get enough money to disappear. He needed the money. He needed a gun.

Frank looked at his watch. It was still early, before eleven. If he could get started soon he might be able to hitch a couple of hundred miles before dark. He didn't know whether to head for Canada or Mexico. Or maybe out to the cattle or lumber country, where he could lose himself and never be found. But so long as he left New York he was safe temporarily. Frank walked with more determination to the bus stop. He would still beat the rap. He had to. He was too young to die. And if he had to die he was going out fighting.

As he waited for the bus the hatred and fury that he felt for Black Benny drove everything else from his mind. Benny had done this to him, and now he was going to become a fugitive because of Benny. Then it would be Benny's luck to squirm clear of the murder charge and drop the entire blame on him. Because if there weren't any fingerprints on the gun Benny could claim that Frank had done the shooting. That wasn't any good. Benny had to be made to pay. The bastard. The drunken bastard.

The bus swerved toward the curb and Frank entered, paid his fare, and sat staring out of a window. It was Benny's fault. Only Benny's fault. Not his. It wasn't his idea to go back to school. Benny had been waiting for him with the car, not he for Benny. It was even Benny's idea that they should act like wise guys when Mr. Bannon questioned them. It was because Benny had bought the bottle and they had become half tight that Bannon was dead. And

206

whose idea was it to go back to the school? And who wouldn't throw away his gun? And who had slugged Bannon with the gun and then shot him? Not he. Benny. Benny the wise guy, who thought he was a hard guy and wanted to be a killer. Now he was on the spot, not Benny. He was the one who had done most of the alibiing to the cops, had kept them from tripping them up, from confusing them so that they would tell incriminating, conflicting stories. And for all of this he had nothing to face but the chair, or maybe life. Frank saw prison: its gray monotony, its closeness, its stifling of freedom. Look how long the month of June had been. How much longer would thirty —no, fifty—years be than a month?

Frank yanked the signal cord as the bus approached Amboy Street. Benny had to be paid off. He entered a shabby little candy store on East New York Avenue and looked up the telephone number of the police station. Now Benny was going to get his. The troublemaking bastard. Carefully he placed his handkerchief across the telephone mouthpiece and dialed the station number.

"Hello," he said in a disguised and muffled voice, "I want to speak to Lieutenant Macon. It's important." Frank waited as the connection was made. "Hello," he said again, and his voice trembled and the telephone receiver was damp in his hand, "I want to talk to Lieutenant Macon. . . . Yes, Macon."

Frank peered out of the booth. The only customers in the store were two little girls buying colored jelly beans. No one would walk in and see him in the booth, but to play safe he shifted about so that he stood with his back against the glass panels in the door. Perspiration dampened his lips and nose, and he rubbed them against the handkerchief that covered the mouthpiece. He started as he heard Macon's voice and he gulped before he was able to speak.

"Detective Macon," he began, "I'm a friend of Mr. Bannon's. . . . Yes"—Frank nodded—"the teacher who was murdered. I wanted to call you before this but I was scared. Yeah, scared. The guy who knocked him off is one of them tough Jews. A killer." Frank congratulated himself. This would help throw suspicion from him as the informer. If he played it right they'd only get Benny, and when Benny tried to implicate him he would deny it. That was the angle! The out! Benny was the killer!

At the other end of the telephone line Macon signaled for Gallagher and Wilner to listen in on the extension telephones. He winked at them and made a circle with his thumb and index finger. The case was breaking.

"So you know who did it." Macon spoke into the telephone. "Can you tell us?"

"I can," Frank said. "I used to go to the same church with Mr. Bannon and we were good friends, but I was afraid to talk before now."

"We'll take care of you," Macon said. "You don't have to be afraid. Who did it?"

"I—it—it——"

"You want to tell us at the station? We're at East New York and Rockaway." Macon spoke quietly.

"No," Frank faltered. "His gang is liable to get me. They're killers. I'll tell you who did it and that's all."

"All right." Macon nodded at the telephone. "Who did it?"

Frank struggled to speak.

"Who did it?" Macon asked again, and covered the mouthpiece of the telephone with his hand. "Gallagher," he whispered, "start tracing that call!"

Gallagher nodded, hung up, and left the room.

"Don't be scared," Macon said soothingly. "Who did it?"

Frank's mouth was dry and his tongue felt as if it did not belong to him. He had to go through with it. Benny had got him in trouble and Benny had to be paid off. It was Benny or him. He wet his lips and spoke directly into the mouthpiece. "Benny, the kid they call Black Benny, did it. He shot Mr. Bannon." And as he informed, Frank wanted to recall the words, but it was too late.

Macon's face was triumphant, and Wilner tried to smile but found it difficult to do so. "Thanks," Macon said. "So he did it? We suspected him."

"He did it," Frank repeated hoarsely.

"O.K." Macon played his trump card: "You better come in, Frank. We want to talk to you too."

Frank slammed the receiver onto the hook, stuffed his handkerchief into a pocket, and ran out to the street. He stood on the sidewalk, dazed, turning about, not knowing where to go. Macon had been too smart for him. There was no escape. Blindly he ran into the hallway of his tenement and up the stairs. He flung open the kitchen door, and his hands trembled as he opened the bureau drawer and searched under his clothing for the wallet. He sighed with relief and hope as he found it and skimmed rapidly through the compartments. The money was there, though now, as he looked at it, twenty dollars was so little. But he could still buy that gun. There was only one reefer in the cigarette case, and the paper wrapper of the reefer was old and wrinkled. For a moment he debated whether he ought to save it for a tight spot, but then he decided that he was in as tight as he could ever be, and so long as he felt the way he did about shooting it out with the cops he ought to smoke it now. With a gesture of defiance he struck the match, lit the marijuana cigarette, and blew the first puff of smoke at the mirror. He looked all right. His eyes were narrowed and drawn at the corners and his lips twitched, but he knew he would get away. He had to get away, but he regretted squealing to the cops. What he should have done was buy the gun and knock off Benny. That would've been best. That way he would've paid the bastard off, and he still wouldn't have ratted. But it was too late. The cops were going for Benny, and the heat was on for him.

He jerked erect as he heard the front door open and Alice's light step in the kitchen.

"Oh." She was startled as she saw him standing in the doorway. "I didn't know you were home."

Frank dragged on the cigarette and felt the first pulses of false courage surge through him. "Yeah," he replied. "It's me. I'm clearin' out."

Alice barred the kitchen door. "No!"

"I got to, baby." He laughed. "I'm in a jam. The cops must be lookin' for me now."

He derived a perverse joy from seeing the sorrow in his sister's face.

"Yeah," he went on, "in a jam. You know what I done?"

Alice struggled to speak.

"I'll tell you," he went on. "I just told the cops who killed Mr. Bannon."

"Frank!" Alice screamed.

Frank advanced toward her and drew back his fist. "Don't yell," he warned her, "or I'll flatten you. I told them Benny did it, but the cops want me too."

Alice's relief was explosive. "Thank God!" she said.

Frank took one last luxurious drag on the reefer and threw the butt into the sink. "Don't thank nobody," he said to her. "I was with Benny when he shot him. The cops are lookin' for me. I gotta get goin'."

Alice's world sank into the sea. She looked at her brother with a fear and despair that aged her. She struggled to speak, to cry out, to say something, to call aloud, but she could do nothing but stand against the kitchen door, rigid, stiff with despair and fear.

"I'm sorry, kid," Frank said. "You better let me go."

"No," she whispered. "We'll save you. Somehow we'll save you."

"Save me," he laughed, "for what?"

"We'll save you." Alice stood with her back against the kitchen door. "You didn't mean it. I know you didn't mean it. We'll get a lawyer; we'll get all the lawyers you need, only don't run away and make it worse. Don't run away," she repeated.

Frank hesitated. "You think so?"

"Yes," Alice whispered, "we'll get lawyers. Mom 'n' Pop'll come home and we'll tell them."

"That's no good." Frank took his cigarette case from his hip pocket and then put it back again as he realized it was empty. "You heard Mom on Sunday when she called me a murderer."

"Don't say it!" Alice shook with sudden nausea.

"A murderer," Frank repeated hollowly. "She called me a murderer."

"Don't say it!"

"A murderer." The phrase was hypnotic and he had to repeat it again. "A murderer."

Alice looked about her. There was nothing she could do.

"If you love me"—Alice stretched out a hand—"if you love Mom 'n' Pop you'll stay so we can help. It was an accident, wasn't it?" she plunged on desperately. "So maybe you won't get so long in prison and then you'll come back and we'll be waiting here for you."

"That's all, sister," Frank flung at her. "Come back to this? To this!" He pointed about him. "To this dump and these flats and houses? To these streets? To Brownsville? To this?" he screamed at her, and his face was a contorted mask of fright, disgust, and frustration. "I'd rather die! Hear me, die!"

"We'll save you," Alice whispered. "Save you. Momma, Poppa——" Her voice broke. "Momma! Poppa!" She called desperately, as if by some strange miracle her cries would bring her parents to her.

"Get outa my way." Frank grasped her shoulder.

Alice flung herself at him. "No," she wept, "no! Stay! Stay! You can't go. They'll kill you! They'll kill you for telling on Benny!" She locked her arms around him as he struggled to break free, and suddenly Frank hit her a short jolting blow on the jaw. Stunned, she released him and staggered to the table.

Frank looked at her. "I had to do it, baby. I'm sorry. Don't worry, I'll get away."

The sight of his sister weeping upset him. Hesitantly he approached her and then realized that he was losing time he needed desperately.

"Say good-by to the folks." He jammed his hat on his head, and as she did not reply he turned again to her. Alice sat hunched over the table with her head pillowed on her arms, crying, her thin shoulders shaking, her heart twisted into a knot of grief.

Somehow he could not leave Alice, and as he hesitated again he heard the thin metallic shrill of the police sirens as the scout cars raced into Amboy Street and blocked off Pitkin Avenue and East New York Avenue.

"The cops," he gasped. "The cops!"

Alice looked up. "I'm glad," she said.

"You little bitch," he snarled wildly, "glad that I'm gonna burn?"

"We'll save you," she said wanly. "We'll help you."

Frank's eyes rolled in his head. His tongue flicked his lips and, dumb with fear, he raced out of the flat up to the

211

roof. Cautiously he peered over the edge of the roof and saw the cars blocking the entrance of the tenement and the crowds of people, thin streamers of heads, arms, and legs converging and surging against the police lines around the tenement. Hopelessly he passed his hand across his eyes and thought of the suspense, fears, and uncertainties that had made of his days and nights an anguish and rack of misery, and which had corroded and rotted the guts out of his friendship for Black Benny, until in his all-consuming hatred, his mortal funk, he had betrayed Benny and had trapped himself beyond all hope of escape. He thought of Betty, of her bright smile, her firm young breasts, her soft lips and mouth whose kiss and caress he would never know again. He thought of July, freedom, the sea, the escape that almost had been his. He thought of living, clean sweet air, broad fields and rivers, clean streets and houses.

And as he stood at the edge of the roof, uncertain and afraid, suddenly he was struck a staggering blow in the back of his head that sent him stumbling against the roof ledge. The pain was a throbbing club that beat in his brain, and reeling and helpless, he turned about slowly and saw Crazy Sachs advancing toward him. Crazy wore brass knuckles on his right hand, and in his brutal, insane face there was the red lust of the killer. Weakly Frank raised his hands to ward off the next blow, but Crazy hit him a jarring blow that deadened the muscles of his arm, and as he dropped his guard Crazy's left cut into his face.

"I was listenin' to the radio," Crazy hissed, "and you squealed on Benny!"

Frank choked, and a thin spume of blood flecked his lips. "Let me alone," he gasped, and tried to run, but Crazy blocked his escape.

"Now I gotcha." Crazy's voice was triumphant. "Gotcha!" He swung again, and the brass knuckles broke Frank's nose. "Gotcha for everything!"

Frank was blind and helpless with pain, and Crazy rushed him, pounding killing blows on his head and shoulders, blows that broke his flesh and muscles and bone, that left him gagging with an incessant drumming pain. Suddenly he grabbed Frank by the throat and forced him back over the ledge.

People in the street began to scream and to point at the struggling figures on the roof. They could see the threshing boys and the slow, inexorable stiffening of Crazy's arms as he choked Frank and forced him back over the roof ledge. From the surrounding windows the people screamed for help, shielding their eyes, wanting not to look or see, and yet fascinated by the deadly tableau on the roof.

As Crazy continued to force Frank back and over the roof edge, his arms were grasped by his mother.

"Leon!" she shrieked. *"Zindele,"* she implored, and tugged vainly at her son. "Leon! Let him go. For God's sake, let him go! Leon! Leon!" She clawed at his clutching fingers. "Zindele, zindele!"

Crazy's breath came in great heaving gasps and he looked at his mother, who stared at him with dead, rigid eyes. In her face and eyes there was no longer the love and affection he had always known, and she appeared like a woman made of wax, whose features have been frozen into an expression of terror beyond belief.

Snarling, Crazy shoved his mother aside and with one last blow and curse he hurled Frank from the roof. With flaying arms and legs Frank fell and hit the rail of the third-story fire escape, then caromed out in an arc toward the street, screaming his life away.

Everything Happens With
Boys&Girls Together

William Goldman's
bold, shocking novel of our times!